### *"Marry me, Alex."*

Her body went rigid in his arms. She clenched the material of his shirt in her fists as if she wanted to shake him, only she didn't—merely held on as if her life depended on it.

"Talk to me, Alex, please. Tell me I'm a jerk for not talking to you for fifteen years, for trying to waltz back into your life like nothing happened in between. Tell me it's outrageous. Tell me you would never consider marrying—"

"You're a jerk for not talking to me for fifteen years." She nodded in agreement. "For waltzing back into my life like nothing happened in between. It's outrageous." She closed her eyes. "So outrageous I can't believe I'm even considering it."

Reese froze. She was considering it?

Dear Reader,

As Silhouette Books' 20th anniversary continues, Intimate Moments continues to bring you six superb titles every month. And certainly this month—when we begin with Suzanne Brockmann's *Get Lucky*—is no exception. This latest entry in her TALL, DARK & DANGEROUS miniseries features ladies' man Lucky O'Donlon, a man who finally meets the woman who is his match—and more.

Linda Turner's *A Ranching Man* is the latest of THOSE MARRYING McBRIDES!, featuring Joe McBride and the damsel in distress who wins his heart. Monica McLean was a favorite with her very first book, and now she's back with *Just a Wedding Away*, an enthralling marriage-of-convenience story. Lauren Nichols introduces an *Accidental Father* who offers the heroine happiness in THE LOVING ARMS OF THE LAW. *Saving Grace* is the newest from prolific RaeAnne Thayne, who's rapidly making a name for herself with readers. And finally, welcome new author Wendy Rosnau. After you read *The Long Hot Summer*, you'll be eager for her to make a return appearance.

And, of course, we hope to see you next month when, once again, Silhouette Intimate Moments brings you six of the best and most exciting romance novels around.

Enjoy!

Leslie J. Wainger
Executive Senior Editor

Please address questions and book requests to:
Silhouette Reader Service
U.S.: 3010 Walden Ave., P.O. Box 1325, Buffalo, NY 14269
Canadian: P.O. Box 609, Fort Erie, Ont. L2A 5X3

# JUST A
# WEDDING AWAY
## MONICA McLEAN

Published by Silhouette Books
**America's Publisher of Contemporary Romance**

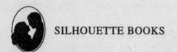

SILHOUETTE BOOKS

ISBN 0-373-07993-1

JUST A WEDDING AWAY

Copyright © 2000 by Monica Caltabiano

Visit us at www.romance.net

Printed in U.S.A.

**Books by Monica McLean**

Silhouette Intimate Moments

*Cinderella Bride* #852
*Just a Wedding Away* #993

## MONICA McLEAN

gave up a jet-set career as a management consultant to pursue her dream of writing romance novels full-time. "What can I say? I'm a sucker for a good love story and a happy ending." A former stockbroker, to boot, she has a B.S. in business law and an MBA in finance. Though she claims McLean, Virginia, as her hometown, she has also lived in New York, Pennsylvania, Maryland, North Carolina, Georgia, Ohio, Michigan, Minnesota...and Texas, if you count living in a hotel (ah, the life of a consultant). She is married—no kids, no pets, no plants—and lists good food, good company and good clothes among life's pleasures.

For my family—my husband, parents and sister—
for pulling together during the darkest days of 1998.

And for the first loves and heartbreaks that inspire artists
to rewrite their tales with happy endings time and again.

With special thanks to the following individuals:

Melissa Martinez McClone, a superbly talented
author and priceless friend, for sharing my crazy,
fictional world and believing in my vision for this
story even when I didn't.

Lynda Curnyn, a brilliant and insightful editor, for
investing your time and expertise in me.

Karen Solem, agent extraordinaire, for seeing potential.

Wendy Corsi Staub, master-of-all-fiction-trades,
for early encouragement and troubleshooting.

Danielle Girard Kraus, suspense diva,
and her father, John Girard, M.D.,
for consultation on Alex's medical condition.

My fabulous critique partners:
Jean Brashear, Chelle Cohen, Inglath Cooper,
Shelley Cooper, Tracy Cozzens, Anne Ha,
Lynn Johnson, Connie Marquise, Julia Mozingo,
Carol Opalinski, Roxanne Rustand, Suzanne Thomas,
Joe Thoron, Virginia Vail.

# Chapter 1

Closed For Private Party. Alexandra Ricci glanced at the red and green sign in the window of the restaurant and pulled her wool coat tighter around her. Through the glass, she could see people talking, laughing, and having a good time, while her reflection stared back at her.

Always on the outside looking in.

Taking a deep breath, she squared her shoulders and pushed open the heavy oak door. As she stepped inside, a rush of heat swirled around her. The halls were decked with boughs of holly, and the uplifting melody of a live band floated in the air.

*Okay, get a grip. This isn't so bad.*

One hour maximum. How hard could it be? She'd mingle with a few colleagues, then hightail it out of there. "Face time," her father called it. She was up for promotion in the spring, and everything else being equal, higher-ups tended to remember people they actually saw on occasion.

Ridiculous, she told her father. Everything else was hardly equal, as he'd reminded her from the time she was four years old and the doctors diagnosed her as highly gifted left brain.

"Do you know how many people would kill to be in your shoes?" he would ask. Every time, she would muse how she'd trade places with any of those nameless, faceless people in a heartbeat. To be ordinary, like everyone else...

Always, the impossible dream.

"Coat check?" a tuxedo-clad woman asked from a booth.

Alex hesitated, then nodded. She couldn't very well blend in and try to polish her people skills standing around in her coat. "I—I'm not planning to stay long."

The woman handed her a ticket. "Just bring that back whenever you're ready. I'll be here."

"Thank you." She straightened her waist-long French braid and simple, black velvet dress, took tip money from a silver-beaded handbag and placed the bills in the empty glass on the counter. "Happy Holidays."

The woman brightened. "To you, too. Enjoy the party."

She would try. She owed her father that much. She owed herself, she thought, taking in the colorful ornaments hung with care on a ten-foot evergreen and picturing her own empty house.

No tree. No decorations. No celebrations of any kind for almost two years.

As if in a trance, she crossed to the tree and fingered the edge of a gold star. It was time to stop mourning, time to get on with her life and rejoin the living. And there was no time like the present.

With a last glance at her reflection in the window, she

rounded the corner, plucked her nametag from a table and joined the festivities.

At the punch bowl, she scanned the room and spotted a group of women standing around a table. Perfect. With determined steps, she started across the dance floor.

Twenty feet. Eighteen. Fifteen and three quarters. Almost there.

Her heart started racing. Her upper lip dewed with perspiration. Her steps faltered, then stopped. She stood in the middle of the dance floor frozen halfway between the table and the Exit sign, feeling as naked and exposed as a goldfish in a glass bowl.

Growing up, kids often teased her because she was...different. Her father told her they were jealous, but she never believed him.

"Mind over matter, Alexandra," he would often say when she'd run home in tears. "Learn to control your emotions, or you'll subject yourself to ridicule all your life. Toughen up, or they'll eat you alive."

And so she had learned: Tough cookies didn't crumble.

Alex could not give in to the insecurities of the little girl who still lived inside her. Punch glass in hand, she lifted her chin and started again for the table.

Ten feet. Seven and a half. Four, three, two...

"Hi." She forced a confident smile that belied the butterflies in her stomach. "I'm Alex Ricci. Physics department." She pointed to her nametag. "May I join you?"

"Yes, of course." A pretty blonde—Connie Berns from the English department—stepped back to allow Alex entry into their circle and made introductions.

A few sweeping glances assessed her attire. She might have worried if she hadn't made her selections from a holiday issue of a popular fashion magazine. Dress, shoes, accessories, even new makeup. Dressing Up a Wallflower:

Understated Elegance. R-r-rip. She'd taken the page to the mall with her.

"We were just discussing the trials and tribulations of the working mom," Connie said with a you-know-how-it-is roll of her eyes.

Alex's chest tightened. She forced an oh-sure-you-bet smile and clutched her handbag a little closer.

"I'm having problems with my middle child," said one woman. "When she was a baby, she'd eat anything. Hits first grade, and all of sudden, we're in this picky phase."

A murmur of understanding followed from the group.

"She won't eat anything the rest of the family likes. I don't know what to do." She tossed up her hands. "My kids are thin as rails. They *need* to eat more. But I don't have time to fix separate menus every night. If they all decide they want to order à la carte, I'm dead."

"Do you have children, Alex?" Connie asked.

"No." She swallowed past the lump in her throat and gave a polite smile. "No children."

Several gazes dropped to her hands, and she surmised from their sympathetic expressions, a few figured out she was a widow from the gold band she had transferred to her right hand.

"Look who's here." One woman grabbed the arm of another.

The second woman's gaze followed hers. "Is it him?"

"Him whom?" Connie craned her neck. "Who's here?"

"That drop-dead gorgeous lawyer."

"The new guy?"

"Yeah, he only teaches one class. Took over mid-semester for a professor out on disability, and the powers that be twisted his arm to keep him on another semester."

"You should see the waiting list," a third woman piped

up, standing on her toes to get a better look. "All of a sudden, everyone's clamoring to take Business Ethics."

"Smart and cute, a deadly combination."

Alex, too, turned to see the subject of their ogling. In the blur of faces, a tall, dark-haired man stepped within her path of vision. His ebony tuxedo, snowy white shirt and perfectly centered bow tie matched those of others, and she almost scanned right past him except his impressive, broad shoulders made her glance up to his face.

His face... She blanched. Her pulse thundered in her ears, and her palms broke into a sweat.

*Reese Collins.*

Oh, dear God. It couldn't be. *Drop-dead gorgeous lawyer. Only teaches one class.* No. Please, no. This couldn't be happening. As if it wasn't hard enough to avoid him in an upstate New York town with a population of eighty-thousand. A college campus of ten-thousand? Forget it!

At that moment, familiar steel-blue eyes locked with hers, and a wave of lightheadedness seized her.

She whirled, turning her back to him, and prayed he hadn't recognized her. What were the chances? He'd seen her only once in the past fifteen years. Could he spot her in a crowd after all this time? *Could he ever?*

"He's coming this way!"

She raised a shaky hand to smooth her French braid. She wouldn't let his presence bother her. No, not at all. She was a grown woman, not a teenager.

"All right, single moms. Line up for a spot on Studmuffin's dance card."

Damn. Where had she put that business card from the M.I.T. dean? Boston sounded really good right about now. The heck with the family legacy at Sycamore University. She didn't need to follow in her father's footsteps, or his father's before him.

"He's looking at me."

"I think he's looking at me."

*Just shoot me now.* Alex raised her eyes heavenward and willed the ground to open up and swallow her. At a firm but gentle hand on her elbow, her back stiffened. The gaggle of women went silent beside her, their eyes practically bulging from their sockets.

"Alex." His voice was deeper now, more gruff, but just as compelling as she remembered.

She turned to face him, took an incremental step back and tried to muster surprise. "Reese. Hi."

"Hi, yourself. I was hoping to run into you." He gave her the same slow, easy grin he must have given her at least a thousand times as a teenager, and the air stilled in her lungs as it had on each and every one of those occasions.

"Evening, ladies." Reese tipped his head toward the women, then turned to her, oblivious of his new fan club. "How've you been?"

"Good. Fine. You?"

If he found anything strange about her monosyllabic responses, he had the good grace not to comment. "Can't complain," he said with a shrug.

"I…didn't realize you were teaching a class."

If she had, she never would have come tonight, never would have even contemplated it. She had avoided him since the funeral nearly two years ago, since the tragedy that took her husband and Reese's brother and sister-in-law, bringing Reese back to Sycamore after more than a decade away. She'd avoided him for this exact reason…

She didn't move. She couldn't speak. She simply stared into familiar steel-blue eyes and felt herself sucked into a vacuum of time and space where she and Reese weren't two adults who might as well have been strangers, but two teenagers—best friends—at a party.

Loud music. Cigarette smoke. Couples necking. And Reese, as always, cajoling Alex into relaxing in a place she didn't belong. She tutored him in math; he taught her about life outside the classroom. She was the awkward misfit, and he was the charming heartthrob—the object of many a teenage girl's fantasies, Mr. Popularity, everybody's friend.

Only she had noticed his careful, subtle efforts to keep others at a distance. To her, Reese Collins always seemed alone, even in the middle of a crowd of admirers both male and female. Despite hoards of acquaintances, he had no close friends—until her.

"We have a lot to catch up on, Alex," he said now, and the velvety sound of her name on his lips made shivers dance up and down her spine. His gaze never left her face. "You look great."

"You, too." Her voice came out scratchy and hoarse. She took a sip of punch, hoping not to choke.

The women resumed their chatter, obviously thinking to give them some privacy. But the privacy Alex craved at that moment was the empty house she never should have left.

Her gaze shifted between Reese and the door, at once attracted and put off by the man she had spent fifteen years trying to forget.

Reese lifted a hand to return the wave of a man across the room. "District Attorney," he explained. "Wife teaches history."

She nodded mutely, realizing the slash of his dimple was right where she'd last seen it. But there were other changes. His legs were longer, his shoulders broader than the boy she remembered. He'd grown at least two inches in the intervening years since they'd been neighbors, and she had to tilt her head back even farther to look up at him. Faint lines now crinkled from his eyes to his temples and bracketed his mouth when he smiled.

He had aged well, damn it.

"How are the girls?" She asked the question that had nagged at her to swallow her own conflicting emotions and pick up the telephone.

His brother's girls—three little orphans, now Reese's wards.

"Getting bigger every day," he answered with a proud smile.

"That's great. That's really great, Reese." *Can I leave now?* She didn't want to ask about his wife, didn't want to hear about their wonderful marriage or the joy his brother's girls brought to their lives. Least of all, she didn't want to know anything about the woman who had managed to steal Reese's heart, the woman who had succeeded where countless others had failed. Herself included.

"Want to see their pictures?" He pulled his wallet from his jacket pocket, and before she could think to protest, flipped open to a portrait of three, elementary-school-aged girls, each one dark-haired with captivating blue eyes and a vibrant smile. "That's Elizabeth—she's oldest. Middle's Nora. Youngest is Jayne."

They could have passed for his own daughters.

*His own daughter.*

A giant fist inside her squeezed tight, threatening to cut off her oxygen supply. "They're beautiful," she said, willing her voice not to shake. "Just as I imagined."

She couldn't get enough air into her lungs. She felt hot, dizzy and nauseous all at once. She had to get out of there, away from him, away from the past and all its painful memories. What was done was done, and there was no way to undo it.

She threw an anxious look at the door. "Reese, I—"

"Care to dance?" He inclined his head in the direction she'd just gazed.

"No. Thank you. I don't think that's a good—"

"You're right. Bad idea." He combed a hand through his hair and glanced toward the bar. "How about a drink?"

She pursed her lips, remembering the last time they drank together—the end of their friendship.

"A nonalcoholic drink," he amended, as if reading her mind.

Before she could formulate another protest, Connie backed into her with a none-too-subtle cough and jolted her forward. Despite appearances, the women were still tuned to her station and listening with rapt attention.

"I—I could use more punch," she said, holding up her empty glass. Excusing herself from the group, Alex started for the bar. The weight of Reese's gaze bored between her shoulder blades. He obviously wasn't going to give up. She might as well exchange polite chitchat and get it over with. Then, they could go another fifteen years without speaking.

Reese could do this. Nothing to it. Two old friends having a drink. What could be simpler?

A root canal maybe. But, hey, it was all relative.

If only Alex didn't bolt for the exit. She looked as jittery as if he'd asked her to the altar instead of the wet bar...not that the former hadn't crossed his mind.

Ever since his mother raised the issue of the girls' custody, he'd had more than a few desperate moments. But none that desperate. At least not yet.

*Anyone but you, Alex. Anyone but you.*

One fateful night years ago, he'd taken advantage of her friendship and suffered the consequences—a lesson he hadn't forgotten. He knew better now, knew friends and lovers didn't mix. But even after fifteen years, he still hadn't figured out a way to apologize.

*So Alex, about that time I got hammered and lost control...or was it that I lost control and then got hammered? Well anyway, you know the night you lost your virginity, and I got caught with my pants down?*

Ah, hell. What were the chances she still remembered?

He took their drinks out to the three-season room where Alex waited. One look at her face, and he knew she'd contemplated ditching him while he wasn't looking.

*Damn.* She remembered, all right.

"Nice view." He indicated the castle-sized brownstone, perched atop a steep, snow-covered hill.

"The Hall of Languages." She nodded. "It's quite beautiful."

"Yes, it is," he agreed, but he was no longer looking out the window. "Here." He handed her a wineglass, clarifying, "They ran out of punch glasses."

"Thanks." She accepted the drink but made no move to take a sip, instead holding the glass in front of her like a cross to ward off vampires.

Instinctively, he backed away several inches, and she relaxed somewhat, turning her attention to the task of wrapping the napkin around the stem just so.

She wasn't going to make this easy for him.

Not that he blamed her.

Reese took a long pull from his bottled water and squinted at the Hall of Languages, trying to find words to break the ice that had been frozen for well over a decade.

As always, he couldn't look at the brownstone castle for longer than a few seconds without memories of his brother intruding. As boys, they would sneak out to go sledding down its steep hill. Midnight madness they'd called the tradition they started the winter Reese came to live with the Collins family as a foster child.

Twelve years old, two years older than Jeff, Reese had spent most his life shuffling from foster home to foster home, yearning for a family to call his own. From the very first night he'd slept in one of the twin beds in Jeff's bedroom, he had wished for Jeff's life. And now he had it.

*Be careful what you wish for…*

"Midnight madness?" Alex had followed his gaze.

"Yeah." Reese pinched the bridge of his nose.

Her intuition should have surprised him, but it didn't. Once upon a time, she'd been one of the best friends he'd ever had—the only one who'd ever slipped past his guard.

What started out as a punishment for him—private math tutoring—soon turned into a game. Thirty solved algebraic equations in return for an hour of cross-country skiing. Three dozen geometric proofs in exchange for a snowball fight. The unit circle in trig qualified for a movie.

Reese had no shame—he bartered basketball games, parties, four-wheeling in the country. He figured if Miss Priss expected him to sit still and endure the endless torture of her textbooks, she was going to have to take a walk on the wild side and live a little in return.

Before he knew it, his relationship with Alex had shifted from resigned tolerance to amusing pastime to genuine friendship. Then it had fallen apart—thanks to him—and he'd be damned before he crossed that line *with anyone* ever again.

"I imagine your midnight traditions aren't the same without Jeff," Alex whispered, taking a step toward him before appearing to remember herself and stop short.

His gut constricted at the knowing expression in her

enigmatic brown eyes. He studied the planes of a face he'd once known as well as his own, taking time to reacquaint himself with every feature. Winter pale skin with a tinge of coloring from her Italian ancestors. High cheekbones swept up from a pert nose and lips that didn't smile nearly enough. Waist-long, dark brown hair worn in a French braid.

So familiar, yet so different. The girl he knew was gone, but in her place was this woman who bore an aching resemblance.

"They say you can never go back again." He spoke not only of his brother but of the past he and Alex once shared.

"Reese, I…" She pursed her lips as if debating whether or not to confess some great sin. He could just picture Alex at the confessional on Sunday.

*Bless me, Father, for I have sinned. I ate an entire bag of chocolate chip cookies in one sitting.*

Yep, that was the extent of Alex's sins, he imagined. No transgressions marred the pit of her soul. Unlike his.

"Never mind." She gave a weak attempt at a smile.

He remembered the hoops he used to jump through to make Alex smile. Really smile. He never could resist the challenge of getting the professor's daughter to loosen up.

A muscle twitched in his jaw. "You never returned my calls after the funeral."

"Didn't I?" Alex shrugged and tossed her French braid over her shoulder. "Must have had other things on my mind, sorry."

"It was understandable. Then. Seems everytime I've seen you since, you've been running in the other direction."

"Really?"

"Really."

Her gaze flickered to his, and he thought he detected a

glimmer of guilt. "I haven't been to the house in a while," she admitted, in reference to her childhood home, directly across from his.

He'd moved back after the funeral. His parents had sold their house to Jeff when they retired to Florida. It was the only home the girls had ever known, and though Reese felt strange living there again, he was leery of uprooting his nieces after all the upheaval in their young lives.

"Dad usually comes to my place," Alex said. "When he's around, that is, which isn't much these days, what with all his travels. Ancient ruins, tropical rainforests, African safaris—the usual footloose and fancy-free, retired-scientist activities. He's in Australia right now."

He could tell from the strain in her voice she was struggling to converse with him. It was the same way when they'd first met. How he'd prided himself when she finally let down her defenses. Then he'd gone and robbed her blind.

"I wasn't sure you'd show tonight," Reese said, his voice thick.

She lifted her shoulder in a delicate shrug and circled the rim of her glass with an index finger. "Me, neither."

Finally acknowledging it wasn't going to get any easier, he drew a deep breath and expelled it with a hiss. "Alex, I know we didn't end things on a positive note. We were young and stupid. You were young, and I was stupid."

Her eyes clouded, and her chin lifted a notch. "You were never stupid."

"Except in math."

"You passed that calculus test," she said, a hard edge of conviction like granite in her voice.

"As I recall, you were the only one who believed it." He'd never forgotten what precipitated the night he and Alex made love—his math teacher's accusation he'd cheated and the resulting suspension. For a boy who'd been accepted to a prestigious, Top Ten university that fall, the incident had rocked his entire world.

His adoptive parents, both lawyers who subscribed to the notion of "innocent until proven guilty," took one look at the crib sheets found underneath his desk and rendered their own guilty verdict. Even Jeff had his doubts. Only Alex had believed in him. But then, she'd been his tutor. She had every reason…

"Alex, about what happened…"

"You know, we really don't have to talk about this."

"Yeah, we do. This apology's been a long time coming. I'm sorry things got out of hand that night. I crossed the line with you. I never should have—"

"I got you drunk, Reese. I practically poured the bourbon down your throat. I had no idea… I didn't know…" She shook her head. "I knew how upset you were. I should have known."

*Upset* was being kind.

Reese could still remember the shock and wonder he'd felt the day Clay and Kitty Collins told him they wanted to adopt him. No one had ever made it any great mystery to him—not the social workers, not any of his foster parents—that only to the extent he could be the son they wanted, would any family keep him. Though he'd always tried his hardest, he inevitably fell short somehow, some way.

When Kitty called him into the den *alone* one evening, he figured that was his cue to start packing. But for some reason he would never understand but forever be grateful, they had made the decision to keep him—something no one, not even his birth mother, had been able to stomach.

He had vowed on that day never to disappoint them, or make them regret their decision, or shame them in any way. Then, five years later, in the span of twenty-four hours, he'd managed to do all three.

In time, they would have come around to believing he didn't cheat on the exam, but when Kitty walked in on him with Alex, his fate was sealed. They yanked him out of his private, college preparatory high school and shipped him off to a military boarding school to finish out the rest of the year. Though they never talked about the incident again, he would never forget the look of horror on his mother's face.

"You were a good friend, Alex," he said, words long overdue, "and I took advantage of you. There's no sugar-coating it. It never should have happened."

He saw the hurt in her expression at that moment, and age-old self-recrimination resurfaced as he'd always known it would whenever they got around to this conversation. He wouldn't blame her if she couldn't forgive him. He'd turned to Alex in desperation, because she was the only one in the universe who believed in him without question.

"I owed you, Alex."

"You didn't owe me."

"I did, and that was no way to repay you. I regretted it right away."

"I know." She stared into her punch.

He wanted to reach out, to trail his knuckles across her cheekbone and along her jawline, to trace the curve of her lips. But he could no sooner act upon those impulses now than he should have then.

"Can we move past this?" he asked. He knew better than to ask for forgiveness. She'd already given him enough. He wouldn't ask for more.

"You don't owe me, Reese. The past is in the past.

There's nothing either of us can do but move forward.'' She bit her lip and extended her hand.

''Thanks.'' He engulfed her hand in his. It felt cool in his warmth, and he automatically curled his fingers.

It wasn't like Alex to initiate physical contact. He recalled that night when he'd taken her hands and placed them on his bare chest. He'd never wanted to think of Alex in that way, could have gotten physical satisfaction from numerous other sources. But that night, it had to be her.

Only her.

One second, she'd been in his arms—the same innocent way she'd been dozens of times before. And in the next, everything had changed. The damage done.

As if she too remembered, Alex quickly withdrew her hand and lowered her gaze to her glass, absently stroking the stem.

Reese's gaze flickered between the idle motion of her wedding band and the Hall of Languages, memories of his brother once again intruding.

*If anything ever happens to Karen and me, I want you to raise our girls.*

*Nothing's going to happen—*

*Promise me, Reese.*

He stared at Alex's wedding band. She wasn't married anymore. It had been two years…

*No.* He clenched his fist. This wasn't about him; it was about her, about righting a past wrong. If push came to shove and his mother pressed for custody, he would not, could not think of Alex as a viable solution.

''Alexandra is different from other girls,'' Frank Ricci once told him, which Reese translated to mean *hands-off* in layman terms. ''She has a higher purpose than you or I.''

"Reese?" Alex's eyebrows knitted together. "Is something wrong?"

A knife twisted inside his gut. *Anyone but you, Alex. Anyone but you.*

"No, nothing." He smiled and shoved his hand back in his pocket, but the skepticism in her frown told him she wasn't convinced.

He never could fool her. That was the problem. She always saw too much, always honed right in on whatever he was trying to hide, like a Geiger counter detecting the slightest radioactivity.

"Life's ironic sometimes," he admitted. "Who'd have thought one day I'd be raising Jeff's girls, living in his house, even working at his university?"

"I hope you aren't blaming yourself. You didn't wish for this. No matter what you think."

Amazing. Fifteen years, and she could still write a dissertation on his psyche in her sleep.

Unlike his wife of three years, who couldn't begin to fathom why he would want to give up their yuppie lifestyle, who didn't want to be saddled with the burden of motherhood under *any* circumstances.

Unlike his mother, who wanted to yank the girls from the only home they'd ever had, so they could go live with her in Florida in some retirement community. She claimed they needed a female influence, which he couldn't dispute. But he wondered if it wasn't more than that, if once again he wasn't good enough.

He shoved a rough hand through his hair.

"Reese? Are you sure…?"

"You're right," he said, not giving her a chance to ask again, not wanting to lie to her again. "Time just kinda slips by, doesn't it?"

"Yes," she whispered. "It does."
*Fifteen years in the blink of an eye.*

Despite the cold, Alex felt flushed, her stomach tangled
in guilty knots. Thirty seconds alone with Reese and age-
old memories felt as fresh as yesterday.

The good, the bad and the ugly.

She hated that his presence still affected her. She wished
he would move, so she could deliberately choose the other
direction. She wanted to run far, far away. Yet she stood
rooted to her spot. Part of her reluctantly wanted to be
there, wanted to feast on his rugged, handsome face and
drown in the deep rumble of his voice one last time.

It was just physical, she told herself. She was a lonely
widow, and he was and always had been the most attractive man she'd ever known.

A surface-level attraction. That's all she felt, nothing
more. Nothing different from lusting after Val Kilmer in
the movie *The Saint.*

Nothing as it once had been.

"So." Reese rocked back on his heels. "Mom told me
you moved out to Skaneateles. What's that? Twenty, thirty
minutes of commute time in good weather?"

She averted her gaze at the mention of his mother. "I
didn't realize Kitty was keeping tabs on me."

"And I suppose Frank never told you anything about
me?"

"Well, maybe a few things. I knew you left your law
firm on the West Coast to move back here and take care
of the girls, but I didn't realize you were teaching a class.
That, um, caught me by surprise." A mild understatement.

"Just found out tonight, huh?"

She nodded.

"Not to worry. I'm working on the stuffy part, trying
to fit in with all you intellectuals." He schooled his fea-

tures into a model of seriousness. "How am I doing so far?" He stroked his chin thoughtfully.

Alex grinned despite herself. "Don't quit your day job."

"Might have to," he said, and this time when he smiled, his eyes didn't crinkle at the corners. "Teaching law works a whole lot better than practicing sixty-hours-a-week when you're doing the single parent thing."

*The single parent thing.*

Blood rushed in her ears, amplifying the pounding rhythm of her heart. "Wh-what single parent thing?"

Reese stared somewhere over her shoulder. "Leslie and I separated last year. The divorce went through a few months ago. It's a done deal."

"I didn't realize. I had no idea." Alex swallowed down the hard lump in her throat.

He shrugged. "Irreconcilable differences."

There had been a time when he would have told her the whole story, spilled it out, sparing no details. And she would have listened, making the appropriate sympathetic noises, and tried not to read too much into his latest self-sabotaged relationship. She had felt privileged to be his only confidante and knew better than to let her one-sided attraction interfere with their friendship.

With one fateful exception.

Alex's stomach clenched. She wrapped her arms around her waist in reflex. "I almost called...so many times...to ask about the girls. But I didn't know...I wasn't sure..." She blinked. "I never imagined you were raising them alone. I'm so sorry."

*Sorry about your marriage, sorry I never called, sorry for much more than you'll ever know.*

A moment passed during which neither of them spoke

nor turned to leave, then Reese broke the silence. "So, when can you come over?"

"When...?" Her tongue stuck to the roof of her mouth.

"I'd like you to meet the girls."

"But I thought..." *She thought they were saying the goodbyes they'd never said.* Her gaze darted around the three-season room, looking for something, anything on which to focus besides Reese's expectant face. In desperation, she checked her wristwatch. "Oh, wow. Gosh, I didn't realize the time. I have to go. Albert's waiting for me."

"Albert?"

"Albert Einstein," she clarified. "My cat."

"Wait." Reese reached out, placed an unrestraining hand on her arm before she reached the door. "I'm sure Albert will understand if you waited five more minutes. Can't two old friends get together for dinner?"

Friends. That's what they'd been all right, all those years ago. Just friends. As simple and as complicated as that. Thanks, but no thanks. She'd expended her quota of heartbreaks in a lifetime.

"This month's bad," she said.

"When's good?"

*Never.* "I—I don't know."

"Can I call you?"

"Sure." She forced a smile, trying to forget the years when he hadn't. Never called. Never wrote. Never crossed the damned street to say hello to her father or ask about her. Just up and left one day, put an entire continent between them without looking back.

For years, she'd harbored the hope he'd grown pudgy, bald and otherwise unappealing. Anything but a man who would still make her heart race or her palms sweat if she were to run into him again. A man who could make her question the contentment of a comfortably staid marriage. Or a man who made her long for the very things she could never have, while selfishly overlooking that which she did.

Mind over matter, her father had taught her. But her mind had little say in the matter of Reese Collins.

She was glad she'd never seen him while Tom was alive. She had feared her reaction and prayed their paths never crossed. They hadn't—not even once—until that bleak, desolate day at Oakwood Cemetery. At the funeral service for the twenty-two plane crash victims—students and faculty returning from a college bowl game.

"Alex..." The sound of his voice was exactly as she remembered it. Deep, warm and somehow soothing. The same qualities that had struck a chord of unbearable nostalgia on that miserable, frigid afternoon.

Those steel-blue eyes had captured hers across the snow-covered graves. And afterward, though they hadn't spoken in thirteen years, he had approached her with the familiarity of their teenage days, as if no time had passed at all. But then, he didn't know everything. Because she hadn't told him.

She'd barely been able to look at him under the weight of three sets of eyes—her father's and his parents'—but she remembered his voice.

*You aren't alone in your grief, Alex... If you ever need to talk...*

She hadn't—she wasn't one of his obligations, and she never would be. So she had clutched her father's arm and leaned into the strength of the first man she had ever loved as she mourned the death of the last...and tried to forget there had been another, far more powerful, in between.

She walked away from him now as surely as she had then, determined to put the past behind her where it belonged. "I have to go, Reese."

"Running again?"

She froze, one hand on the three-season room's door.

"Go on. Run away." His voice held a note of challenge.

She laughed then, a short, bittersweet puff of air, and whirled to face him. "Like you're one to talk."

"Touché." He grinned—that aggravating, unnerving, bone-melting grin. "Your eyes still sparkle when you're ticked."

"Oh, brother." She rolled said sparkling eyes.

"Come on." He crooked his head. "I'll walk you to your car."

"No, you don't have to do that."

"I want to."

She glared at him. "You're one of the most stubborn men I've ever known. Has anyone ever told you that?"

"Yes. You." That insufferable grin again. "Though I prefer persistent myself." He winked and opened the door. "After you."

She bit her lip and resisted the urge to belt him. So many feelings once buried now surfaced. She wanted to beg his forgiveness for the decisions she had made, the actions she had taken. She wanted to kick his shins for staying away, for breaking her heart. But more than anything, she wanted a friend again. She wanted *her* friend again.

She hadn't realized how empty her life had become until she came to the party tonight, until she stood in a group of working mothers—yet another place she would never belong.

The culmination of loneliness she'd ignored for years hit her full throttle. She *did* want to have dinner with Reese. She *did* want to meet the girls. What could it hurt? Her heart again? No, not that. Fifteen years ago, she'd loved and lost enough to make her immune for a lifetime.

As they crossed the dance floor toward the exit, Alex

felt the gazes of the women on her back and knew well the direction of their thoughts. The night might as well have been a time warp back to the parties of their youth where everyone had wondered the same thing: What's a cool guy like him doing with a nerd like her?

She felt Reese's hand at the small of her back as he guided her out the door and stole a sidelong glance at his devastatingly handsome profile as he retrieved their coats.

Outside, the snow fell in big flakes, floating like parachutes. She turned her face to the night sky and filled her lungs with the crisp, dry air.

"Lunch." The single word tumbled out before she could stop it.

Reese accepted her counteroffer with a nod, blowing on his curled fist as they walked toward the parking lot.

"You still don't wear gloves," she noticed.

"And you still change your mind at the last minute. Feels strange, doesn't it? After all this time…"

"In a lot of ways, yes. But in some ways, no."

"Same here. Sometimes you don't realize you've missed someone until you see them again."

*And sometimes you never forget.*

# Chapter 2

"Do you go by Dr. Ricci?" Reese asked as they neared a dark blue Swedish import. Snowflakes swarmed around the street lamp like soft, huge moths, and packed snow crunched under their feet.

"Professor Ricci works for me." She pressed a button on her key ring, simultaneously disarming the security system and unlocking the doors. "I'm not hung up on my doctorate like some people."

"To note, *some people* didn't get their doctorates when they were twenty-two."

"Well, believe it or not, I also answer to Alex on occasion," she muttered.

"Wow, no kidding? Your first name? Nothing like playing fast and loose, huh?" He opened the driver's door for her.

Without a word, she reached into the back seat and pulled out an ice scraper. Her eyelashes were spiked with tears from the wind, and she wore a wry smile.

"Want a ride, wise guy?" She whacked the instrument into his stomach. "Start scraping."

*Know when to quit this time, Collins.*

Reese took the proffered scraper and brushed several inches of fine powder off her car with the quick strokes of one used to the task, then returned the instrument.

"I'll walk. It's not far."

"Are you sure? You're all dressed up and everything."

"I like the cold air." He needed it. "Thanks anyway." As she slid into the front seat, he picked up the hem of her coat before closing the door. With a wave, he turned, shoved his hands in his pockets and started down M Street.

When he rounded the corner, he stared up at the snow-covered slope where he and Jeff had sled down every winter. Every muscle in his body tensed, and he broke into a sweat even as he breathed icy air into his lungs.

Reese had envied his brother, as he'd envied all the natural-born children in the foster families in which he'd lived. Every night, he had wished to have been born into their lives, instead of his own, born into a family where he belonged unconditionally, instead of being passed around like a collection basket at church. Instead of having to sing for his supper, the threat of being out on the streets looming around every corner.

He had wanted an unattainable dream—not the reality in which he now found himself. But now, it was too late. Too late to thank Jeff for being the best brother a guy could have. Too late to tell him he loved him.

Too late to repent for the sin of envy.

Now, all Reese could do to repay his brother was to raise Jeff's girls to the best of his ability, as his brother had wanted. And for that, he would do anything.

Even if it meant remarrying.

With a low groan of anguish, he accelerated his brisk walk to a run and didn't stop until he reached home.

The sound of the girls' laughter drifted through the mudroom door. Elizabeth was ten. Nora, eight. Jayne, six. Reese leaned back against the door, stopping to regain his breath before he pulled off his galoshes and heavy coat and entered the foyer in his stocking feet.

"Hi, Uncle Reese!" Elizabeth ran down the staircase, chalky blue goop covering her face. "We're playing beauty salon in your bathroom. Is that okay?"

He smiled, kissing the crown of her head. "Depends on the mess I find when I get up there."

"We'll clean up. Tiffany's giving us facials." His model-in-the-making turned one way and then the other, showing off her wares. "Isn't she the best baby-sitter?"

"Smells like toothpaste."

"It is!" she squealed with delight.

"So maybe you can smear some of that on a toothbrush?" He held up his watch. "Seeing as it's past time for bed…"

"Five more minutes. Please, please, please?"

"All right, all right." He surrendered. "I am such a sucker for a pretty face."

"Why, thank you." She beamed, exposing a row of pearly whites amid the blue paste, before running up the stairs. "Almost forgot." She backtracked two steps. "Grandma called."

Reese stiffened. "She did? What did she say?"

"Nothing much. I told her you were out and you'd be back late. She said she'd call back. No biggie."

He watched Elizabeth dart back into his room, heard the peals of ensuing laughter.

No biggie. Right.

With a grimace, he yanked the bow tie from around his neck.

*No biggie except Grandma wants to take you girls away from me, and I need to find another wife.*

Alex trudged across her snow-covered driveway toward the pale green house illuminated by spotlights. Funny how the outdated appearance no longer bothered her. She and Tom had bought the house furnished at a great price—a "fixer-upper" that required a slew of repairs and renovations.

In the beginning, she could hardly stand to look at the spring-green carpets, rust-colored accents, and other trendy fashions of decades gone by that dominated the house. She started redecorating right away, replacing the furniture piece by piece as they could afford, while Tom attended to more practical concerns such as the antiquated plumbing and ventilation systems.

But all that stopped nearly two years ago. Tom died, and Alex no longer cared about color schemes. Albert didn't seem to mind, and who else was there to impress in the big, lonely house that would never know children's laughter?

"Albert! Here, kitty. I'm home." At the sound of her grand entrance, two glowing eyes appeared at the top of the stairs, and a tabby came bounding down. Purring, he wound himself around her snow-dusted legs. "Aw, did you miss me terribly? I knew you would worry if I didn't come home on time. And not just because I'm your meal ticket, right?"

Alex rubbed his ear, then shrugged out of her coat and started to hang it in the hall closet when she reconsidered. Drifting into the living room, she flung the garment over the back of a yellow and rust, floral-printed sofa.

She'd never been one to tolerate clutter, had been taught from an early age that a cluttered house indicated a cluttered mind. But tonight, for some reason, picking up after herself seemed pointless, the niceties of hanging a coat in a closet a total waste of time and energy.

Who would know if she threw her clothes on the floor? Who would know if the house was untidy?

"Who would know?" She sat down, pulled off her shoes and pitched them into the empty room. She watched as one hit the far wall, leaving a spot on the gold foil wallpaper.

For a moment, both she and Albert stared transfixed on the mark. Then she got up and crossed the room, bent down and rubbed her hand over the smudge. But instead of removing it, she smeared it further. Without further thought, she reached for the wallpaper seam and pulled the tarnished strip off the wall.

"Hmmm…what do you think?" she asked, tilting her head to the side. "I am nothing if not *gifted*."

Albert blinked.

"Oh, lighten up, kitty. You're entirely too rigid." She crumbled the scrap into a tight wad and tossed it across the floor for Albert to chase.

Walking right by the bookshelves Tom had built for her cookbooks, she took a can of soup from the pantry. Where once she prepared fragrant and hearty homemade soups and stews in the winter, she now used a can opener for most of her meals—one can for her and one for Albert.

After emptying his into a bowl and hers into a saucepan, she tossed the cans into the sink, leaving until later the task of washing them out for the recycling bin.

*Simplify if you must, but flagrant disregard for order? Alexandra, you know better.*

Her father's quiet, logical voice rumbled through her

mind—always the steadfast voice of reason. Thousands of miles away yet Alex could still smell the cherry tobacco of his pipe and picture him glancing up from his newspaper, one eyebrow raised in question.

Automatically, she reached for the cans and rinsed them out. She knew better all right—her father had been fastidious in her instruction. Since his wife had died during childbirth delivering Alex, his mission in life had been to impart his wisdom to their only child, his protégé.

From endless theories about the universe's earliest moments to the groundbreaking insights of Niehls Bohr, Marie Curie, and her favorite Albert Einstein, Alex had soaked up her father's teachings like a thirsty sponge. And with every step forward in her intellectual development, she stepped further away from her peer group.

Until Reese, she had only the vaguest inkling what she was missing. Until Reese, emotion had played no role in the physical structure of matter. Until Reese…and the tiny life that had grown inside of her…the tiny life that had been taken away from her much too soon.

Alex gripped the handle of the saucepan and closed her eyes against the ever-present burning of unshed tears. Her father's calm, rational voice echoed in her mind.

*You must work on your will, Alexandra. This flagrant loss of control will be your downfall. A sure sign of weakness. Run along now. Mop up those tears.*

The telephone rang out in the silence of the kitchen. Albert jumped from his now-empty bowl, as if he, too, hadn't expected the disturbance.

"Sorry, kitty. Probably a wrong number." Alex ran a shaky hand through her hair, drew a steadying breath and grasped the receiver on the third ring. "Hello?"

"Alex, are you okay?"

"Reese." Her voice caught in her throat. "Yes, I'm

fine. I was just thinking of… I didn't expect… The phone startled me.'' She snapped her mouth shut and wound the cord around her finger.

''I've got the news on. Skaneateles is getting hit pretty hard. I wanted to make sure you got home okay.''

''I did.'' She kept her voice casual, though the phone cord threatened to cut off the circulation in her finger, and she wasn't so fine or in control all of a sudden. ''I thought it was heavier than usual, but I can't really tell anymore. You know—if you've seen one blizzard, you've seen them all.''

''Six inches in two hours? Not too many of those. Be careful if you're going out again.''

''I'm not going anywhere anytime soon, but thanks…for your concern.'' She wanted to tell him she'd changed her mind about lunch, about having him in her life again. The pain of the past was alive inside her, like an open wound that would never heal.

''Alex?''

''Yes?'' Her fingers clenched around the telephone receiver.

''Thanks again…for everything,'' he said with the slightest note of hesitation…or apprehension, as if he knew what she was thinking. ''It was good seeing you tonight.'' The rich timbre of his voice reached right through the telephone line to wrap around her heart.

*Mind over matter, Alexandra. Mind over matter.*

She bit her lip. Heaven help her, she didn't want to want him again. She didn't wish for this. *She didn't.*

''You, too.'' The truth tumbled out, as if on its own volition. She clamped a hand over her traitorous mouth.

''See you around.''

She nodded mutely, though he couldn't see her, and hung up the phone. She slid her back down the wall until her bottom hit the cold tile floor. She drew her knees to her chest, wrapping her arms around her legs. Huddling into a ball, she rocked back and forth.

"Albert, I'm sorry. You have to leave for a minute." She tossed his favorite catnip toy into the dining room and closed the door behind him.

The tears began in silence, running unchecked down her cheeks to dampen her face. Sniffles followed, punctuated by short gasping sobs. And finally, hiccups.

In the shadowy darkness of the kitchen, where no one could see her and no one would know, Alex lost her already-precarious battle for control.

She cried for the lonely, isolated girl of her youth, and the shell of a woman she'd become. She cried for her six-year marriage to a man for whom she'd felt nothing more than platonic affection, and for the tragedy that had taken his life. She cried because ignorance was bliss and knowledge was crippling, because in two hours' time she'd rediscovered everything missing in her life and everything she'd tried so hard to deny she'd ever wanted.

And when her muscles grew stiff with the bone-deep pain of abandoned hopes and dreams, she cried for the babies she would never conceive.

And for the baby she had.

Reese hung out in the back of the auditorium until Alex finished the last minute of her lecture. As the students filed out, he treaded up the aisle like a salmon swimming upstream. Stopping in front of the overhead projector, he waited for Alex to look up.

She wore a navy blue cable-knit sweater with a matching turtleneck and a long, tan corduroy skirt, the tips of her boots peaking out from under the hem. Despite her casual attire, she had an air of sophistication that set her apart from the common man or woman, made her come across as unapproachable. No students hung around after class to ask questions, not even with finals in a week.

Occupied with the task of gathering her transparencies, she didn't notice him for several minutes. When she finally glanced up, her eyes brightened. "Reese. I didn't see you. How long have you been here?"

"About a minute. I didn't want to make you nervous if I showed up for your lecture."

"I would have been," she admitted lowering her lashes.

His stomach hitched in a knot. On the surface, Alex might have appeared a woman who lived her life on autopilot, merely going through the motions, existing without living. But her eyes told a different story, an occasional glimpse suggesting something vibrant and alive hidden in those enigmatic depths, something that begged to be set free.

Or so he'd thought.

He should have known better than to act on the subtle shift in Alex's behavior that night. He'd spent four long years trying to ease her out of her scholarly shell, and some inner voice had whispered, "Tonight's the night."

He shouldn't have listened. He wished he hadn't. Because one thing had led to another, and in the end, the only one whose reserve had cracked wide open was him. And that had scared him more than anything else.

Never before had he needed someone so desperately—never before and never again.

The stale air in the auditorium felt suddenly asphyxiating.

"How about that lunch? Unless you've already eaten. It is kinda late, but I thought you could meet the girls."

Her expression turned apprehensive. "Today?"

"Yeah, they're coming home to change for dance, and

I need to get out of this suit before my class." He carpooled twice a week with a woman who worked part-time at the same law firm and had asked her to drop him off on campus today. The firm wasn't his first choice, but they were so desperate for good people, they allowed flexibility in schedules.

A match made in mutual desperation.

"I—I don't know if I can make it today." She pursed her lips. She did that a lot when she was thinking—pursed her lips just short of a pucker.

The expression made him think, too. About things he didn't want to think about, things that probably never even crossed Alex's mind.

Reese told himself he didn't care. He couldn't *afford* to care. They were colleagues now. Any renewed friendship would remain just that—friendship.

"I'm going to head over. You know where to find the place if you decide to come." He glanced at his watch. "Should be there for the next two hours." Without waiting for her reply, he turned and strode from the auditorium.

Pushing open the outside door, he inhaled deeply, relishing the sharp bite of frosty air. He didn't want to think about Alex's pucker, or notice things like how the sapphire studs on her earlobes matched her sweater. He didn't want to contemplate things that might or might not have lain beneath Alex's exterior. And he definitely didn't want to wonder what else she'd matched that he couldn't see.

His wayward thoughts didn't fall within the parameters of his relationship with Alex—past or present.

"Reese, wait!" Alex shouted across the quad, but he was too far away to hear her. Careful not to slip on the ice, she rushed after him, her long French braid bobbing against her back. "Reese!"

He glanced over his shoulder, spotted her and stopped. He wore a long, black cashmere coat, and his impressive stature positively radiated power. She imagined he made a formidable opponent both in and out of the courtroom.

"This doesn't qualify as changing my mind, I'll have you know," she said when she'd caught up with him. "You didn't wait for me to make it up in the first place."

He didn't say anything but reached for her book bag and slung it over his shoulder along with his soft briefcase.

Their gazes met and held for an instant before returning to the sidewalk where they navigated over the snow and ice that had accumulated since the last shoveling. They walked the length of University Avenue in silence, past snow-covered tennis courts and around the corner.

He was angry with her. She could tell. With Reese, there were two kinds of quiet: quiet companionable and quiet angry. This was the latter.

"I, um, I know I didn't say this before," she said, taking his extended arm as she stepped over a patch of ice. "But I've always envied your people skills. You…you've always been so good—reading people, knowing what they want, giving them what they expect. I understand things up here." She tapped her temple with her gloved finger. "And in here." She indicated her heart. "But something's lost in the translation."

"Analysis paralysis." Reese nodded. "That genius brain of yours tends to overthink things, so you psyche yourself out."

"Maybe I could sit in on one of your classes? See how you do it? I'm up for promotion in spring, and lecture's my weak link."

He shrugged. "Anytime."

A few more blocks, and they came to the tree-lined street where Alex had lived her entire childhood and grown into adolescence. In the neighborhood where several university-affiliated families dwelled, and houses rarely went on the market, her friends had been few and far between.

Then one summer when she was twelve, right before her freshman year in college, the owners of the house across the street decided to retire to Arizona and sold the place virtually overnight. Soon the Collins family relocated from the other side of campus. Jeff was her age, Reese two years older. Both quickly garnered the reputation of the neighborhood's best athletes.

She recalled a day she'd watched from the sidelines, pretending to read a book as the team captains picked their team members for softball. Reese ran over and plucked her from the curb. He tugged her over to where the other kids gathered, and when they groaned in protest, he insisted he and Alex were a package deal.

"Take it or leave it," he said, already turning for home, his brand-new bat in hand. And because they'd wanted him so badly—not to mention his bat—they grudgingly had let Alex play as well.

As she studied his profile now, her throat tightened at the memory of a boy who had gone out of his way to include the social misfit…and the man he had become.

She sighed and swatted at the branches of a snow-dusted fir. "I wish you wouldn't give me the silent treatment. You know how I hate it."

His gaze flickered her way, and he shook his head. "You frustrate me."

"Well, you're not alone." *And you don't even know the half of frustration, Reese Collins.*

He stopped walking and dropped their bags in the snow at his feet. "Look, do you think I'm out of line, asking you over? Because if you do, just say so. I can't read your mind."

"Out of line? I don't understand."

He blew out an exasperated puff of air, his gaze intense and unwavering. "I look at you, Alex, and it's like the last fifteen years are a blip. I feel like I could pick up right where we left off, but we both know that isn't possible. We aren't the same people anymore.

"But this déjà vu to the nth degree—I can't shake it. I don't know how I'm supposed to act. Like a stuffed-shirt colleague? An old boyfriend? Or a guy who's known you since you were twelve and snapped your training bra?"

She caught her lower lip between her teeth, the sting of the dry winter wind making her eyes water. Were she and Reese so different after fifteen years?

He was still a chameleon, changing his colors to adapt in any environment. How she'd envied his uncanny ability to blend into any given surrounding. She knew too well the struggle of trying to meet expectations...to be the desired child, friend, spouse...to measure up to someone else's yardstick.

And for those very reasons, she still cringed at the thought of being the recipient of Reese's misguided sense of duty. She didn't want him to have to adapt—not around her. She wanted him to be himself—the person he became when everyone left, when he was alone in bed at night. That image had fueled her teenage desires...and haunted her for the past week.

She'd never told him back then, could never show him. Not when he didn't feel the same way. Not when he regarded her as just a friend. Not when she plain didn't know how.

No, it was easier to pretend she didn't care, to hide behind a cloak of indifference, to avoid risking her heart.

It was a double standard.

"I want you to be you," she told him now. "Just have

patience with me, okay? You know I have trouble—'' She gestured with her hand in an effort to find the right word.

"Communicating?'' he supplied.

"Yes.''

"Expressing yourself?''

"Yes.''

"Eating messy food in front of me?''

She pulled her scarf over her nose and mouth. "This is so unfair. There must be some statute of limitations on how many old vices you can bring up within seconds of each other.'' She wagged her finger at him. "If you were a true friend—''

Reese laughed and picked up their bags in one fell swoop. "Save the lecture for your students, Miss Priss. Let's get moving before we turn into Popsicles.''

"Call me Miss Priss one more time, and I'm going to start calling you—''

"Your Honor?'' He looped an arm around her shoulder to prod her along. "I kinda liked it when you used to call me that.''

"It was sarcasm.''

"Nah, you were flirting. Admit it.''

"You're still a pain,'' she mumbled under her breath, folding her arms as she started down the street.

"What's that, Alex?''

"I said I have a pain.''

"Uh-huh. That's what I thought.'' He glanced down at her and winked, a broad grin on his face.

She scowled back. But inside her a warmth unfurled, one that took the bite out of the winter chill as they walked in silence—the companionable kind—down the street.

"Looks like everyone has their decorations up.'' She noted the trees in the windows and the houses lined with lights. "I love all the red and green everywhere. I know," she quickly added. "You'll have to take my word for it."

Reese stared at her with equal measures of wonder and disbelief, as if she were someone near and dear to him who'd returned from the dead. "You remembered I'm color-blind."

She nodded. In truth, she was pretty floored herself by all the things she remembered. Small things she hadn't thought about for years rushed back with vivid clarity, as if they'd happened only yesterday.

She saw her own childhood home first. A big, white colonial with dark green shutters. Reese's house was on the other side of the street—a large English Tudor with a cobblestone chimney.

How many times had she escaped there? Whenever the walls threatened to close in on her and her father's over-protective nature bordered on oppressive. She had always known she could run away, run to Reese, and his smile alone would lift her spirits.

To her, his house had always felt so warm, friendly and inviting. She never realized how good Kitty Collins had been at keeping up appearances, for Reese had never given Alex any indication. She had found out on her own. And she'd never forgotten.

"Thanks." She stepped through the wooden gate Reese held open for her and proceeded up the front walk.

"Watch your step."

"I'm fine," she said the second before she started to slide on the icy pavement.

His hand shot out and grasped her elbow, steadying her before she lost her balance. Without asking, he guided her to the front door, making sure she didn't slip.

He had the most impeccable manners of anyone she'd ever known—not "good breeding" in a snotty sense, but a certain politeness that permeated his personality. A constant awareness of others, a deliberate effort to see to others' comforts, to put their needs first.

He'd been that way for as long as she'd known him, and she remembered how his behavior had surprised her at first. Her father had never done ''the little things'' for her, nor had she for him since she didn't know any better, so Alex wasn't used to it.

''Sorry it was so slick,'' Reese apologized, releasing her arm to insert the key into the lock. ''I didn't have time to salt this morning. I hear that song *Wipeout* in my mind every time I leave the house.'' He shoved the door open and gestured for her to precede him. ''I can't believe you commute from Skaneateles when you could crash at your dad's place in the winter.''

''It's not so bad.'' She stepped into the mudroom. ''Of course, I would have told you differently the other day when it took me over an hour to get home.'' She shrugged out of her coat, and he took it from her, hanging it beside his on one of six bright-colored pegs.

Now Reese Collins had always looked good in everything, anything and nothing, but today he wore a finely tailored, navy blue suit and a blue-and-yellow striped tie. Blue and yellow were his favorite colors since reds and greens bled into browns.

Her gaze swept over legs that seemed to go on forever, before settling on the tasseled dress shoes at his feet. He could have passed for a professional model, yet he seemed unaware of the full impact of his magnetism with women.

''…not even when the weather's nasty?''

''Hmmm?'' At the tail end of Reese's question, Alex lifted her gaze, having forgotten the subject.

''Your father's place.'' He hitched his chin toward the

house across the street. "You don't even stay there in bad weather?"

"Well there's Albert, of course." She rubbed her arms, knowing her cat wasn't the only reason. "Oh, I don't know." She lifted her shoulder. Like so many emotions, she didn't know how to explain the stifling claustrophobia or echoes of "rules" that still followed her from room to room. "I guess I feel like a kid all over again whenever I'm there."

Reese grinned. "You were never a kid."

He was right. She'd had the body of a child, the intelligence of an adult, and the maturity of neither. A stranger in a strange land, she'd never fit in with other kids of her age, nor with adults. Only with Reese had she ever felt at ease.

Not normal—she could never be that—but accepted, for who she was. Even when he teased her, it wasn't as though he was laughing at her. Rather he was trying to get her to laugh with him. And it always seemed so important to him, as if he measured his entire self-worth by his ability to make others happy.

Maybe he did, but she'd never wanted him to "perform" for her. She never would have forced him to assume a role he wouldn't voluntarily have chosen—a fact on which Kitty Collins had never missed an opportunity to capitalize.

"So how does it feel living here again?" Alex asked, bending down to unlace her boots.

Reese shrugged and shucked his own shoes with little effort. "It's the girls' home now—the only one they've ever known. Need a hand?" He'd obviously noticed her struggle to remove her remaining boot.

"Yes, please." Flushed, she smiled in embarrassment. "I'm not too good at this when I'm standing up."

''Hold the doorknob,'' he instructed and reached for her extended foot. ''Ready?''

''Ready.'' She gripped the brass knob, expecting him to yank the boot off her foot. Instead, he held her calf in his left hand and with his right, wiggled the heel until it slipped off her stocking foot. Automatically, she curled her toes.

Reese dropped her foot on his hard thigh, but he didn't let it go. ''Cold?''

She nodded.

In response, he cradled her foot with both hands and began to rub. Vigorously. Heel, arch, toes. Every inch massaged with his strong fingers until Alex felt the ensuing warmth of his touch through her ragwool socks.

Out of nowhere, the sensations escalated. His bowed head was so close she could have reached out and threaded her fingers through the dark locks of his hair. The familiar touch of his hands fueled a long-suppressed need hidden deep within her.

*Her need for him.*

Awareness hit her like a jolt of electricity, sending currents dancing up her leg. Her eyes widened, and her lips parted as she sagged against the doorknob, an ache unlike any other rippling through her limbs.

''Enough,'' she said in a weak voice that sounded far too breathless, even to her own ears.

''What?''

''I—I think that's enough.'' She retrieved her foot, unable to look at him. ''Thanks.''

''Sure. Door's open. Behind you, Alex.''

''Right. Oh. Okay.'' Her hands fumbled on the knob. She spun around and pushed into the house, stopping short at the barrage of once-familiar sensations that assaulted her.

The ceramic tile at her feet. The crystal chandelier two stories above. The curving staircase with its polished mahogany balustrade. The smell of cinnamon, cloves and firewood. All reminders of winters at the Collins's house. Reminders of Reese. Reminders of wanting and needing, of things she could never have. And things she could never forget.

"It's exactly the same," she whispered.

"Not quite. Take a look in here." Reese gestured toward the family room.

With hesitant steps, Alex followed him, trying to calm her reeling senses. She took a deep breath and braced herself for the last sight she'd had of the Collins's home.

She was a grown woman. She could handle this. She could. She poked her head inside and nearly stepped back.

The room looked nothing as she remembered. Different carpet and furniture, what she could see of it. Books, toys, games, newspapers—all in disarray, as if a tornado had swept through. A Christmas tree stood in the corner, trimmed with an array of handmade ornaments—so different from the perfectly trimmed, artificial one Kitty insisted made for better cleanup.

Alex pointed to the blankets covering a cluster of chairs and assorted tables on their sides. "Nouveau decorating?"

"Yeah, we call it early twenty-first century indoor fort *à la* Collins."

"I don't have to repeat that, do I?"

"I don't think I could."

"Good, so what is this?"

"This," he indicated with a flourish of his hand, "is the Play Zone. Nothing's ever in order until someone loses a shoe. Only then do we clean up. House rule, though I admit to deliberately hiding a shoe on occasion. That's between you and me, okay?"

"Mum's the word." She stifled a laugh. "Your mother would die if she saw this."

Suddenly, his easy grin faltered, and a look of anguish crossed his face before he could hide it.

Beside him, Alex tensed. She recognized that look from long ago. She'd spent enough time watching him, observing his behavior. She had known when something was wrong, when she glimpsed the shadows no amount of charm could conceal. Only she'd never known how to broach the subject.

*You could have tried the direct approach.*

Alex swallowed and rubbed a clammy hand down her skirt. "What's wrong, Reese?"

"Nothing, Alex." The words slid off his tongue so easily. Too easily. Years of practice.

Her gaze narrowed, but at that moment, a door slammed, and from the mudroom came a chorus of "Uncle Reese! We're home! Hello!"

His eyes lit up, and a wide grin spread across his face. "They're home."

"I heard," she said, bemused by the immediate change in his expression.

He crossed the foyer and flung open the front door, his arms spread wide. The girls hurled themselves at him, chattering nonstop, each recounting the highlights of her day. Reese smiled and nodded, and though Alex doubted he could follow all three threads of conversation at once, the girls obviously basked in his attention.

After a moment, the littlest one noticed they weren't alone. "Who's that?" She pointed one short, chubby finger at Alex.

"That," Reese replied, grasping her finger, "is my friend Alex. Why don't you come in and say hello instead of *pointing* at her.'' He growled and pretended to bite the errant finger.

''Uncle Reese!'' she squealed with laughter, yanking back her hand. ''Hi, Alex.''

Greetings followed from her sisters as they spilled into the foyer, slamming the door shut behind them.

''Elizabeth, Nora, Jayne, meet Alex. Alex, my nieces, in descending order.''

''Hi,'' Alex said, her voice strained. ''It's so nice to finally meet you.'' Her gaze eagerly sought and soaked up every little detail, from their heads to their toes. Overwhelmed by a sudden barrage of maternal instincts, she crossed her arms to suppress the urge to touch their cheeks and count their fingers and toes. ''You're every bit as beautiful as your pictures,'' she told them. ''More.''

''So are you,'' Elizabeth said. ''You're the same Alex who used to live across the street, aren't you?''

''That's me.''

Reese frowned. ''I don't remember telling you that.''

''You didn't. Dad did. I saw pictures.''

Alex couldn't decipher the expression that crossed Reese's face in the instant before it disappeared.

''So, your Uncle Reese says you're off to dance class this afternoon?''

They nodded.

''What kind of dance do you take?''

''Jazz.'' Elizabeth spun across the tile in an eclectic dance move.

Nora hesitated then pirouetted in her sister's wake. ''Ballet,'' she said softly, her gaze skittering away.

''Tap.'' Jayne bounced up and down as she flashed a grin that revealed two missing front teeth.

''Three very distinct personalities,'' Reese summarized.

''I can tell.''

Jayne cupped her mouth and leaned toward Elizabeth, who had stooped to scrounge around in her book bag. "I like her hair," she whispered loudly enough for everyone to hear.

"So tell her," Elizabeth returned, shaking her head.

"I like your hair." Jayne beamed.

"Thanks." Alex self-consciously tucked a stray lock behind her ear.

"Uncle Reese, can you do my hair like hers?" Jayne pointed, then quickly curled her finger into her fist and grinned from ear to ear.

"That French thing? Are you nuts? You're lucky I can do this much." He tugged her plain braid.

Alex took a step forward, clasping and unclasping her hands. "I'd be happy to do your hair for dance class."

"Now don't let them bamboozle you—"

"No, really. I don't mind."

"Yes!" Jayne exclaimed, grabbing Alex's hand midair and swinging it. "Uncle Reese, you watch her and then you can practice on Heidi again, like you did—"

"Uh, Jayne," Reese interrupted, covering her mouth in obvious embarrassment. "I'm sure Alex doesn't need to hear about my shortcomings in the hairstyle department."

Jayne pried free. "It's not his fault," she explained, holding up her uncle's hand for prominent display. "See, his fingers are too big."

Alex nodded, trying to keep a straight face. "I can see where that would be a disadvantage. So who's Heidi?"

"My doll. She's got long, long beautiful hair just like yours. Uncle Reese says he likes long—"

"On that note," Reese tried again. "Anyone hungry?"

"Me!" came the chorus.

"Well, let's hustle then." He clapped his hands. "Gotta get fed, dressed and packed before Dr. Rothermel gets here. Move, move, move. Carpool,'' he explained to Alex as the girls ran for the kitchen. ''The Rothermels have three girls, too, and we often do slumber parties after dance.''

Alex nodded and wrapped her arms around her stomach as a bittersweet longing pulled deep inside her.

How many times had she wondered how Reese would have reacted had she confided in him all those years ago? As she stared into his proud eyes, she knew without a doubt—he might not have wanted her, but he would have wanted their child.

The daughter Alex had lost.

# Chapter 3

"Oh, Al-ex," Reese called from the kitchen. "Could you come here for a minute?"

They'd eaten chicken-salad sandwiches and apple slices, after which the girls had gone upstairs to change into their dance clothes. Alex sat at the table in the breakfast nook where she'd just finished braiding Jayne's hair.

"Coming." She got up and walked into the kitchen when the small hairs on the back of her neck rose in recollection of the way Reese had drawn out the syllables of her name. In times past, such a pronunciation precipitated trouble, and Reese's mischievous grin served as confirmation.

"Oh, no." She held up her hands to ward off his approach. "Whatever it is, no."

His grin widened. "Why, Alex. You have such a suspicious nature."

"You're up to something. Whenever you say my name like that…"

"Really? And here I thought I was being subtle. So much for old techniques, huh?" He pulled a tin from behind his back, opening it to reveal a mound of chocolate chip cookies. "These are for you. We baked them last night."

"Oh, Reese." She shook her head, recalling the last time he'd exploited this particular weakness of hers and the utter lack of control with which she'd gobbled up the sinful delights. She could still taste the chocolate on her lips, feel the silken texture of the morsels against her tongue. She all but sagged against the counter.

"Is that a yes?" He took a step forward.

She took a step back. Attempting to raise her gaze to his in silent protest, she got as far as his mouth and the easy grin she had never forgotten.

With a start, Alex realized her subconscious had stored away other details, such as the texture of his mouth against hers and the taste of him on her lips.

Out of nowhere, long-lost sensations spiraled back to her, rendering her once again frozen, unable to move or react. Helplessness suffused her as she remembered that night—one of unbearable pain and unmistakable pleasure as she'd teetered on the edge of losing control, hanging on by sheer force of will.

*Mind over matter, Alexandra. Mind over matter.*

"I—I can't." She swallowed, backing away another step. "Really." Her breathing had grown labored at the memory. "I…I won't be able to stop," she voiced the truth she'd always feared. Not about cookies but about Reese.

"We'll make more," he offered.

She shook her head and clasped her hands together.

"All right, then I'll just put a few right here on this napkin, in case you change your mind." He broke off a piece and popped it into his mouth, his eyebrows dancing up and down in mock suggestion.

Alex forced a nonchalant smile that belied the shifting and settling inside her. As a boy, Reese Collins had made her yearn for things she couldn't name, much less imagine. As a man, his appeal had only magnified. And as a woman, Alex knew exactly what she wanted—even if she still had no idea how to express it.

*This flagrant loss of control will be your downfall. A sure sign of weakness, Alexandra.*

She could no sooner squelch the voice that held her back than she could deny her fear of the truth in its admonition. What would happen if she lost control so completely she could never pull herself back together? What if she made a fool of herself in the process? What if there was nothing left afterward, not even a tiny scrap of pride?

She couldn't risk it, not when she'd finally achieved the steadfast discipline she had pursued for an entire lifetime. She couldn't sacrifice the fruits of her labor. She *had* to resist the temptation—the unbearable lure—of that very first bite.

"Alex?" came a soft voice from the entryway. Nora stood there with a hairbrush and ponytail holder in her hand. "Could you please braid my hair, too?" she asked, a note of hesitation in her voice.

"Yes, of course." Welcoming the distraction, Alex gave what she hoped was a warm smile. She took the handle of the proffered hairbrush in one hand and with the other scooted the napkin on the counter in Nora's direction. "Would you like a cookie?"

"No, thanks. Uncle Reese said he's going to get you to eat messy food in front of him again by hook or by—"

"Uh, Nora." Reese made a slashing motion across his throat.

"Whoops." She covered her mouth with both hands and suppressed a giggle. "Sorry."

Alex shook her head. "That's all right, Nora. Your uncle Reese has already made his intentions perfectly clear. He gets an *A* for effort."

"Don't you like cookies?" Nora asked.

"Oh, I like them. I like them too much—that's the problem."

Nora giggled. "Like Angelica. She loves cookies."

"Angelica?"

"A cartoon character," Reese supplied.

"Oh." Alex nodded, wondering how it felt to be part of a family with children, to watch cartoons and understand all the inside jokes only families shared.

"We'll make more." Nora parroted her uncle's earlier-spoken reassurance verbatim.

"This is a plot, isn't it?" Alex's gaze shot to Reese. He leaned against the kitchen counter, casually hooked one ankle over the other and appeared to inspect something on the ceiling. She half-expected him to start whistling to complete the "don't-look-at-me" ensemble.

He'd changed into faded jeans and a flannel shirt with a small, blue-and-gray-checkered pattern, the swirl of colors matching his eyes almost exactly. The top two buttons of his shirt remained undone, revealing a white thermal undershirt underneath. And the sight of his muscular, denim-clad legs made her fingers tingle.

Dangerous. He was every bit as dangerous as those innocuous-looking chocolate chip cookies. Both threatened her control—once she started, she could never get enough.

"All right. Come on, Nora. Why don't we sit at the table?" she offered with a determined smile, gripping the hairbrush a little tighter.

Cookies forgotten, Nora returned her smile with a shy one of her own. "Can you make it like yours?"

With sudden clarity, Alex realized Nora was nervous, and the realization brought a lump to her throat. She'd spent her entire life studying and trying to emulate the social patterns of others—the way they walked, talked, dressed. Never once had anyone wanted to emulate *her* in any way besides her mind.

"I'll do my best," she promised, gently reaching around to lift Nora's chin to a conducive angle. "Stay right there for me, okay?"

When she released her hold, Nora remained steady.

"Perfect. Let's see what we can do with all this beautiful hair."

Nora ducked her head, but the curve of her smile raised the apple of her cheek which she couldn't hide.

Alex began with three sections, trying to focus her attention on the task at hand. As with Jayne, it was difficult at first to braid someone else's hair, even though she did her own every day. But soon enough, she got the hang of it and deftly wove the soft strands.

As with Jayne, she tried not to think about another little girl who might have grown up to ask Alex to braid her hair, tried not to imagine what she would have looked like, sitting in the chair in front of her. Tried not to imagine Nora was that little girl, or that she was her mother.

Tried and failed on all counts, for Alex couldn't help but mourn the simple mother/daughter rituals she had always wanted but would never have. Nor could she help a pang of bittersweet envy for the precious gifts Reese had received in his happy, healthy little nieces.

"There." She secured the braid with the elastic band. "Now, since you're taking ballet, your teacher will probably want to see your neck, so we'll just take this end and tuck it right up underneath.'' She stepped back to survey her work and smiled. ''Oh, Nora. This look really suits you.''

''Really?'' She lifted a hand to the back of her head. ''Is it like yours?''

''It's even better. Go take a peek in the mirror and see what you think.''

''Okay.'' She scrambled out of the chair, then turned around, her face beaming with delight. ''Thank you, Alex.''

Like the first sip of hot chocolate on a cold winter day, something soft and sweet unraveled inside her, warming nerves that had gone numb and stopped feeling long ago.

''You're welcome,'' she said, wrapping her arms around her midsection to savor the sensation as she watched Nora's retreat.

A minute later, a squeal of excitement echoed from down the hall. ''I like it!''

''I'm glad!'' Alex laughed and lifted her gaze.

Reese lounged against the wall, arms folded across his broad chest, a slow grin spreading across his face.

Her own smile froze, and her heart skipped a beat, then thudded erratically. She cleared her throat. ''If you're still thinking of how you're going to get me to eat those cookies—''

''I'm not.''

''Oh. Well, what then? You're looking at me funny.''

''Just noticing.''

A shiver danced up her spine. ''Noticing what?''

''How good you are with my girls, especially the shy one.'' He nodded toward the hallway. ''Nora doesn't come out of her shell for just anyone, you know.''

''Thanks.'' Alex shrugged and held up the hairbrush. ''I

never did any typical little girl things when I was growing up. This was…fun.''

''Can I ask you a personal question?''

Pinpricks of apprehension rose on the back of her neck, but she nodded, more out of curiosity than courtesy.

''Did you and your husband want children?'' His smoky blue eyes probed hers, as if her response mattered to him on a personal level, as if he somehow sensed the secret she'd carried all these years.

But that was impossible. He couldn't have known. Only one other person could have told him, and she wouldn't have dared to implicate herself in the process.

Reese had a right to know about their baby—he'd always had that right. But if ever Alex was going to tell him, the time had come and gone over a decade ago. She'd had her reasons then, as she did now, and though they differed, the outcome remained the same.

She couldn't tell him what happened, couldn't heap sorrow upon a man who had known enough pain and loss in his lifetime. Nor could she face the possibility of his blame, when the burden of her own weighed like a ton of wet sand at the bottom of her heart.

There, she carried the guilt, remorse and anger she had never expressed to another soul—not even her cat. And she never would—even if she could—because once the pieces of her broken heart unraveled, they would fragment into so many tiny bits, she would never, ever retrieve them.

''I always wanted children,'' she confessed with a sad smile. ''Unfortunately, fate had other plans.''

''Leslie didn't want children. I didn't think I did either until—''

The peal of the telephone cut him off, but he made no move to answer it.

"Go ahead," Alex encouraged. "I'm not going anywhere."

"You sure?" At her nod, he caught the receiver on the third ring. "Mom. Hi. What a surprise to hear from you," he said, but his tone contradicted his words.

Alex went ramrod straight, envisioning the woman on the other end of the phone. Her hands gripped the sides of the chair. She held herself perfectly still, hoping if she didn't move, didn't make a sound, Reese wouldn't mention her presence.

"Your ears must've been burning. Alex and I were just talking about you earlier."

Her hands started to shake.

"Alex Ricci, who else? Do we know any other Alexes?" An excruciating pause.

A cold bead of perspiration trickled between her breasts. She could picture the expression on Kitty Collins's face, her practiced smile faltering for a moment, then curving right back into place.

"Yeah, I know we haven't seen each other in ages." He glanced at Alex and winked.

She forced her own smile and clamped her hands together. She recalled how Reese's mother had brought her flowers at the hospital and told her she'd made the right decision. *Decision,* as if she'd had a choice instead of an ultimatum. *Right,* as if good had prevailed over evil.

But then, Kitty had made her preference known even before Alex's medical complications came to light. And the irony of condolences from a woman who had urged her to give up her child made Alex retch the first solid food she'd eaten in days. Even now, her stomach still roiled at the memory of that visit.

"Hey, Mom?" Reese switched the receiver to his other

ear. "I'm sorry to cut you off, but this isn't a good time. Can I call you back tonight?"

Alex shook her head, motioning to the door.

Reese nodded emphatically, gesturing for her to stay put. "What was that? No, I haven't checked yet, why?" His face suddenly turned ashen.

An eerie silence filled the room as Reese closed his eyes and raised a hand to his forehead.

"All right," he whispered. "Yeah. Bye." He hung the receiver in its cradle.

"You…you didn't have to get off on my account."

"No." He combed his fingers through his hair before turning to her. "I had to get off on mine. You just gave me an out. Thanks." That look again. Pain and regret.

"What's wrong, Reese?"

"Nothing, Alex." He shoved his hands in his pockets. "Nothing I can't handle."

A car honked outside, and the thudding of little feet echoed from the foyer.

"Sit tight a minute. I'm going walk the girls out and check the mail."

"Okay." She forced a smile but couldn't help the knots in her stomach as she wondered what screw Kitty Collins had turned to cause the change in her son's behavior.

Reese opened the mailbox to find a large envelope awaiting him. He tore it open, knowing the contents full well. Even then, he couldn't stop the sharp bite of anger that ripped through him when he yanked out the custody papers.

*How could she do this?*

With a vicious oath, he slammed the mailbox shut and raised his arm to chuck the envelope as far as he could throw it, but he knew it would only come back down.

In some remote corner of his mind, he had hoped it would all blow over, that she wouldn't really go through with it, and life would go on uninterrupted.

But life never turned out the way he planned.

Reese tipped his head back and stared up into the gray winter sky, inhaling deep lungfulls of frosty air. As a kid, he'd always believed once he became an adult, things would change, and he would gain control of his fate. But time kept proving the more things changed, the more they stayed the same.

He turned his gaze to the house, envisioning Alex sitting inside, waiting for him. With weary steps, he trekked back to the mudroom and methodically removed his boots. He hung his coat and pushed into the house with every intention of proceeding to the kitchen, only to collapse onto the fourth step of the staircase.

He didn't know how long he sat there, holding his head in his hands, before he sensed her presence and glanced up.

She stood in the foyer, her eyebrows furrowed. She didn't say anything at first, just looked at the envelope in his hands, then up at him.

"I...I should go." Her voice held a note of hesitation as if she'd deliberated saying something else.

He nodded. "Thanks for coming."

"Thanks for inviting me. Your girls are great."

"They liked you, too."

"Maybe...we could get together another time?"

"Yeah." Reese clamped down on his jaw. He didn't let on to the possibility his days with the girls were numbered.

Alex clasped her hands together and started for the door, then paused and turned back to him. "Did you know," she asked very softly, "I could see your front door from my bedroom window? See, there." She drew aside the drapery and pointed to her childhood home. "It helped me sometimes to know you were so close, to know I could come over here if I wanted. You had such a knack for saying the right thing, and I...I always wished I could do that for you."

She let the curtain fall away and turned toward him, one hand outstretched. "Reese, if there's anything... I know I don't have your gift, but I can listen."

"Thanks." He dropped his gaze to the envelope, telling himself he didn't want Alex to listen, didn't want someone to talk to, someone to confide in.

He wanted to be alone, to work through his problems, to deal with things on his own, in his own way, as he always had. Before Alex. After Alex. Here and now.

Hadn't experience proven time and time again there was only one person he could count on when the going got tough? Only one person who would never leave, never send him away when he screwed up?

People came and went. Only the man reflected in the mirror every morning remained his companion through thick and thin. All these years, he'd never allowed himself to need anyone else. Not his brother. Not his ex-wife. No one. It was the only way he could shield himself from the eventual and inevitable loss, the only way he could survive, walk away intact, if not unscathed.

The front door creaked open, followed by the swish of Alex's corduroy skirt. It wasn't until the door creaked shut that something tightened in Reese's gut.

Alex never left him. He left her.

He pinched the bridge of his nose and squeezed his eyes shut, but it didn't help. Nothing would. Not when the solution to his problem had just walked out the door.

"This is crazy." He sighed in disgust, but when he opened his eyes and raised his gaze, he realized Alex hadn't left. She stood with one foot in the mudroom, her hand poised on the doorknob, her gaze locked to his with electric intensity. He shook his head in an attempt to break the spell, but it didn't work.

"What the hell's going on?" he asked, more to himself than to her. "We haven't been friends for fifteen years."

She gave him a wobbly smile and raised her shoulder in a delicate shrug. "It doesn't feel like fifteen years. It hardly feels like fifteen minutes. It feels like I should put my boots on and run across the street before my father realizes I'm not in my room."

He swallowed, unable to form a coherent thought as the reality of her words gripped him by the throat. He tore his gaze away and stared at the envelope clutched in his hands.

"Goodbye, Reese."

He closed his eyes and gripped the envelope tighter. "Don't go." The words sounded thick and hoarse on his lips.

The door banged shut, and for a moment, Reese didn't know whether to feel disappointment or relief that she'd left. But when he glanced up and saw her standing there, her presence felt like a balm.

"She wants custody of the girls," he confessed, unable to keep the truth from her any longer, unable to resist the appeal of having someone to talk to, someone who would listen—someone who was everything he swore he didn't need.

Later, he would kick himself. Later, he would put up every damn barrier known to man. But for now, he'd release the vise around his chest one measly notch, just enough to catch his breath before it tightened again.

"Your mother?" Alex's eyes widened.

"Yeah." He raked a hand through his hair. "Now that

the divorce is final, she's given up hope of a reconciliation.''

"I...I don't understand. She really liked your wife."

"Not so much Leslie as her *female influence.* My mother doesn't think a man should be raising three girls alone, and I can't say I don't understand where she's coming from."

"With all due respect, Reese—that's possibly the most absurd statement I've ever heard. Granted, I've only spent an hour watching your interactions with the girls, but it's obvious to me you're managing quite well on your own."

"For now. But what happens when they're teenagers? I mean, never mind dating—I already told them *that* wasn't going to happen until their thirties. How's a guy supposed to deal with that woman stuff? I get hives just thinking about it."

"You learned to braid hair, didn't you?"

"Right. And look who they preferred." He crooked a grin and waved his hand at her, but she didn't return his smile. If anything, her expression grew more serious.

"Those girls adore you, Reese. Anyone can see that."

"Yeah, well, it's mutual. That's why I can't stand the thought of turning their lives upside down. Not when they're starting to get their sea legs back. You should have seen them after Jeff and Karen died. It's been a long, hard trip, getting to this point."

"You can't let Kitty raise those girls. You know Jeff wouldn't have wanted—"

"I know." Reese clenched the envelope in his fist. "I know. But unless I..." His gaze dropped, and he shifted uncomfortably under the weight of hers.

"Unless you what?"

He didn't answer, didn't know whether or not to tell

her, didn't want her to think she was his only option. Because she wasn't. She couldn't be. Not again.

"Reese, if there's anything I can do, anything at all—"

"No, Alex." He met her gaze directly. "There's nothing."

She pursed her lips. "I see. So what's in the envelope?"

With a sardonic grin, he raised the item in question. "Custody papers. She drew them up last week. Sent me a copy to sign. That's why she called. Remember, the folks are lawyers, too. We could all sue each other until global warming eliminates winters in upstate New York."

Alex shook her head. With short, brisk steps, she bridged the distance between them, leaned over the steps, and snatched the envelope from his hands.

She withdrew the sheaf of papers and flipped through the pages, her expression one of mounting outrage. And then, like a car downshifting, her expression went back to neutral.

"I can't believe this," she said, her voice steady though her hands trembled.

"What's not to believe? She's got the girls' best interests at heart."

"No, she doesn't," she whispered between her teeth, the undertone of vehemence surprising him. "She just has a really convincing way of making you believe she does."

He had to pry the papers from her ice-cold hands, as if her fingers had frozen around them. "Since when did you develop an aversion to my mother?"

"Since I finally saw her as a whole instead of the sum of her parts."

"What's that supposed to mean?"

"Nothing." She waved away the change in subject, but the uncharacteristic tone he'd heard in her voice churned his stomach.

"Alex, did my mother say something or do something to you that I don't know about?" He wouldn't have put it past her. His mother had a way of burning people with her sunshine.

*Do you have any idea how fortunate you are, Reese? You shouldn't even be here. You shouldn't be living and breathing. You shouldn't exist. Yet here you are.*

His mother's voice played like a broken record in his mind. It was his fourteenth birthday, and she'd given him a new ten-speed bike earlier that day.

"I haven't seen her in years." Alex crossed her arms and nodded toward the envelope. "What happens if you refuse to sign? Do you think she'd actually take this to court?"

"It's not going to come to that."

Her gaze narrowed, searching his. "You have something in mind. What is it? What are you going to do, Reese?"

He drew a deep breath and expelled it with a hiss. "Remarry."

## Chapter 4

Reese's one-word reply sounded terse and clipped, even to his own ears, so he wasn't surprised when Alex's eyes went wide as saucers.

"I don't have a choice," he explained. "My mother's right—"

"*Your mother* is a fraud."

The bottom fell out of his stomach, as if she'd tripped the lever of a trap door he had hidden beneath the carpet, sending him spiraling into the dungeon.

"Alex, what exactly do you know about my mother?"

She bit her lip and appeared to struggle with indecision. Finally she said, "I know she's an alcoholic."

Reese shuddered and closed his eyes.

"After you left, I happened to stumble in on happy hour. Your father tried to intervene, but Kitty was..."

"A mean drunk," he finished, the scene playing in his mind's eye like a bad rerun. "Her...episodes weren't all that frequent, but once she got going..."

"She couldn't stop."

He nodded. "She's been sober since Jeff died."

"Bully for her." Alex's smile didn't reach her eyes, and he had the distinct impression she knew something more than his mother's closet alcoholism.

He drew a breath and braced himself. "What exactly did she say to you?"

She looked away. "Nothing worth repeating."

Panic reared up and kicked him in the throat. He studied her face, looking for any traces of revulsion, anything to indicate his mother's loose lips had sunk his ship, but there were none. Only anger. At his mother.

Whatever disparaging remarks she might have made about him, Alex hadn't bought them. Relief sluiced through him as a death row prisoner handed a reprieve.

"I'm sorry, Alex. I never wanted you to see that side of her."

She nodded. "I've read that families of alcoholics seldom speak about it, even among themselves."

"It's true. My father would put her to bed, and the next day, she'd be fine, and we'd all pretend nothing had happened." It was easier that way, easier to pretend his mother loved him as she loved her real son, that she hadn't truly said all those ugly things about him.

"Just tell me one thing…" Alex's voice trembled, and she rubbed her arms, as if bracing herself. "Your chicken pox scars… Are they…from her?"

He always suspected she'd questioned his canned explanation for the cigarette burns, but he could honestly say, "No, Alex. Neither of my parents was ever physically abusive." Not his adoptive ones.

She relaxed somewhat, then stiffened again. "It was only verbal then." He nodded reluctantly, and she drew her arms tighter around herself. "I am so sorry for what you and Jeff must have gone through…"

Not Jeff. Just him. He was the one who'd always needed to earn his keep.

Reese gave a wry grin. "Don't sweat it. Like I said, it didn't happen all that often. I've survived worse."

She opened her mouth as if to speak, then closed it again and pursed her lips. Unspoken questions still hung between them. She wouldn't ask about his past, knew the subject was off-limits. But those brown eyes continued to search his, looking for answers he would rather die than cough up.

*Don't look too deep,* he wanted to warn her. *You won't like what you find.*

Her nostrils flared. "I'll never forgive her."

"You don't have to."

"Let her sue, Reese."

He shook his head. "I can't."

"Why not?" She narrowed her gaze. "Because you feel an eternal debt of gratitude to her for taking you in?"

He jerked back as if he had a bull's-eye painted on his forehead and Alex had thrown the winning dart.

"I'm sorry." She closed her eyes. "I didn't mean to say—"

"What you were thinking?"

Her gaze dropped to her boots and stayed there, as if she found something incredibly fascinating about them.

Reese blew out a breath. "In answer to your question, I'm not going to fight her for two reasons. One, I don't want to drag the girls through a custody battle, even if I know the outcome—I won't do that to them. And two, can you honestly tell me that as close as you are to your father, you've never yearned for a mother?"

She frowned and crossed her arms.

"I didn't think so. That's why I intend to rectify the situation—my way." He hitched a thumb toward his chest. "My mother and I both have the girls' best interests—"

"Please, spare me." Alex winced and held up a hand, as if to shield herself from the sight and smell of dirty socks in a gym locker. "I can acknowledge your desire for a female influence for the girls, but let's be clear on one thing. Your *mother*," she enunciated, "isn't doing this for the girls. She's doing this for *herself*.

"Maybe she's lonely down there in Florida, and she wants her grandchildren around. Maybe she's taken a cold, hard look at her life and noticed something missing." Her words were slow yet purposeful, with an edge Reese had never heard before.

"She is missing her son. She took Jeff's death pretty hard, like the rest of us. But it doesn't seem to have gotten any easier for her."

"The guilt." Alex nodded, as if she understood from personal experience. "Even though she had little choice, little control over her child's death, I'm sure it still eats at her as a mother year after year." Her eyes took on a distant look, and her arms curled around her stomach. "You wonder what you could have done, what you should have done to prevent it."

"Makes sense."

Her gaze snapped back to his, once again sharp in focus. "Just remember, there's a reason you have custody and not her. Your brother wanted it this way."

He squinted and rubbed his temple. "Not to belabor the point, Alex, but I was married then."

"Marriage cannot be your only option," she shot back, a deep crease between her eyebrows, her jaw set in a firm line of determination.

Reese could almost hear the hard drive of her computer-like brain as it whizzed through different combinations and permutations in an attempt to break some hidden code, crack the safe, find a miraculous solution.

"Don't blow a fuse. I've already found the feasible set. With a sum total of one, even I can figure out the solution." He dragged a hand through his hair. "There's no other way, Alex. If I want to avoid a custody battle *and* provide them with a female influence, I have to remarry."

"Sleep on it," she implored. "You'll think much clearer in the morning."

"I've been sleeping on it for over a month. It's not going to get any clearer than this." He raised the envelope, then flung it across the foyer with a sigh of disgust.

Alex watched it skitter across the floor, then turned to Reese. "I suppose you'll ask a girlfriend then?"

He crooked a weary grin. "You offering?"

"I am asking," she clarified in a clipped tone, "if there's someone in particular you have in mind."

He leaned back against the carpeted steps, bracing his weight on his arms. "No, Alex. There's no girlfriend."

Something flickered in her eyes, almost imperceptibly. Something that looked surprisingly like relief. Then just as quickly, it was gone.

"So, you'll have to find one." She shrugged, but her rigid posture contradicted her show of indifference. "How hard can that be for you?"

Reese raised an eyebrow. "Flirting again, aren't you?"

She glared at him.

"No? Oh, well. Wishful thinking." He winked.

Alex's hand fluttered to her throat, and she turned toward the window. "I know what you're doing. Don't think I don't. You're trying to knock me off balance because you don't like sitting in the hot seat. You'd rather have me there, so you say these things…even though you don't mean them…when we both know I'm hardly your type.''

She had that right. She never had been his type. Too studious. Too serious. Always trying to get into his head, instead of laughing at his stupid jokes, like the other girls.

Even now, she still saw too much. Knew just where to poke, where to prod. Knew the chinks in his armor existed, even if she didn't know the exact locations. Not to mention, her uncanny ability to hog-tie him in the damned hot seat.

What the hell had he been thinking, inviting her over, inviting her back into his life? For all intents and purposes, he'd cut his losses and moved on. Now here he was, starting up yet another tab, like a guy who'd finally managed to pay off his credit cards only to celebrate with a shopping binge that landed him right back in the hole again.

*Anyone but you, Alex. Anyone but you.*

She turned slightly and crossed her arms. ''I suppose you have a little black book or something.''

''Uh…'' Reese tapped an index finger to his temple, feigning an attempt at recollection before responding with a curt, ''No.''

''Don't take it personally. I just imagined you might use some kind of system to keep track of all the women.''

''All *what* women?''

''The ones who came before and after your marriage, I'm sure. You hardly lacked for companionship in high school. I had trouble keeping up with the names of your girlfriends back then—there must have been a new one every other week. I can't believe you'd actually slow down in college, or that you wouldn't pick back up after your separation.''

He stared at Alex's impassive profile. She was like a human video camera, seeing and recording the world around her with little or no interaction. Even if she didn't understand the mechanics behind the actions and reactions, nothing slipped by her camera lens.

He neither confirmed nor refuted her conjecture—she was right about college but wrong about the past year.

"I don't want a girlfriend, Alex. This isn't for me—it's for the girls. They need a permanent fixture in their lives— nothing transient, nothing conditional." *No one who will leave when they mess up.*

"A permanent fixture. I see. And are you planning to use that for the opening line of your personal ad? You know." With one hand, she indicated the "headline" of an imaginary newspaper. "That catch phrase in bold, capital letters. *Permanent Fixture Wanted.*"

"Look, Alex. It's not your problem. I wasn't even going to tell you—"

"Of course you weren't going to tell me." Her voice rose a notch. "Do you have any idea where you're even going to find this wife?"

"I don't know." He shrugged. "A holiday party? Can you fix me up with any of those women you were talking to?"

She fixed him with a glare as dirty as any he'd ever seen from her. A few huffs and puffs to go with the flaring nostrils, and she'd make one hell of a fire-breathing dragon.

"What?" he demanded, trying to figure her out. "Why are you giving me the evil eye? Look what I found last time." He hitched his chin toward her. "Maybe I'll get lucky again. Third time's the charm. Damn." He snapped his fingers. "May have to go to a few more parties."

Alex bit her lip and turned back to the window, her hunched shoulders rising and falling with every breath. "You joke at the most inopportune times."

"Hey, I'd rather laugh than cry, and I figure those are my options at this point."

She didn't respond. In the reflection of the glass, he saw her close her eyes briefly, read the tension in her rigid posture. It had been a long time since anyone had worked themselves into a furor on his behalf. He remembered the last time as if it were yesterday—Alex's outrage at his suspension from school.

She was different that day, the fire in her eyes unmistakable. She was alive and vibrant and more beautiful than he'd ever remembered. His own personal cheerleader, the only one in his corner. He hadn't been able to resist the change in her, hadn't been able to stop himself. He'd wanted desperately, and he'd taken without thought of consequences.

*Like father, like son?* He'd always wondered, like so many other unanswered questions about his natural parents.

Reese levered off the staircase and walked across the foyer, coming up behind her. Her long braid hung down her back, framed between her slim shoulder blades, the curl at the bottom a few inches above her waist.

He started to reach out, then hesitated, deliberating whether or not such an action could be construed as crossing the line. Finally, he dropped his hands to his sides.

"Alex, don't do this," he said quietly.

"Don't do what?"

"Don't get bent out of shape on my behalf." *Don't make me care for you. Don't make me want you, need you this time. It can't happen again—I won't let it.* "You offered me conversation. I took you up on it. But this isn't your problem."

"I know it's not. I know." She glanced over her shoulder, gnawing on her lip and looking too damned much like the girl he once knew, the girl who would have done anything for him if he'd asked.

Even if it was something she hadn't wanted.

He didn't want to deal with this…whatever this was…already happening between them again. He hadn't meant to stir things up, but he had, and now he had to walk away.

Before she did.

But when he should have stepped back, he raised his hands to her shoulders. And when her muscles tensed beneath his palms, he flexed his fingers, holding her in place, kneading at the stiffness until gradually, she eased up.

For a moment, he could have sworn she subconsciously leaned into his touch before she righted herself again.

"Alex…" He lowered his hands to the sides of her upper arms and turned her around to face him.

As a teenager, she'd barely come up to his chin, and now she appeared even shorter, her nose about even with his breastbone. She stared straight ahead, and he carefully reached for her chin, lifting her head. He wanted her to look at him, but she shifted her gaze, first left then right, anywhere but him.

"Alex, please." He hated the twinge of desperation in his voice, hated the way she made him vulnerable in a way no one else ever could.

She frowned and bit her lip, raising her gaze to his as if with Herculean effort, as if it pained her to do so.

Reese remembered how she had frozen up on him on that night long ago, how no amount of coaxing had helped. In all fairness, his coaxing skills had vastly improved since then. But still, he wondered…

Was it his imagination that she'd wanted him, or had she changed her mind at the last minute?

As if in response to his silent question, Alex winced and

closed her eyes. The familiar tightening of rejection closed his throat, and he let his hand fall away when in a flash, her eyelids fluttered open.

Something changed, shifted in some minuscule way, as it had that night, and Reese found he couldn't pull away as he'd intended. Her eyes searched his face—his eyes, his nose, his mouth. Slowly, he watched the transformation. Her eyes darkened, her breathing turned shallow and her eyelids hooded with an almost drowsy quality.

Reese's gut clenched in response. On any other woman, he would have interpreted her actions as desire. And when her lips parted, he felt the slow burn of temptation ignite low in his belly. Damn if he didn't want to lean down and taste her, to tilt that mouth upward and slide his tongue inside, to see if she was still as sweet as he remembered.

But this was Alex, and he had mistaken her actions before. He now knew better than to lump her into a category with any other woman, knew better than to lull himself into a false sense of security around her.

Reese swallowed and forced the words past his lips. "I don't want to involve you in this any further."

She blinked and stepped back, her gaze skittering away. "I see."

He could have let it go at that. He could have let her believe whatever she believed, instinctively knowing she was wrong. He could have leveraged the misunderstanding and forced her out of his life again.

And he could have lived with the memory of her face, of the pain she tried so hard to hide, for the next fifteen years, as he had for the last.

"I don't think so." He reached out and caught her arm. "Alex…" He blew out a heavy sigh and dragged a hand through his hair. "You were my best friend," he admitted with wary reluctance.

She smiled then, really smiled for the first time since
he'd seen her again, and it hit him like a blow to the solar
plexus. "You were my *only* friend, Reese."

A fierce jolt of possessiveness slammed through him.
Without thinking, he yanked her into his arms—one quick
tug, but she didn't hesitate. She wrapped her arms around
his waist, her cheek against his chest, her hands against
the small of his back.

He closed his eyes and drank in the heady rush, like an
old, favorite beer. Too good. Way too good.

"Damn," he whispered.

Once, he'd believed she was safe, that their friendship
posed no threat. Until the night he'd held her naked body
in his arms. And then, he'd realized she was more dangerous to him than any.

If he wasn't careful, she would sneak under his skin and
rub up against his soul. She would burrow so deep into
his mind, he would never be able to get her out. His need
for her would become crippling, something he could never,
ever allow to happen. And yet, in that moment, he knew,
beyond a shadow of a doubt.

Alexandra Ricci was his worst fear and his only hope.

He swallowed convulsively, wrenching the words free.
"Marry me, Alex."

With a whimper akin to pain, the body in his arms went
rigid as a wet sheet hung out to dry in a subzero Sycamore
windchill. He closed his eyes, remembering the last time
he'd evoked the same reaction. No doubt about it—in desperate times, Reese Collins was a selfish bastard.

She pulled back, the slumberous quality vanished from
her eyes, replaced by a laser-sharp precision. "Beggars
can't be choosers, can they?"

He winced. "That didn't come out right. I didn't plan
this, Alex, I swear. I wasn't even going to—"

"I know you weren't. I *know*." She clenched the material of his shirt in her fists, as if she wanted to shake him, only she didn't—merely held on as if her life depended on it. "You'd rather die than ask me, but you don't have a choice. You have an obligation to the girls, and I'm your last hope."

He didn't say anything. Neither did she. He felt her knuckles press against his abdomen, felt her deathgrip as surely as if her slim fingers had wrapped around his throat and cut the flow of oxygen. Could she feel his heartbeat thudding like a jackhammer?

By gradual degrees, she detached herself from his shirt, smoothed a hand down her hair and gave him a tight smile, her usual reserve back in place. "I have to go."

With a choice profanity, Reese shoved a hand through his hair. "Alex, I'm sorry."

"I know you are." With a halfhearted smile that didn't reach her eyes, she shook her head and turned for the kitchen. "I changed my mind." After a minute, she returned to the foyer with the tin of cookies tucked under her arm. "I seem to be on a roll here."

Reese frowned. "Did I miss a segue?"

"In for a penny, in for a pound," she said by way of explanation, only her explanation made no sense to him. "I'll return the tin. Thank you and goodbye."

He swore and followed her into the mudroom. Without a word, she reached for her coat. Reese grasped the collar and held up the sleeves for her to ease into them.

"Talk to me, Alex. Please."

She frowned and plucked her boots from the corner. He lent his knee, so she could tie the laces. She gave him a wary glance, then propped her foot on his jean-clad thigh, her lips pursed in a tight line.

"I don't believe this," he muttered. "You get on my

case for the silent treatment and now this. Can't you wag your finger or something?''

No response.

''Tell me I'm a jerk for not talking to you for fifteen years, for trying to waltz back into your life like nothing happened in between. Tell me it's outrageous, Alex. Tell me you would never consider marrying—''

''You're a jerk for not talking to me for fifteen years.'' She nodded in agreement, removing her second boot from his knee. ''For waltzing back into my life like nothing happened in between. It's outrageous.'' She closed her eyes. ''So outrageous I can't believe I'm even considering it, so get away from that door and let me leave right now, before we both say things we're going to regret.''

His hand froze on the knob. ''You're considering it?''

''*Right now,* Reese.''

He turned the knob, and a gust of bone-chilling wind assaulted them. He felt nothing. ''Did you just say what I think you just said?''

''Yes. I mean, no. I mean, get out of my way. I'm leaving. Goodbye.'' She shoved past him, cutting through the snow to avoid the icy walkway.

*She was considering it?*

Heart pounding, Alex ran across the street and up the snow-covered steps to her front porch. Not *her* front porch any longer, she reminded herself, placing the tin of cookies between her feet as she searched her bag for the house keys.

Wafts of steam rose from her nose and mouth. She couldn't seem to catch her breath, could feel Reese's gaze on her back and wanted nothing more than the temporary shelter of her father's house.

Impatiently, she jostled the bag, hearing a jangle from

all the way at the bottom. Rooting through the contents, she grasped the key ring, found the right key and steadied her hand to slide it into the lock. Inside, she slammed the door shut and collapsed against the wooden barrier, her chest heaving up and down.

*Alexandra, where have you been? Don't you have a presentation to prepare?*

Just like that, she was sixteen again, her father's voice ringing in her ears. Sixteen and more in love than words could express with the boy across the street. The boy who made her palms sweat and her heart race. The boy who thought of her as just a friend.

The boy she could never have.

*Marry me, Alex.*

She drew a sharp breath and raised a trembling hand to her lips. She could still feel his big, hard body beneath her hands and smell him in her clothes—clean, like soap and shampoo and something else, something she'd smelled before when her face pressed against his skin, something that was totally his.

She remembered the first time she'd ever been close enough to notice, the time they'd gone camping at nearby Mallard Lake. It was right before her fifteenth birthday— she had just finished her undergraduate studies, and Reese, then seventeen, his junior year in high school.

Alex's father was away at an out-of-town conference, and Reese had made only the vaguest of references to the attendees of the overnight excursion, allowing his parents to think it was a few of his basketball buddies.

They had stolen away on a Friday afternoon, with the euphoria of two teenagers playing grown-ups. Only after nightfall, with the falling temperatures and lumpy ground, had Alex wished they had settled for a day trip.

''The ground's shaking with your shivering,'' Reese had

whispered in the darkness of their pitched tent. "You're not asleep, are you?"

"Not even close."

A deep sigh. "I'm sure I'm going to regret this." A long pause. "You want to get in here with me?"

"Yes." She bolted out of her bag and climbed into his, without any thought past her cold and his warmth.

"Great," Reese muttered, folding her into his arms. "Typical Friday night. Most guys are out with their girlfriends, trying to get to third base in the back seat of their dad's car. But not me. No, I'm a lucky guy. I'm roughing it with my best friend. Any warmer there, Alex?"

"Umm-hmm." She snuggled closer, pressing her face to his neck.

"Glad to hear it. Say, can you maybe turn the other way?"

"Umm-hmm." She wiggled around, turning her back to him as she pressed against his warmth.

"Thanks." His voice was unusually curt.

For long minutes, she held herself perfectly still and tried to fall asleep, but the ground was so lumpy she could already feel bruises forming. She shifted a little, but it didn't help. She tried again, but to no avail. One more time—

"Alex." Reese's voice sounded like he was clenching his teeth. "Are you warm enough now?"

"Yes, but—"

"Then quit squirming and go to sleep."

"I'm trying. It's just the ground's all bumpy, and there's a rock in my back." She wiggled and reached behind her, her hand finding and wrapping around the hard object. At Reese's swift intake of breath, she froze, her eyes going wide in the dark.

"Alex," he all but yelled. "Move your hand before I evict you from this sleeping bag."

"Sorry." She yanked back her hand and folded it under her chin, her body as rigid as the rock that wasn't a rock.

Reese gave an exasperated sigh. "It's not your fault. Just stop squirming, and it'll go away."

"O-okay."

Alex's cheeks felt hot at the memory. She could still remember how she had felt that night, sleeping in Reese's arms, her body pressed so close to his. Every nerve ending in her body had buzzed alive, literally hummed for the first time, awash with wild, crazy needs she couldn't put into words or even coherent thoughts.

Not then.

Then, she'd been too young to understand, too wrapped up in a world of numbers and scientific proofs to pay attention to the changes in her body, to acknowledge herself as a woman—not in any biological or genetic sense, but in the way her body responded to a man's.

Not just any man's.

No, she'd had fifteen years to ponder that primitive yearning, to wish she had never known it, to pray she could get it back one day...all the time knowing only one man had ever made her feel those things.

The man who had just asked her to marry him.

*To marry him.*

Alex dropped her bag in the foyer, grabbed the tin of cookies and raced for the staircase. She took the steps two at a time. At the end of the hallway, she opened her bedroom door and peered inside.

It was exactly as she'd left it. Not an item out of place. Three walls of floor-to-ceiling bookshelves, a loft-bed over a mahogany desk, a burgundy leather couch, and an armchair. Hardly typical of the average child's bedroom, but then, Alex had never been average.

For several long seconds, she stared at the once-familiar room, the "library" in which she had grown up, in which she'd spent countless hours "absorbing knowledge."

Gone were the canopy bed with the white lace fringe, the matching comforter and curtains, the pink-and-white striped wallpaper. Gone were all remnants of the little girl who had been diagnosed as gifted at age four.

But one look at her bedroom, and Alex confirmed what she had always known: She wasn't gifted, she was cursed. She had accepted her fate long ago. And now, to wave the impossible dream in her face...

She shivered and hugged the tin closer. With brisk steps, she crossed to the window and stared outside. At the familiar Tudor across the street, at the view etched in her memory forever. Of ordinary people living ordinary lives. Of all she'd wanted and all she could never have.

*Marry me, Alex.*

She lowered herself to the window seat and curled her legs beneath her. How many times had she sat here, staring out this same window and imagining those exact words on Reese's lips?

The impossible dream...only this was no dream.

Reese needed a female influence for the girls, a wife for the sole purpose of retaining custody. He'd made it quite plain she was the last woman on earth he would have chosen, but he didn't have a choice. He was marrying for the girls, not himself.

It didn't matter that she wasn't his type, that she never had been and never would be. He didn't want *her* but what she represented—a means to an end.

Marriage to Reese would never be the real thing—she'd known that as a teenager, pregnant with his child.

To him, she would always be the girl-next-door. He might treat her like a princess, but he would never think of her as more than an obligation. He could never feel anything for her beyond friendship and gratitude.

He would never love her the way a man loved a woman…

With trembling hands, Alex opened the tin and took a cookie from the mound inside. Lifting it to her lips, she took the first bite. Delicious. She chewed slowly to savor the sensations and prolong the end, but the end came too soon, as it always did.

She eyed the tin again, then very deliberately closed the lid and folded her hands. Steeling herself against the inevitable, she drew a breath of determination and sat stock still. After a few minutes, the desire for more abated, though it did not cease.

*Marry me, Alex.*

She turned her gaze to the familiar Tudor, lacing her fingers tighter until her knuckles went white. No matter how many determined breaths she took this time, or how still she sat, the longing didn't lessen in the least.

Perhaps it was her penance to live with the impossible day after day, to have her control challenged every waking second. Because if anyone owed anyone, Alex owed Reese—she couldn't change the past, but she could change the future.

She could ensure Reese didn't lose any more children.

Had the time come to repay her own debts?

# Chapter 5

Reese was losing it. Hands braced on his thighs, he sat on the edge of his bed and stared at the telephone. He wanted to call her. He wanted to give her space.

For all the reasons he'd wanted anyone but Alex, he'd caved under with the realization she represented a known threat versus the unknown threat of a total stranger. He had the girls to think about, not just himself.

True, she made him feel like a bug under a high-power microscope, but he knew her, and on some gut level, he trusted her. Enough to know she wouldn't jerk the girls around as Leslie had—as his mother would—with approval contingent upon "good behavior."

But could he trust her not to leave when her microscope finally revealed him for the true specimen he was?

*She never left you. You left her.*

Fifteen years ago, Reese had made his decision before Alex could make it for him. He'd walked away before she could push him. And he'd stayed away because it made him feel the separation was his choice—not her demand.

She'd never left him because he'd never given her the chance. What would happen if he gave it to her this time?

The phone rang as if on cue, and Reese's jaw clenched in reflex. His fist hovered in the air an instant before coming down on the receiver.

It stopped midring under his hand.

He released his grip and drew his feet up on the bed. Stretching out, he leaned his head against the headboard and listened, every muscle in his body tense and alert.

Not a moment later, "Uncle Reese! Grandma's on the phone!" Elizabeth bellowed at the top of her lungs.

His mother. Not Alex. He should have guessed as much.

Eyeing the phone, he braced himself and lifted the receiver. "Hi, Mom. Sorry I couldn't talk earlier."

"No problem, dear. No problem at all." Her voice held a strange undercurrent. "So how is Alex?"

"She's fine. She's still Alex."

"I'm sure you had a lot of things to catch up on…"

Was it his imagination, or was his mother subtly pumping him for information?

"What did you two talk about after all these years?"

So much for subtle. "Mother." He stared at the phone, wishing he could see the expression on her face, so he could get a read on her.

"I was just wondering." She laughed, a hollow tinkling sound. "Nothing earth-shattering, I take it."

His mind went to the custody papers shoved in the kitchen drawer, and he gripped the receiver tighter. He had nothing to lose by telling her. At the least, he could plant the seed, stall her plans and buy himself more time.

Reese cleared his throat. "Actually, I asked Alex to marry me." Silence. "Mom? You still there?"

A delicate cough. "Tell me I'm hearing things."

"You're not."

"Reese, don't you think this is a little...sudden?"

"We've known each other twenty years."

"You can't count the gap."

Not the reaction he'd expected. Reese frowned at the telephone. His mother had always liked Alex. She'd sung praises of her genius to the point where he and Jeff made gagging gestures. It was *her* idea for Alex to tutor Reese, insisting, "*B*s won't get you into the college of your choice," when she really meant the college of *her* choice.

"Alex is hardly a stranger, Mom."

"I realize that," she snapped.

"What's the problem then? Something's obviously bothering you about this."

"You're right. There is. And I suppose I should tell you." A long pause. "I didn't like the idea of you taking advantage of a teenage girl any more than I like the idea of you taking advantage of a widow."

Reese's cheeks stung as if she'd slapped him. "I thought you'd be happy—"

"Happy? To have my son marrying on the rebound?"

He released a short spike of laughter, though the inconsistency of her logic didn't escape him. "Let's get something straight here. Are you worried about Alex or me?"

"Both."

"Then let me reassure you I am *not* on the rebound."

"Fine, that doesn't change the fact she's still a recent widow. This doesn't look good, Reese."

"To whom?"

"To everyone. People are going to talk."

"Let them."

"Think of the girls, Reese."

"I have. They like her. A lot. And it's not like the grave's still warm, Mom. It's been two years."

"Yes, thank you for reminding me."

He punched the pillow in exasperation, then forced himself to calm down. No point defending something that wasn't a done deal. "She hasn't said yes."

"Well, thank goodness for small miracles." His mother sighed dramatically. "We'll discuss this in person, Reese. Your father and I are flying up in two weeks for a wedding in Skaneateles. We get in Friday night. We leave Sunday morning. We're staying at the Sherwood Inn. I'll fax our itinerary. In the meantime, why don't you invite Alex to dinner Friday night." An order, not a request.

"I'll pass, thanks."

"Reese, really." She sounded incredulous. "She lives right down the road. I'd *like* to speak to her before you go through with this."

"To ask her intentions?"

"Something like that. I'm hanging up now," she announced, followed by a click.

Reese dropped the receiver into the cradle and stared dumbfounded into space for several long moments. He was never going to figure his mother out—aside from the fact there was no pleasing her. That much he knew.

But something else bothered him, something his mother had said that struck home. He *had* taken advantage of Alex that night. And now, in asking her to marry him, he was doing the same damn thing all over again.

He'd conveniently put Alex's point of view on the back burner. But the pot had started bubbling again with his mother's accusations. The reality that surfaced made Reese see the critical ingredient missing from his logic.

Quid pro quo—something for something.

He sprung from the bed and gazed around the room in

bewilderment. How could he overlook something so obvious? He and the girls might have needed Alex, but what could they possibly offer in return? So she liked the girls. Enough to be saddled with them for a lifetime?

A hollow, sinking sensation washed over him. For as long as he'd known her, Alex had but one goal in life: the ruthless pursuit of higher learning. She'd chosen the steadfast role of the observer, and no amount of persuasion could change her into an active participant.

She had no reason to compromise her lifestyle, no reason to sacrifice her routines, no reason to forsake precious hours away from her livelihood.

No reason to stick around for the long haul.

Reese sank back onto the bed and flopped against the pillows, one arm slung over his head. Back to square one.

"Oh, Uncle Reese!" a small voice piped up. "Where art thou?"

"In here, Jayne," he called.

She poked her head in the door. Seeing him, she scampered in, dove onto the foot of the bed, and crawled on top of his chest. "Whatcha doin'?" she asked with a big grin, her eyes alight with playful curiosity behind wire-rimmed glasses.

"Nothing much." Reese returned her grin with one of his own, swiftly shifting mental gears so she wouldn't pick up on his tension. "How about you? Wearing Nora's old glasses, huh?"

"Yep, I'm writing in my diary." She plunked the book on Reese's chest with a thump. "Don't I look smart?"

"You always look smart, with and without glasses." He untucked the frames from behind Jayne's ears and eased them off. "It's okay if you want to wear glasses for playtime, but you don't want to wear ones with someone else's prescription in them."

"How come?"

"Because they'll mess up your own vision." He crossed his eyes and stuck out his tongue in mock imitation. "We'll get you some clear lenses in here."

"And then I can wear them?"

"Then you can wear them," he promised. "So how come you want glasses all of sudden, anyway?"

"I dunno." Jayne shrugged. "Elizabeth showed me and Nora a picture of Alex when she lived across the street, and she was wearing glasses. Daddy told Elizabeth that Alex was smart. What does it mean when it says induce vomiting if swallowed?"

Reese bolted upright, knocking both Jayne and her diary off his chest. "Did you swallow something, honey?" he asked, propping her into a sitting position. "It's okay if you did. I just need to know." He tried to keep the panic from his voice as his hand automatically went to her stomach, ready to flip her over.

Jayne frowned. "I didn't swallow anything. I just don't know what that means...induce vomiting. Nora doesn't know either, and Elizabeth said I can't come in unless there's blood—she's doing homework."

"And you're *sure* you didn't swallow anything?"

She shook her head and opened her mouth.

Reese peered down her throat. "Because you know, you wouldn't get in trouble if you did. You'd get real sick though. That's why I'd need to know, so I could help you. You understand?"

"Yes, but I really didn't. I just copied the label from the laundry soap. I'm writing big words in my diary, so I can sound smart. See." She showed him where she'd written the term, running her finger along the words as if they were raised dots of Braille.

Reese hugged his niece with a sigh of relief, feeling as

though he'd aged thirty years in thirty seconds. "You are smart, Jayne. You are one smart cookie. And your daddy would have said so, too."

"Really?"

"Really."

She grinned, her tongue lolling to the side.

"Okay, let's see what you have here." Reese turned the diary toward him. "Induce vomiting means 'make someone throw up,' so if you'd swallowed that stuff, we'd have to make you puke."

"Oh," Jayne said with a pensive nod, then, "Ew, gross."

"You sure?" He poked her belly. "We could do it just for kicks."

"No!" she squealed as she jumped from the bed.

"Hey, I forgot to tell you. Grandma and Grandpa are coming to visit."

"Goodie!" she exclaimed before disappearing.

Yeah, goodie. Reese slumped back on the bed, one arm slung over his head.

Alex drew a breath of determination and entered the classroom. Reese wasn't there yet, so she made her way to the back row. Unlike her huge, theater-style lecture hall, the small classroom with its three rows of concentric horseshoes afforded nowhere to hide. Would the students notice a stranger in their midst?

"You're new." A perky brunette in a dark green parka answered Alex's unspoken question as she took the seat beside her. "Thinking of taking this class next semester?"

"Oh, no." Alex pulled a spiral notebook and a pen from her book bag. "I..."

"You should. It's a great one."

"Is it? Why do you say that?"

"You'll see when you see the professor." She gave Alex a coquettish smile as she pulled off her parka.

At that moment, Reese strode into the classroom, his legs looking impossibly long and far too appealing.

Alex couldn't help the tiny catch in the back of her throat, the shivers that raced up her spine, or the reflexive curl of her fingers over her notebook's spiral.

"Yep" came the voice beside her. "That's just the start."

Great. She finally fit in with a student, and it had to be a co-ed with a crush on her professor. Alex forced a polite smile, suppressed the urge to strangle her newfound companion and slumped down in her seat.

Reese didn't see her right away; but she knew the second he did she could read the startled expression on his face before he covered it up with that trademark easy grin.

"Dimples," the brunette felt compelled to point out. "You gotta love a man with dimples."

"Yep," Alex mimicked, a little too breathlessly for her own liking.

She hadn't wanted Reese to see her until after the class. They hadn't spoken in a week. Had he changed his mind about needing a wife?

Giving herself a mental shake, Alex placed her palms on either side of her seat and straightened her spine. Now wasn't the time to dwell on her personal life. That would come later. For now, she would observe teaching methods—nothing more, nothing less.

Yet a voice in her head asked when she'd ever *had* a personal life to distract her, when her existence had ever consisted of more than tireless study and endless research.

Even her marriage had been an extension of work. She and Tom had collaborated on various research projects with single-minded focus. It was the common interest that brought them together, the bond that held them together.

Only once, long ago, had Alex ever felt there was anything "more" to her than her brain. And only once, had a person made her ache in so many places other than her mind.

"Everyone have a good week?" Reese's voice boomed in the classroom, and the din of chatter gave way to murmurs, grunts and enthusiastic nods.

*Focus, Alexandra. Focus.*

"Great." He leaned a casual hip against the edge of the instructor's table and folded his arms over his broad chest. "I expect everyone's hanging out at Bird Library from open to close, right? Pounding the books, preparing for finals."

Muffled laughter. A few groans.

"Yeah, that's what I thought." He straightened and reached for a single sheet of paper. "So, did *anyone* have time to read the last case on the syllabus?"

A few hands went up. Not nearly enough, in Alex's estimation. Bunch of slackers. She crossed her arms.

"Feinstein. Why don't you brief your fellow colleagues."

Alex noted Reese picked one of the students with his hand raised. She would have chosen from the attendance list at random. Let them sweat a little.

"Okay, so this guy's wife's on her deathbed, and he needs to get her this drug to save her life, only it costs a fortune. No way, no how's he gonna come up with this kind of money. On the other hand, it costs the pharmacists *bupkis* to manufacture the drug—just a zillion percent markup 'cause they got a patent. He's got two choices—steal the drug or let his wife die."

"Excellent brief, Feinstein." Reese nodded. "And very

brief this time. Duly noted.'' He pretended to scribble on his hand.

Chuckles from the students. The two on either side of Feinstein slapped his shoulder and punched his arm respectively. Ah, primitive male bonding rituals.

"So." Reese crooked his head and peered around the classroom inquisitively. "What should the guy do? What would *you* do? And, more importantly, *why?*''

A student in the back row raised his hand.

"Jenkins."

"Question." He appeared thoughtful. "Is it a happy marriage?''

Muffled laughter.

"Yeah, is she a looker, or what?'' piped another student.

More laughter.

Alex rolled her eyes.

"Is she a looker?'' Reese repeated, raising one finger to his lips in careful deliberation, before looking directly at Alex. "She is *unbelievably* beautiful.''

Peals of laughter. A few wolf whistles. Alex stopped breathing.

In that second, she realized what separated Reese from the rest, what had always made him different from the others. It was the way he looked at her. Or rather, the way he didn't. Not as a person looked at a librarian, or a scientist, or any other "expert" or provider of information.

Reese looked at her as a human being, as a regular person instead of a freak of nature with a computer-chip for her brain. And in his eyes, she saw herself as flesh and blood like everyone else, a woman like any other, with the same emotions and desires coursing through her veins.

Alex barely heard the rest of the lecture. She was too caught up in the rapport Reese exhibited with his students, his uncanny ability to involve them in discussion, the way he treated them as colleagues.

Back and forth their discussion went, opinions voiced, challenges flew. Some frowned, some smiled, everyone participated. Every now and then, Reese asked someone to clarify or delve deeper into a particular line of reasoning. Other times, he prompted them in a different direction with a simple question that sent up a flurry of hands.

"All right." He glanced at his watch, and Alex realized with a start the hour had flown by. "Let's recap here. Last week we looked at a few models of moral reasoning. How do today's arguments fit into those models?"

The brunette nudged her notebook toward Alex, revealing copious notes scrawled all over the page. "You can look off of mine if you want."

"Thanks." Alex peered around the room at the notebooks of others and noticed they were much the same.

A vicarious sense of pride warmed her heart. Reese was, quite simply, magnificent.

After class, a few students milled around, lining up to talk to him. Alex lingered a while, then realized she'd likely have to take a number if she wanted any time with him before finals. Fighting her disappointment, she packed her belongings, sidled past the group and aimed for the door.

She didn't get two steps past Reese before he reached out and caught her sleeve. With a raised index finger, he excused himself from the conversation.

"Trying to slip out the back, Jack?" Though his voice was teasing, the expression in his eyes was not.

"No, of course not." Her gaze shifted from him to the students, then back again. "I can see you're busy."

Reese turned to his students, flashed a smile and tapped

his watch. "I've got office hours in twenty-five minutes. Anyone who can't wait until then?"

They shook their heads.

"Great. I'll catch you upstairs." With that, he scooped his papers up in one hand, draped his free arm around Alex's shoulder and steered her out the door.

Alex tried to match his nonchalance and pretend it was the most natural thing in the world for a drop-dead gorgeous man to escort her to the lobby while a dozen pairs of eyes watched on with interest. Once they reached the elevators, she relaxed somewhat.

"Hi," she greeted, a bit belated.

"Hi, yourself." His arm dropped from her shoulder, and he pressed the up arrow. "I didn't expect to see you here."

"You didn't? But you're the one who said… Oh, wait. That was before." Before he'd asked her to marry him. "I'm sorry. I should have checked with you to make sure—"

"Alex." He rubbed the back of his neck. "It's fine. You made me nervous, that's all."

*She* made *him* nervous? The mere notion was so preposterous it made her chuckle under her breath.

Judging from Reese's frown, he obviously didn't see the humor in the situation. "What's so funny?"

"Nothing." She covered her mouth with one hand in a feeble attempt to camouflage herself.

"You're laughing at me!" He looked incredulous.

"With you," she reassured, squeezing his arm. "I'm laughing *with* you."

He glanced down at her hand, then back up, his gaze warm on her face. "In that case, do it again."

At the husky timbre of his voice, Alex dropped her hand and rubbed the sudden gooseflesh on her arms. "Honestly, if that was nervous, I'll have to stop at the bait and tackle shop on the way home to eat worms. You were great. Beyond great. You have such a wonderful rapport with the students. You make it fun for them to learn. Of course, you do have the benefit of a small classroom.''

The bell for the elevator dinged, and the doors slid open. Reese held the door as the bodies shuffled out.

''You have to make your own fun, Alex—large or small audience. All you need is practice.''

''I don't know… I've been practicing for five years.''

''Not with me you haven't.'' He gestured for her to precede him into the empty elevator.

She stepped inside then spun around, coming face-to-face with the wall of his chest. Her gaze swung upward, but whatever words she would have said died on her lips.

In that split second, she could have sworn something flashed in Reese's eyes. Something raw and primitive that reached deep inside her. Something that siphoned the oxygen from her lungs, leaving her light-headed and breathless.

And then, before she could analyze it further, it was gone. Just like that.

Reese crossed to the other side of the elevator, jabbed the button for the sixth floor, and folded his arms. Alex stared down at her feet, the weight of his gaze heavy on her as the elevator rose.

On the third floor, the doors opened to admit a tall, distinguished gentleman with slicked back gray hair. ''Dr. Collins.'' He nodded to Reese and then to her.

''Dean Olicker.'' Reese nodded back.

''Enjoyed your article in the *Stanford Law Review*.''

''Thank you.''

''Miss the west coast?''

''Not really. I've got everything I need right here in Sycamore.'' Reese's gaze went to Alex.

Hers flew to the electronic display over the door, focusing intently on the numbers lighting up one by one.

On the fifth floor, the Dean stepped out. "Take care."

The doors swished closed, and suddenly their quarters felt a lot smaller, their bodies a lot closer, the air much thinner. Alex moistened her lips and willed the elevator to hurry up and reach their destination. At long last, the elevator stopped at the sixth floor, and Reese stepped out, leaning his back against the doors to allow Alex's passage.

"After you," he said simply, eyeing the space between them.

"No, that's okay." Alex swallowed. "Why don't you go ahead, lead the way. I—I don't know where—"

"Left." He smiled—the lazy, sensual smile of a Cheshire cat. "I'll be right behind you."

"Thanks." Alex drew a breath and braced herself as she walked within inches of touching him. She tried not to think about the proximity of his body, the molecules of heat he radiated, the density of the air between them.

Tried and failed on all counts.

Exhaling, she spun around. "I can't do this."

"Do what?" Reese lifted a strand of her hair and tucked it behind her ear.

She swatted at his hand. "Pretend everything's fine, and it's the good old days, when it's not."

He sighed and folded his arms. "What do you want from me, Alex? Do you want me to be your colleague? Your friend? What? I told you before—I can't read your mind."

"Yet you expect me to read yours," she shot back in frustration. "I'm sorry." She closed her eyes and tried for an even tone. "What I want, Reese, is for you to tell me what *you* want for once."

He looked startled, as if no one had ever put the question

back to him, but he covered it up with the smooth flash of a dimple. "I thought that was kind of obvious the other day." He reached for the doorknob to his office.

She caught his arm. "*Nothing* is obvious with you. You're the master of mixed signals. First, you tell me there's nothing I can do to help you. Then, you tell me you plan to remarry but have no candidates. You finally get around to asking me, and then you say you're sorry."

"I was. I am. Damn it, Alex." He raked his fingers through his hair. "This isn't easy—"

"Okay, let me make it easier for you. Let's begin with *what* you're actually sorry about. Is it something in particular, or everything in general?"

"A lot," Reese whispered. "I'm sorry about a lot of things."

"Which tells me *nothing,* as usual. Nice sidestepping, though. You've got that down to a fine art. Anyone ever tell you that?"

"No." He sighed and folded his arms. "No one's ever noticed besides you."

"Yes, well, they tell me I'm smart like that." She frowned and rubbed her temple. "But what I'm really struggling with here is that niggling little question of whether or not you still want a wife. Can you help me out?"

Reese leaned a casual shoulder against the wall and raised an eyebrow. "Nothing's changed, Alex. Are you offering?"

"Yes, Reese," she answered in a breathless rush before she could change her mind. "As a matter of fact, I am."

And for the first time in history, that trademark easy grin slid right off Reese Collins's face.

# Chapter 6

*Holy Mother of Pearl.*

"Yes?" Reese repeated, barely managing to keep the astonishment from his voice. "Did you say yes?" At her nod, he swallowed. "Just checking."

*Yes!*

Like a last-minute upset in the Superbowl, a jolt of unexpected victory shot through his veins. He told himself to play it cool. As if he'd had total confidence in the underdog winning all along. As if he'd had some hot tip the odds were grossly miscalculated, and he hadn't wagered his entire life savings on pure speculation.

*Yeah, right.*

He fumbled for the knob, pushed open the door and jammed his hands in his pockets to hide how badly they were shaking.

"Nice." Alex gazed around his office. It was one of the larger ones and afforded a panoramic view of the campus.

Reese barely noticed. Two years ago, he'd occupied a

posh corner office in one of the most prestigious buildings in downtown San Francisco where he'd had a breathtaking view of the bay. Been there, done that. He didn't miss anything about his former life. Except maybe sushi. On occasion.

He closed the door and considered the woman in front of him, the woman who had at one time been closer to him than any girlfriend, any friend, any family he'd ever had.

"Why?" The single word leapt from his lips. So much for playing it cool.

Alex frowned. "Why?"

Uh-uh. He wasn't buying the befuddled act. If there was one thing he'd never underestimated, it was Alex's methodical, no-nonsense approach to problem-solving. The exact same question must have run its course through her brain, and damn if his self-preservation instincts would let him venture down this path without knowing the answer.

"Why would you marry me?"

"It was your idea, Reese."

"I know that. What's in it for you?"

She lifted a shoulder in a shrug. "Why, to spend the rest of my life with you, of course."

"Of course." He nodded, then shook his head. "Try again."

"Private tutoring. I want you to teach me how to do what you did in there."

"Yeah. Right." Was she out of her mind? Bartering teaching lessons for holy matrimony? Like there was nothing wrong with that picture?

"Well, I should go. You have office hours." She gave a tight smile and attempted to sidle past him.

No way. No freakin' way. It *couldn't* have been that

easy. Nothing in life was *ever* that easy, least of all anything concerning Alexandra Ricci.

He moved to block her path. "Why, Alex?"

"Reese, really. I told you—"

"I know what you told me." He frowned. "I'm waiting to hear something that doesn't insult my intelligence."

Her eyes clouded, and she turned toward the window, her hands clutching the ledge on either side of her. "I want children," she admitted in a small voice. "Preferably with two parents since I never had that benefit. I'm thirty-one years old. I'm not particularly interested in dating, and I'm not getting any younger. My choices are somewhat limited. Actually, they're very limited."

*She wanted children.* Reese turned that piece of information over in his mind and found it didn't quite fit the puzzle. Close, but not a perfect match. She was still holding back on him. He felt it in his gut.

"In fact, you might not be so interested in me as a candidate for motherhood after I tell you..." She glanced over her shoulder, worrylines creasing her brow.

He braced himself. "Tell me what?"

She raised one shoulder in that inconsequential shrug of hers. "You know I've never been...normal. You know how I was raised...like an adult for most of my life. I don't know anything else. You said it yourself the other day. I was never a kid. I don't even know what it means to *be* a normal kid. I can read books on the subject, but I can't relate firsthand."

She was rambling. And fidgeting. She did both those things when she was nervous. And when she was beating around the bush.

"Where's this going, Alex?"

Just then, the phone rang.

Reese closed his eyes. "This is getting to be a habit with us."

"Oh, dear. Would you look at the time." She held out the face of her watch. "Your students will be here any minute. We'll talk about this some other time."

"No." Reese unplugged the phone. "We'll talk now."

"That could have been important."

"So is this. I've got voice mail."

Alex sighed and rubbed her arms. "I just don't know how qualified I am for this role. I don't know what kind of mother I would make. I don't know if I can *be* the kind of mother the girls need…"

Reese shook his head, trying to wrap his brain around what she was saying—more importantly, what she *wasn't.* Women had a tendency to do that—some kind of female conspiracy to make the poor guy read between the lines.

He obviously needed a secret decoder ring because he couldn't tell if Alex was giving him a disclaimer, making a counteroffer, or reneging on the whole box of cornflakes.

"Look." He sat on the edge of his desk and folded his arms. "I don't know where you're headed, but let me tell you something about the other side. When a *normal kid's* separated from his natural parents, he loses the freedom of being normal. The natural source of unconditional love and acceptance is gone, and it's difficult if not impossible to replace.

"No matter how stable your life, no matter how secure, your carefree nature is compromised. You can feel pressure and obligation and insecurity not common to the *normal* kid. So if you're trying to fit the idea of marrying me to a bell-shaped curve with a normal distribution, keep in mind the whole family's a bunch of outliers—not just you."

For some reason he didn't understand, moisture shone in Alex's eyes.

"Impressed I passed statistics?" he asked.

"No, it's not that. It's just..." She shook her head. "You never talk about the years you spent as a little boy."

A sudden heat crept up his neck. "I wasn't talking about me."

She nodded and bit her lip.

"I wasn't," he said with more force than intended.

"I didn't say anything."

"You didn't have to."

One corner of her mouth curved upward. "We could certainly *pass* for an old married couple sometimes."

"Yeah, no kidding." Reese rubbed the back of his neck. "So are you going to confess you overspent the credit card, or what? I'm going to find out, Alex. You might as well spill the beans. I know you're hiding something." His gaze flickered toward the window, certain a bolt of lightning would zap him dead for his hypocrisy any second.

But Alex didn't even try to deny it. Admission was written all over her face. She lifted her hand and appeared to struggle for the right words. "You teach ethics. You know the question, 'If a tree falls in the forest, and no one hears it, did it really fall?' What's your answer?"

Reese shrugged. "If the tree fell, it fell."

"But isn't perception reality?"

"True."

"So if you don't know the tree fell, then in your mind, it didn't happen. And you can go on living your life."

He raised an eyebrow. "You can go on living your life either way, Alex. Unless the tree fell on you."

She sighed and turned away. "This is precisely why ethics gives me a headache. It's far too abstract. There are no right or wrong answers. Everything depends on your reasoning. So I keep thinking, what if I'm wrong? What if my reasoning is flawed?''

"What if you're human after all?"

"Yes," she whispered. "You see, after you left for boarding school, I..." She blinked and shook her head, her face paling. "I can't. Not everything. I just can't."

"Can't what, Alex?"

She wrapped an arm around her stomach as if she was going to heave any minute. "I can't give you anymore children. I had a hysterectomy. I'm sterile."

*A half-truth.*

"Not by choice." Alex felt compelled to add.

"I'm so sorry. I had no idea." He rose from the desk and took a step toward her.

She took a step back. "I—it's not something I usually talk about. I've had a while to come to terms with...what happened, but it's still hard."

Reese's gaze never wavered. Without a word, he lifted his hand to her. A simple gesture. An offer of comfort. Hers for the taking.

*If a tree falls in the forest, and no one hears it, did it really fall?*

*If your baby dies before she's born, but you never knew of her conception, did she really die?*

Alex wrung her hands together. She was wrong never to have told Reese about the baby while she was pregnant, wrong to have made a decision about her life without consulting him. But afterward, was she wrong to have spared him from the grief of her loss? Or was her altruism selfishly motivated, like Kitty Collins's? Was she, too, trying to save face from an unspeakable wrong?

"Trust me, Alex."

*How can I trust you, when I don't even trust myself?*

She took a tentative step forward, followed by another,

until she was close enough to touch him. She stopped and stared at his outstretched palm for several seconds before placing her hand in his. Strong fingers closed over hers, engulfing her in warmth, as Reese eased back down on his desk and pulled Alex forward.

"I can't even begin to understand how you feel," he said quietly. "But I can tell you this. We'll have three girls, Alex, and if you're anything like me, it won't be long before you'll think of them as your own."

*Her own.*

Thickness lodged like a cork in her throat, and she choked back a sob at the bittersweet appeal of helping to raise Reese's girls, the chance to actually be a mother, something she thought was gone forever, banished from the realm of possibilities for her.

Without warning, tears pooled in her eyes, but when she tried to blink them back, a few inadvertently trickled free.

"Ah, hell." Reese brushed the pad of his thumb over her cheek. "I didn't mean to make you cry."

"No, no, I'm not." She hastily swiped at the moisture and struggled for composure. "It's not what you think. It's just that you've always had this knack for saying the right thing." She gave a watery smile and raised her trembling fingers to his mouth.

His lips felt firm and smooth to the touch, and without thought, she found herself tracing the shape, reacquainting herself with the texture.

Reese didn't move, not a single muscle, for the space of two heartbeats. Two long, unsteady heartbeats.

"I don't know how a person manages it time after time." Her eyebrows drew together in equal measures of puzzlement and wonder. "But somehow, you always do." Her hand moved to cup the side of his face.

The touch of her fingers caressing his skin sent a burst

of heat rippling through him. "Alex...?" His eyes searched her face, at once pleading with her to back up, while she had the chance, and urging her to come closer.

But she wasn't looking at his eyes as she leaned forward by slow, aching degrees and brushed her mouth over his. Molten liquid poured through his body at the fleeting contact—a moment of warmth to a man dying of hypothermia. He bit back a groan and clenched his teeth to keep from seeking more.

"Thank you." She drew away to gaze up at him with that slumberous quality that messed with his mind.

She was right. She wasn't his type. And he wasn't hers. They were as different as night and day, orange and purple, salt and sugar. And yet, he was drawn to her, to the promise in her eyes, the promise of mind-blowing passion buried far beneath the surface—a hidden bounty for the man who could draw it out.

When it came to Alexandra Ricci, Reese had always felt like a lone pirate driven in his search of a legendary, sunken treasure no one had ever found—one only he believed truly existed. Not even foiled attempts could thwart his efforts or shake his belief something was out there. Something rare and precious and worth fighting for. He alone knew it, and he wanted it for his own.

No, not for his own, Reese corrected. For the girls. He wanted to tap into Alex's passion for the girls. *They* needed her—not him.

Sudden recognition flickered in Alex's eyes. But when he would have nudged her away, he didn't. And when he would have expected her to retreat, she stayed put. Her gaze dropped to his mouth, and damn if she didn't actually lick her lips.

A white-hot streak of desire surged through him. For a girl who wouldn't have known flirtation if it bit her in the butt, the woman did one hell of an imitation. Part of him rationalized she didn't know what she was doing; the other part wanted to find out for himself.

No, not for himself, Reese corrected. For his parents. *They* needed to believe his marriage was real; therefore *he* had a fiduciary responsibility to see if he and Alex could pull off the charade.

Yeah, that was it—he had to make sure they could fake their attraction, for their families' sake. His hand slipped around to the back of her neck.

"Alex…?"

"Reese…" Her lips parted, and he felt the warmth of her breath, soft and tempting against his chin.

A sudden, sharp knocking at the door jarred them apart like the two teenagers they'd once been, caught in the act. Wide-eyed, Alex backed up several steps, unnecessarily straightening her clothes. Reese rubbed a hand over his face, relief warring with frustration at the interruption.

"Dr. Collins?" The voice on the other side of the door held an undercurrent of urgency. "It's Kristin Santala. I know you're on the phone, but it's urgent."

"The dean's secretary," Reese explained. "What is it, Kristin?"

"It's your niece, Elizabeth. Her school just called. There's been an accident."

In three brisk strides, Reese crossed the room and yanked open the door. "What happened?"

Kristin's gaze flickered briefly toward Alex before returning to Reese. "Nothing life-threatening. She fell and bit her lip. She's in the school's clinic. They think she might need a stitch—"

"Thanks." Reese didn't wait for the rest but shot out the door, making tracks for the elevator.

Behind him, Alex grabbed their coats and scribbled a

note for Reese's students on the dry erase board tacked to
the door. She caught up with him as he gave the elevator
button one last, impatient jab and spun for the stairwell.

"Reese, wait. I think it's here." The down arrow illuminated as if on cue.

He turned, his face pale. "About damned time."

"Did you walk?" she asked, handing him his coat.

"Yeah."

"I'll drive you."

He nodded, clenching and unclenching his fists at his
sides as the elevator doors slid shut. She wanted to say
something to make him feel better, but the right words
wouldn't come. Feebly, she grasped his hand and
squeezed.

"Thanks." He squeezed back, though his expression remained grim. "This is the worst part of parenthood, Alex.
No matter how many spills they take, it never gets any
easier. I get this same sick feeling in my gut every time."

"It'll be okay," she whispered.

He looked down at their joined hands. "I owe you."

Bristling, Alex closed her eyes and withdrew her hand.
She told herself it wasn't her—that Reese felt like he owed
everyone—but it didn't help. She had always wanted to be
the exception, the one person to whom Reese turned, not
out of obligation but genuine desire. She had wanted for
their relationship to be different, for Reese to choose to be
with her because he wanted to, not because he owed her
for some stupid barter trade.

Only once had that ever happened—the day before
Reese left for boarding school. The day his entire life had
crumbled around him, and he'd come to her, seeking comfort.

The day that had changed her entire life.

\* \* \*

For the first decade of his life, Reese had hated the school clinic, to the point where he'd taken extra precautions on the playground and in gym class to avoid careless scrapes and tumbles.

All those nurses with their prying eyes. They could never give a kid a Band-Aid or an ice pack and send him on his way. They had to poke and prod and ask a million questions.

*How did you say you got these bruises, Reese?*

*Fell off my bike.*

*Wasn't that last month? These look fresh.*

*I fell again.*

*Umm-hmm. Why don't you let me take a look.*

*No. No, that's okay. I'm fine. Can I go now?*

Back in those days, Reese had lived in constant fear of a call to social services, yanking him out of yet another foster home. Even in bad times, the monster he knew beat the monster he didn't know hands down. He'd gone from bad to worse enough times to question if "things can only get better" was a prayer or a pipe dream.

But all that ended when the Collins family adopted him. Soon, worries about food, shelter and physical safety turned into things of the past. And after a while, getting sent to the school clinic no longer felt like a death sentence, and no one even questioned his age-old scars.

No one, of course, but Alex.

Whether spoken or not, Alex questioned everything.

Reese turned his gaze from his new fiancée to his eldest niece, one of three reasons he'd ignored his self-preservation instincts and walked straight into the lioness's den. The girls were his priority; he would deal with the rest later.

"Hey there, big girl." He flashed a sympathetic grin.

Elizabeth's red-rimmed eyes widened over the ice pack

she held over her mouth and chin. "Uncle Reese!" She scrambled from her chair and dove into his awaiting arms, clinging to his neck as he lifted her. "Hi, Alex," she mumbled into the ice pack, her gaze darting to the woman at Reese's side.

"Hi." Alex held up a hand in greeting, then indicated the doorway with a nod. "I, um, I'll wait outside."

"How bad is it?" Reese asked, angling for a look.

"It's numb." Elizabeth held the ice pack in place.

"Come on. Let's see."

Eyes downcast, she lowered the ice pack, revealing a small gash under her lower lip that definitely required stitches.

Reese whistled through his teeth. "You know, there are a lot easier ways to get me to let you play ice hockey."

But instead of laughing, Elizabeth's chin trembled. "Is it going to hurt?"

He drew her closer. "Just a tiny bit, like a pinprick. It'll be over before you know it. You can even close your eyes if you want, and I'll tell you when to open them."

"You'll stay with me?"

"Of course."

"You aren't…mad at me?" Her voice cracked, and fat teardrops plopped down her face.

Reese drew back in astonishment. "Mad at you? Why would you think that?"

"Because. You told me to be careful, and I wasn't. And now I have to go to the emergency room and get stitched. All because I was stupid. I can't do anything right."

Her self-derision sliced through his heart. "Now that's baloney, and you know it. You do a lot of things right. If you did any more things right, you'd give your sisters inferiority complexes."

She appeared to consider him, then promptly burst into

tears, burying her face against his neck. For all her outward spunk, of the three girls, Elizabeth rode herself the hardest. Anything less than perfection, and she beelined for the doghouse, convinced she belonged there.

"Elizabeth." Reese lifted her chin and reassured her in the only way he knew, with the words he himself had longed to hear as a boy, "You can't beat yourself up over this. Accidents happen. You don't have to be perfect."

She swiped her nose. "You really aren't mad at me?"

"I'm really not, jelly bean. I'm just glad you're all right. That's the most important thing to me."

"Promise?"

"Promise."

"'Kay." She dropped her head on his shoulder. She wound her arm around his neck, and he held her a little closer, pressing his cheek to the crown of her head.

"Better?" he whispered.

"Umm-hmm." She sniffled. "Can I play ice hockey?"

A chuckle burst from his chest. "Stinker."

"*Your* stinker," she pointed out, an inside joke he and the girls had whenever someone called someone else a name.

"That's right—my stinker." He brushed aside her bangs and dropped a kiss on her forehead. "Would the injured party like ice cream on the way home from the hospital?"

"Yes, please. Can Alex come?"

"She's driving."

"Can she stay for dinner?"

"Maybe."

"Uncle Reese?"

"Hmm?"

"I love you," she whispered, words she hadn't spoken since Jeff and Karen died.

He swallowed around the sudden knot in his throat. "I

love you, too, jelly bean.'' He blinked and stared up at the ceiling. ''I love you, too.''

Alex stole a glimpse at Reese's profile as they pulled into the parking lot of the convenience store. She wondered about the change in his expression ever since she'd left him in the school's clinic. From the time he emerged, holding Elizabeth in his arms, he'd appeared rather... besotted.

It was a look he wore well. Too well.

Her stomach quivered, and a bittersweet ache rippled through her limbs. She tightened her grip on the steering wheel, aborting her flights of fancy before they could get off the ground.

She and Reese had agreed to marry for the benefit of the girls and nothing more—not now, not ever. He wasn't interested in her as a wife but as a mother, and since he couldn't get the latter without the former, he was stuck with the whole package.

If she expected to survive their arrangement with her heart intact, she would best remember those facts, instead of allowing her emotions to run amok as they had in Reese's office. For the briefest of seconds, she'd actually thought he was going to kiss her. Embarrassment stained her cheeks.

''I'll run in,'' Reese said, already reaching for the door handle as the car came to a stop. ''Mint chocolate chip in the back. Rocky Road for the driver?''

*He remembered her favorite ice cream.*

Mutely, Alex nodded. A gust of cold air swept into the car as he slipped out, closing the door behind him. She watched his retreat, then forced herself to look away. In marrying Reese, she would receive far more than she had ever expected. She had no business longing for more.

She turned up the heat, lifting her hand to the vent. "Warm enough back there?"

Elizabeth lay across the back seat, buried beneath the folds of Alex's winter coat. "Yes" came her muffled response, followed by a rustling. When Alex glanced up, blue eyes met hers in the rearview mirror. "Uncle Reese told Grandma he asked you to marry him."

"Oh?" She moistened her suddenly dry lips, trying to think of ways to stall until Reese returned.

"Jayne kinda overheard."

"Oh. Hey. Maybe we should get something for your sisters?" She unbuckled her seat belt. "I can probably catch Reese before he—"

"Are you gonna say yes or no?"

So much for stall tactics. Alex took a deep breath and turned in her seat. Angling her leg for balance, she met Elizabeth's inquisitive gaze. "I've already accepted your uncle's offer. I hope that's all right. We probably should have talked it over with you and your sisters first. I mean, you barely know me, and—"

"We know about you."

"You do?" Alex frowned. "How?"

"From Dad." Elizabeth self-consciously raised her hand to cover her bandage. "He told us about a girl named Alex who used to live across the street. Nora and Jayne don't remember, but I do. And when I met you, I just knew. That Alex was you." She lowered her hand. "We were hoping you would say yes. We'd like you to be our aunt."

"You would?" she asked, her voice filled with wonder.

Elizabeth nodded.

"I...I don't know what to say." An unexpected surge of euphoria welled inside her. She found it hard to believe Jeff had mentioned her to his daughters even in passing, for she had always been far more his brother's friend. But whatever he'd said must have left a favorable impression, and for that, she was profoundly grateful.

"*Thank you,* Elizabeth," she managed. "That has to be one of the nicest things anyone has ever said to me."

"Can you stay for dinner?"

"Maybe." Alex smiled. "Aren't you tired?"

"I napped enough in the waiting room."

"Well, we'll see if your Uncle Reese doesn't already have plans."

"He doesn't. I asked. Here he is," she said as Reese opened the door. "I'll ask again."

"Ask what?" Reese leaned inside and passed them their cones before sliding into the passenger seat with his own.

"We don't have plans for dinner, do we?" Elizabeth prompted, taking a lick of her ice cream.

"Nope. No plans at all. Say, Alex—"

"In that case," Alex interjected. "Maybe you'd like to come to my house for dinner." Her gaze darted to Elizabeth, a broad grin breaking out across her face. "I can't wait to get to know the girls."

Of course she was excited to get to know the girls. Reese was excited she was excited. And he didn't feel any twinges of envy when she leveled that rare, hundred-watt smile at Elizabeth instead of him. None whatsoever. Everything was exactly how it should have been.

With that thought firmly entrenched in his mind, Reese outlined his strategy for breaking the news to the girls. He figured they would sit in the family room, and he would explain how this time his marriage would be different, how the girls could expect more of a mother-figure from Alex.

But all his well-laid plans went out the window the second Alex dropped Elizabeth and him off.

Not two steps inside the house, Elizabeth bellowed at the top of her lungs, "Alex is going to be our new aunt!"

Nora's head popped around the corner. It was a toss-up between which was wider—her mouth or her eyes. "Really?"

"Yes, really," Elizabeth answered before Reese had a chance. "I asked her myself."

"You did?" Reese frowned. "But how did you know—"

"This house has ears, Uncle Reese."

The ears appeared at that moment. "Did she say yes?" Jayne asked.

Elizabeth nodded. "And she invited us to dinner at her house!"

"Tonight?" Excitement bubbled in Nora's usually quiet voice.

"Tonight!"

"Goodie!" Jayne clapped her hands.

Reese cleared his throat. "I, uh, take it you're okay with the idea of me marrying Alex?"

"Yes!" the girls answered in unison, then burst into laughter.

They liked her already. And she liked them. They were off to a good start. On that note, Reese decided to table serious discussion for another time. Not to mention he and Alex still had a lot of discussing to do themselves, so they could get their stories straight and present a united front.

"Well, what are we waiting for?" He clapped his hands. "We have dinner plans. Unless you intend to show up at your future aunt's house dressed like—"

He didn't need to finish. They'd already tuned him out in their mad dash for the stairs.

"Oh, dear." Elizabeth froze midstep, gaping in mock mortification. "What *will* we wear on such short notice?"

"I know. I know." Reese shook his head. "A closet full of clothes and nothing to wear. I don't know how I'm going to survive the teenage years."

"Don't worry, Uncle Reese," Nora said in all seriousness. "Aunt Alex will help you."

"Yes, she will." He smiled as he followed the girls up the staircase, an extra spring in his step. For the first time in a long time, he too felt like celebrating.

They washed up and changed clothes in record time, climbed into the Suburban and started for Skaneateles, a small resort town twenty minutes south of Sycamore.

"Wow." Nora gushed as they drove into town. "You didn't tell us Alex lived on a lake."

"I didn't know." Reese peered through the windshield at the pink horizon. "This is the first time I've been to her house."

"Did she just move here?"

"No, she's lived here for a few years."

"Then, how come—"

"Look!" Jayne piped up, kicking the seat with a loud thump in her excitement. "Ice skating!"

"Hey!" Elizabeth straightened in the passenger seat. "Stop kicking." And then, following her sister's gaze, "Wait a minute. They're not just skating. They're—"

Reese groaned. "Don't even say it."

"What?" Nora asked, straining to glimpse some forbidden activity. "What are they doing? I don't see anything."

"Ice hockey." Elizabeth turned and smiled, raising her eyebrows up and down suggestively. "Uncle Reese is *considering* letting me play."

"Keep dreaming, babe." Reese grinned, turning onto Alex's street. "If the modeling doesn't pan out, you might want to consider law. I can see you milking the poor jury with those baby blues."

"Grandma says we have lawyers in our pants." Jayne giggled, to which her sisters simultaneously burst into laughter.

"Lawyers in our pants!" they repeated, chortling.

It took Reese a minute to figure out what Jayne meant, then he, too, chuckled. "Uh, that's *genes,* sweetheart." He winked at her in the rearview mirror. "Maybe Alex can explain it better than I did."

"Because she's smart?"

"Because she's a scientist."

"She has scientists in her pants?"

"Something like that." He pulled behind Alex's car, cut the engine and unlocked the doors. The clicking of seat belts resounded as the girls released their straps and bounded from their seats.

"Sure is big," Nora whispered in awe.

Reese turned his gaze to the rambling lake house, taking it in for the first time. The paint had peeled in places, revealing a dingy gray underneath. Several rungs were missing from the large, wraparound porch, and a shutter teetered from a second-story window.

But for all its dilapidated features, the house had definite character. He could envision how it would look with a little TLC, its former charm restored.

"Uncle Reese?" Jayne asked. "Can we call her Aunt Alex now, or do we have to wait?"

"Hmm. Good question. Probably better ask her."

"Nora, you ask."

"I'm not going to ask. You ask."

"I'll ask," Elizabeth volunteered.

Muffled giggles floated behind the girls as they trekked toward the house, their animated chatter tinkling through an otherwise-silent, winter evening.

How Reese loved the sight and sound of their happiness.

It soothed an ache buried deep inside him, in a faraway place he loathed to admit still existed, even to himself.

"How come Alex doesn't shovel the driveway?"

"When you and Alex get married, will she come live with us, or will she stay in her own house like Aunt Leslie?"

"Is there a path to the lake?"

"Whoa." Reese frowned, realizing the extent of the logistics he and Alex still had to hammer out. "She only agreed to marry me today. We still have to work out some of the finer points."

"Like when you're getting married," Elizabeth stated.

"And where," Nora chimed in.

"Can we be flower girls?" Jayne wanted to know.

"Yes," he answered with grand flourish of his arm before he pressed the doorbell. "To all three of you."

Alex opened the door to a chorus of cheers. She wore winter-white pants and a black sweater with tiny gold hoops dangling from her earlobes.

"Welcome. Come in. Come in." She stepped back to allow them entrance, and the tantalizing scent of tomatoes and spices wafted outside.

"Yum!" Jayne sniffed the air. "What's for dinner?"

"Pasta." Alex smiled. "I hope you're hungry."

"A cat!" Nora exclaimed. "Uncle Reese, you didn't tell us she had a cat!"

"Uh-oh." Alex's eyes widened. "Is someone allergic?"

"No, we love cats!"

"Well, in that case… Girls, meet Albert Einstein."

"Cool. What's back there?" Elizabeth craned her neck to get a better look.

"Can we explore?" Jayne asked hopefully.

"Make yourselves at home." She smiled as the girls scampered in every direction. "Please excuse the decor," she called out. And then to Reese, "My renovating efforts got waylaid a few years ago. I've been so busy with work. You know how it goes."

Yes, he did. He knew exactly how a person threw himself into his work with single-minded focus to avoid dealing with other life issues. In fact, he had a good suspicion he could pinpoint the time Alex's renovating efforts derailed. And it made him feel lower than slime.

He should have come over when she didn't return his phone calls after the funeral. He should have shown up on her doorstep and asked if she needed anything. Instead, he'd taken her rejection with his tail between his legs, and she had born her grief alone, as anyone could see by taking one look at her house in its state of disrepair.

"I'm sorry." He awkwardly removed his coat and scarf. "I should have come out here sooner. It's been two years, and I—"

"You're here now." Bright, brown eyes sparkled with unconcealed pleasure. "And you come bearing three exquisite gifts. What more could a girl want?" She smiled and led the way to a huge gourmet kitchen.

Reese struggled to think of some lighthearted crack but for once couldn't return her easy banter. He didn't know what more a girl could want, especially one like Alex, but he sure knew what more a guy could want.

Especially one like him.

"Need any help?" he asked, eyeing the spread on the counters, anything to keep from looking at Alex.

"No, thanks. Everything's set." She stirred the sauce with a wooden spoon. "About ten more minutes, okay?" She glimpsed up, still wearing her smile. One look at him, and it faded on the spot. "What's wrong?"

"Nothing." He shrugged.

Her eyebrows knitted together, her gaze searching his face as a forensic scientist examined evidence for answers.

In that moment, he wanted nothing more than to see the light back in her eyes. Not just today, but every day. From the time she braided her hair in the morning to the time she brushed it out at night.

He could live with the fact he didn't put it there, but he didn't want to be the one who snuffed it out. All his life, he'd lived in fear of screwing up, of losing whatever ground he'd gained, of disappointing the people who meant the most to him. He'd limited the number of those people by not forming attachments, and with remarkably few exceptions, he'd succeeded.

Now here he was—with Exception *Numero Uno*.

He could feel himself slipping already into old ways, old feelings he didn't want to have. But whatever happened between him and Alex, he would deal with it, as long as she stayed. More than any fear he might have had for himself, his concern for the girls' security overrode all else.

"It's not just you and me this time," he told her. "Whatever comes down the pike, we have to stick it out— for the girls." He took her right hand in his, displaying her wedding band. "I know we have issues, but I need to know you're with me on one thing." He searched her eyes, looking for any signs of wavering. "This is for keeps, Alex. No one leaves this time. No matter what. I need your word."

She pursed her lips, then nodded once. "No one leaves," she vowed solemnly. "No matter what."

# Chapter 7

"Aw, do we have to leave? Can't we spend the night?" Jayne flashed a toothy grin.

The evening had passed faster than anyone realized. They'd eaten a sumptuous Italian feast, watched the last half of Disney's *Beauty and the Beast,* played beauty salon with Alex's makeup and explored every inch of the house.

Now, after they'd finished dessert, the grandfather clock in the hallway chimed ten o'clock, and the girls' eyelids started to droop.

"Jayne." Nora nudged her with her elbow. "We're not supposed to ask in front of other people."

Elizabeth frowned. "But Alex isn't other people anymore, is she? If she's going to be our aunt, she's like Uncle Reese—family—so we can ask in front of her, right?"

The girls looked from Reese to Alex for answers.

Reese leaned back in his chair and tipped his chin toward her. "Care to take this one?"

"Me? Oh, okay. Let's see." Alex turned her gaze from

one set of curious eyes to the next. "I'd say Elizabeth has a point— If I'm your aunt, then I'm not other people, so you should feel free to ask me anything you want. Of course, I won't always know the answer, but I don't want you to be shy around me, or think you have to be polite, or treat me like a guest. How does that sound?"

The girls nodded and murmured their assent.

"Are we allowed to call you Aunt Alex, yet?" Elizabeth asked. "Or do you want us to wait until it's official?"

Alex looked to Reese, but before he could say anything, Nora jumped in with, "He said it's up to you."

"In that case..." One corner of Alex's mouth tugged upward. "I really like the sound of Aunt Alex."

"Goodie!" Jayne clapped.

"Aunt Alex?" asked Nora. "May we spend the night?"

"You bet." Alex grinned wholeheartedly, pleased with her first foray into parental decision-making. "You're more than welcome, if it's okay with Uncle Reese."

"Can we, Uncle Reese? Can we?" Jayne tugged at his sleeve.

"Whoops." Alex covered her mouth too late. "I didn't mean to put you on the spot, Reese."

But Reese just smiled. "It's fine."

"Yay!"

"Uh-oh." Elizabeth framed her face with both hands. "We didn't pack overnight bags. What will we wear to bed?"

"How about some big, baggy T-shirts?" Alex brushed Elizabeth's bangs and teased, "I don't know how fashionable they'll look. Can you rough it for a night?"

"Why, of course, darling." Elizabeth grinned and patted Alex's hand in her "movie star" persona. "How very kind of you to offer."

"Don't mention it, dear," Alex mimicked in return, to which the girls giggled, and Reese covered his eyes.

"Can we pick our rooms?" Nora asked.

"Sure, if you're finished eating."

"Red!" Elizabeth shoved back her chair and bounded from the table.

"Wait!" Jayne sprung up. "I wanted the red room!"

"Too late. I called it."

"Can we share?"

"What'll you give me?"

"I want the flower room," Nora called, taking off after her sisters.

"Whoever sleeps in the blue room gets to sleep with Albert!" Alex added, to which Jayne promptly changed her mind.

The girls scurried from the room, with Albert bounding after them, their excitement echoing down the hallway and up the stairs. In their stocking feet, the pitter-patter of their footsteps sounded like those of playful kittens chasing each other back and forth across the hardwood floor.

Alex closed her eyes to savor the crackle of energy in a house whose spirit seemed to have awakened after a long hibernation. "Is it always like this?" she asked, propping her elbow on the table and resting her chin in her hand.

Reese stared at the ceiling, as if he could see the girls overhead. "The bickering, yes. The summer camp enthusiasm, no. They're pretty geared up. They like you."

"I'm glad. I like them, too. It's been a long time since I've felt…" She shook her head with wonder. "I don't think I've *ever* felt the way I do with them."

How could she explain the absence of awkwardness and the feeling of belonging? She wasn't in familiar territory, but she didn't feel like an outsider. She still wanted to fit in, but she was already one of the gang. And when she struggled to find the right words to say what she wanted, the girls somehow made it easier. Like a square peg sliding into a square hole, she felt…normal.

"It's extraordinary," she admitted. "I just hope…"

"What?"

"I don't know." She shrugged and picked up her spoon, idly swirling the remaining banana pudding in her dessert bowl. "I'm nervous. I hope I don't fall short once the newness wears off."

"If you're afraid of making mistakes, take it from a pro, there's no way around it." He reached for the box of cookies on the table. "Like everything else, you do the best you can, try to learn from each mistake, try not to repeat the same ones. That's really all anyone can do." He took a cookie for himself and offered another to her.

"Thanks." She took it without blinking, dipped it in her remaining pudding and took a bite. "You make everything look so effortless."

His gaze followed her movements, his eyes unusually somber. "It's all an illusion, Alex."

"Trying to discourage me?"

"Not a chance."

She indicated his empty bowl. "More?"

"No, thanks. I'm stuffed." He thumped his stomach and leaned back in his chair, lacing his fingers behind his head. "It was nice eating with you tonight."

"You, too."

"You know what I meant." A cream-colored fisherman's sweater stretched across his broad chest, making her fingers curl in reflex, itching to touch the soft fabric, trace the contours of hard muscle underneath.

"Yes, I know." She smiled and lowered her gaze. Her self-consciousness, though paralyzing while she was in the thick of it, always seemed so silly in retrospect.

"That's how I knew when I'd won you over—when you weren't embarrassed to eat messy food in front of me."

"Oh, really?" She raised an eyebrow. "Won me over?"

"Yes, really. Won you over." His confident grin dared her to deny it.

She glared back. "There's no need get a swelled head. My self-confidence has improved a bit since I was sixteen."

"So I noticed." His gaze warmed her face.

Alex blinked. Once. Twice. But Reese didn't look away. Clearing her throat, she shifted in her chair and laced her fingers together. The action succeeded in diverting Reese's attention to her hands.

"Tell me about him," he said without looking up, an almost imperceptible tightening around his mouth.

"Whom?"

"Your late husband."

"Oh, Tom." Alex turned her gaze to the band on her right hand, fondly remembering the man who had been her companion for six years. "He was a very kind man. I still have a hard time believing he's really gone, that he's never coming back." She frowned, thinking of the various research projects he'd started and she'd taken over, determined to carry on and follow through in his absence. "I miss him."

"I'm sorry."

"Thank you."

"Does it bother you to talk about him?"

"No, why would it?"

"No reason." Reese propped his fist under his chin, his expression unreadable. "How did you meet?"

"Through our fathers—they were colleagues, as were our grandfathers. Tom was at Cornell when we were introduced. We collaborated on a few papers, found we worked well together and started a joint research project. Tom conceptualized everything—'' She punctuated the word with an all-encompassing gesture of her hands "—before acting."

"Hmmm." Reese stroked his jaw, his eyes alight with humor. "Sounds like someone I know."

Alex shook her head. "He did it even more than I do. Honestly, he made me look downright spontaneous."

"No." Reese dropped his jaw in feigned disbelief.

"Yes." She laughed. "His insights into the complexities of general relativity were second to none. He questioned things I would never even think to question. I think that's why my father liked him so much. He reminded him of himself." She pursed her lips. "I suppose that's why I married him, looking back. Kind of Freudian."

Reese blew out a breath. "You and me both."

"Oh?" She sat a little straighter. "Do tell."

"Leslie and I met in law school. We had the same last name and joked about getting married—how she'd insist on keeping her maiden name, and I'd encourage her to hyphenate. We ended up at the same law firm, worked several cases together and got promoted at the same time. We figured we weren't going to get rid of each other any-time soon, so we went ahead and got hitched."

"Be still my heart." Alex clutched her hands to her chest. "In the romantic tradition of Kitty Collins." His mother had married a law school professor sixteen years her senior, though the two never appeared to have anything in common beyond being in the same place at the same time.

"Exactly. Which would explain the divorce."

"But your parents didn't divorce."

"No need. They manage to give each other space and

# How To Play:

**No Risk !**

**1.** With a coin, carefully scratch off the 3 gold areas on your Lucky Carnival Wheel. By doing so you have qualified to receive everything revealed — 2 FREE books and a surprise gift — ABSOLUTELY FREE!

**2.** Send back this card and you'll receive brand-new Silhouette Intimate Moments® novels. These books have a cover price of $4.50 each in the U.S. and $5.25 each in Canada, but they are yours TOTALLY FREE!

**3.** There's no catch! You're under no obligation to buy anything. We charge nothing — ZERO — for your first shipment. And you don't have to make any minimum number of purchases—not even one!

**4.** The fact is thousands of readers enjoy receiving books by mail from the Silhouette Reader Service™. They enjoy the convenience of home delivery…they like getting the best new novels at discount prices, BEFORE they're available in stores...and they love their *Heart to Heart* subscriber newsletter featuring author news, horoscopes, recipes, book reviews and much more!

**5.** We hope that after receiving your free books you'll want to remain a subscriber. But the choice is yours — to continue or cancel, anytime at all! So why not take us up on our invitation, with no risk of any kind. You'll be glad you did.

**No Cost!**

# LUCKY
**Find Out Instantly The Gifts You Get**
**Absolutely FREE!**
## Carnival Wheel
Scratch-off Game →

**Scratch off ALL 3 Gold areas**

LOSER    WINNER

WINNER    LOSER

LUCKY CARNIVAL WHEEL

WINNER

**YES!** I have scratched off the 3 Gold Areas above. Please send me the 2 FREE books and gift for which I qualify! I understand I am under no obligation to purchase any books, as explained on the back and on the opposite page.

**345 SDL CY4N**                          **245 SDL CY4J**

| | | | | | | | | | | | | | | | | | |
|-|-|-|-|-|-|-|-|-|-|-|-|-|-|-|-|-|-|

NAME                        (PLEASE PRINT CLEARLY)

| | | | | | | | | | | | | | | | | | |
|-|-|-|-|-|-|-|-|-|-|-|-|-|-|-|-|-|-|

ADDRESS

| | | | | | | | | | | | | | | | | |
|-|-|-|-|-|-|-|-|-|-|-|-|-|-|-|-|-|-|

APT.#                CITY

| | | | | | | | | | | | | | | | |
|-|-|-|-|-|-|-|-|-|-|-|-|-|-|-|-|-|

STATE/PROV.                    ZIP/POSTAL CODE

## The Silhouette Reader Service™ — Here's how it works:

Accepting your 2 free books and gift places you under no obligation to buy anything. You may keep the books and gift and return the shipping statement marked "cancel." If you do not cancel, about a month later we'll send you 6 additional novels and bill you just $3.80 each in the U.S., or $4.21 each in Canada, plus 25¢ delivery per book and applicable taxes if any.*
That's the complete price and — compared to cover prices of $4.50 each in the U.S. and $5.25 each in Canada — it's quite a bargain! You may cancel at any time, but if you choose to continue, every month we'll send you 6 more books, which you may either purchase at the discount price or return to us and cancel your subscription.

*Terms and prices subject to change without notice. Sales tax applicable in N.Y. Canadian residents will be charged applicable provincial taxes and GST.

unconditional support.'' He shrugged. ''It works for them.''

''But it didn't work for you?''

''Not when my wife had no interest in raising my children.''

She nodded in sympathy, although she truly couldn't understand how any woman could resist the appeal of those three girls.

Reese stared at the table, an unfathomable look in his eyes. Around them, the air seemed to still, almost hover, like a gathering storm, and Alex sensed the imminent crack of lightning.

''Leslie had her tubes tied,'' Reese whispered, ''without telling me.''

Boom. The bottom plummeted out of her stomach. She felt herself blanch and clutched the edge of the table to hold herself up. ''She...she did?''

''Yeah, a few months after I moved out here to be with the girls, *knowing* I would be raising them.'' Reese gave a sardonic grin. ''We didn't even talk about it. I found out from the insurance claim.''

''Oh, God.'' Alex heard the quiver in her voice. The guilt. It was as if the heavens had cast a giant spotlight upon her soul and asked: what made her any different from Reese's ex-wife in withholding information from him? ''M-maybe there was a medical reason—''

''She should have told me *before* the fact.'' The muscles at the base of his throat worked convulsively. ''It wasn't just her future parenthood but mine at the time.''

''You wanted children.''

''I wanted a say. She cut me out of the loop entirely.''

An agonizing pain seared through her heart, for she knew in that moment Reese would never forgive her deception. Malicious intent or not, it wouldn't matter. *It wasn't just her future parenthood but mine.* And if he found out, he would walk out of her life yet again—this time, for good.

Alex couldn't let it happen. Not now, certainly not now, when everything she'd ever wanted was within her grasp. She couldn't lose her one chance at motherhood, her one chance to spend the rest of her life with the man she—

"I'm sorry, Reese." She grasped his hand in hers and whispered the words that rang in her ears every time she looked into his eyes and imagined the life she had taken from him without his knowledge, "I'm so, so sorry."

*I'll make it up to you. You'll see. I'll be a good mother. You won't lose the girls. You won't lose any more children.*

Reese's steel blue eyes roved over her face, a myriad of emotions reflecting from their bottomless depths. When he spoke his deep voice sounded like gravel spread with honey. "That was then. This is now." He turned his gaze to her hand, flipping his own over, palm up. Strong fingers clasped hers. "The girls are better off. *Way* better off."

She blinked, her heart hammering double-time.

"I want you to move in with us, Alex."

"Reese, I—"

"Obviously, that can't happen until after we're married, so I'd like to get past our nuptials ASAP."

"Right. Of course." A wave of light-headedness seized her. "Excuse me for a minute." She took back her hand and pushed away from the table.

When Reese rose as well, she skirted past him to the island in the middle of the kitchen. Turning on the faucet, she let the sound of splashing water fill the room, hoping to drown out her own inner voices.

"Alex." Reese planted two large hands on the counter across from her where a row of bar stools lined the island.

"What?" She reached for a dirty dessert bowl.

"Leave those. I'll do them."

"You did the last batch."

"All right, but we need to iron out a few things. Can you rinse and think at the same time?" He grinned.

"Yep, smart and coordinated. What more could you want in a wife?" She smiled in self-deprecation and reached for the dish brush.

Reese lowered himself onto one of the bar stools, watching her carefully, as if trying to ascertain how much she could take in one sitting. "On the topic of living arrangements, we can keep both houses if you want."

She nodded. "That would probably be wise."

"I don't mean separate residences, Alex. The girls sensed something was wrong when Leslie didn't live with us, and they were right. When you marry me, we're a family—we live under one roof. The lake house can be for weekends, summers, holidays—that sort of thing. Agreed?"

She lifted her gaze to the ceiling and wondered if the heavens didn't have a sick sense of humor. "Yes, agreed."

"Okay, one other thing." He seemed to be going down some mental list. "There's no tactful way to ask this, so I'm just going to come right out and say it."

Suspicion warred with curiosity, but she grasped the bottle of liquid detergent by the neck and tried to appear indifferent.

"Were you planning on being celibate for the rest of your life?"

She nearly dropped the detergent, missed the edge of the sink and clipped the bottle with a thump on its return. "Gee, I hadn't really given it much thought, Reese."

"Well I have, and it's not an option for me. What are your thoughts on adultery?"

Alex felt the blood drain from her face in shock. *No,*

*absolutely not.* Her fingers clamped around the handle of the dish brush so tightly her knuckles went white, and her hand shook. Even if she wasn't normal, she wouldn't be humiliated further with an unfaithful husband.

Anger supplanted shock with the force of a volcano. No, she couldn't and wouldn't lose control. She forced herself to uncurl her fingers and put down the brush in a civilized manner.

In an even, deadpan voice that betrayed no emotion and would have made her father proud, she said, "You will *not* sleep around on me, Reese Collins. I forbid it."

Relief flooded his face. "Good. We're in agreement."

"We are?" She stared at him, her pulse still drumming in her ears. At his nod, she cleared her throat and reached for another utensil. Cautious as to whether the roller coaster had come to a stop, or started up yet another hill, she asked, "And, to be clear, what is it we're agreeing to?"

"Sleeping together."

The fork slipped from her hand, clanked against the sink and plopped into the soapy water. Visions of long-lost images filled her mind. Part memory, part dream. Sweaty bodies and tangled limbs. Unspoken desires and whispered pleas. Before she could reach for anything else to rinse, Reese was up and out of the bar stool, standing beside her, reminding her this was no dream.

"I won't rush anything else," he promised, lifting her soapy hand to indicate the symbol of her union with another man. "I can wait until you're ready, but it's my ring you'll wear on your left hand, and our parents need to believe what we have is real." His eyes searched hers. "*My* parents need to believe we're in love, Alex."

"Oh, sure. No problem." She snatched back her hand, jerked the faucet to cold and stuck both hands underneath.

She focused on the cascading water and willed her thunderous heart to slow, but it was too much, too fast—their pretend world too close to her own. Her control waned by the minute.

Reese swore and turned off the water. "Look, I'm not saying it's going to be easy. Faking never is." He gazed at her pointedly.

She swiped her hands on the towel and wrapped them around her waist, recalling the night they'd made love.

*Please don't tell me you were faking.*

"Maybe if we practiced, it wouldn't look so awkward."

He thought she was awkward. Clearly, she hadn't known what she was doing. She was sixteen. Did he think she had learned nothing of human behavior over the years, that she would need to practice what came by instinct to others?

"What do you say? Want to try?"

She gave him a dubious look. "Try what?"

He crooked his head. "We could kiss for starters."

"Kiss?" A traitorous tingle of anticipation raised goose bumps on her arms. "Here? Now?" She sounded winded already, imagining his lips over hers, the heady rush of their tongues sliding together.

Reese shrugged. "We're going to have to sooner or later. My parents aren't going to believe—"

She cut him off with an emphatic wave of her hand. "Okay, okay." She didn't want to hear any more cold, clinical rationale, even if it was true. "Let's do it and get it over with. Where do you want me?" She surveyed the counters, the bar stools, the refrigerator door, all the while feeling Reese's gaze intent on her.

Did he think she wouldn't go through with it? She would. She'd show him. She could handle a simple kiss. She wasn't *that* incompetent.

"Right here's fine." Reese's voice sounded strained. He took a step toward her, and she bridged the remaining distance, wanting to prove she wasn't afraid this time.

They came toe-to-toe. Boldly, she leaned closer and laid her palms against his chest. His muscles contracted, and instant pinpricks of humiliation darted through her. She'd messed up already—he didn't want her this close.

She started to pull back when he grasped her hands. Without a word, he tugged them upward and laid one atop each of his shoulders. The movement drew her breasts against him. At the surge of heat from the brushing contact, she sucked in a sharp breath.

*You'll be fine. Remember to breathe.*

She drew her lower lip between her teeth and glanced up, but Reese's eyes didn't meet hers. Instead, he focused on her mouth with that same expression from the elevator—raw and primitive. Hungry.

*For her?*

No, not for her. For pretend. It was an act.

"Kiss me, Alex." His deep voice rumbled in his chest, and his hands lowered to her hips, as if he feared she might leave if he didn't hold her there.

But she was far beyond leaving, far beyond having the good sense to retreat even if she wanted. Which she didn't.

Dear God, was this really happening? Was she really here in his arms? Were her fingers really sliding around the back of his neck as if of their own volition?

Alex closed her eyes and willed herself to make the first move, to act on the impulses coursing through her veins. She felt a nip at her earlobe, the scrape of late-night stubble against her face, and shuddered.

"Kiss me, Alex." Reese nuzzled her neck, his velvet-smooth voice rippling over her senses, sending wave after wave of desire crashing through her body. "Kiss me like we're in love."

Her head lolled back, and a moan of frustration caught in her throat. She flexed her hands on his broad shoulders, afraid to let go of reality, to lose herself in the fantasy, yet equally afraid not to, lest Reese find her inept.

Like two thunderclouds that had built up static electricity, charges leapt between them. And when Reese's hard, muscular thigh brushed against her, she half-expected their heat to set off an electrical spark, making the air explode with a loud boom.

Who was she kidding, trying to psyche herself into kissing him? Alexandra Ricci had wanted Reese Collins for more than half her lifetime. She couldn't deny that fact any more than a magnet could fight its attraction to an opposite pole.

And so she stopped overanalyzing and took action. Stretched up on her toes and brushed her lips over his. Gripped his arms and gave herself up to the sweet agony of being so close, and yet so far. Leaned in to him and savored every texture, every taste, every exquisite sensation of the only man she had ever truly—

*No, don't go there. Admit you're attracted to him if you must. But no more.*

Reese groaned and cupped her face, angling her head, taking over. Was she doing it wrong? Was he trying to help? Uncertain, she pulled back, but Reese's open mouth moved to her throat, drawing a broken sigh from her.

She felt weak in the knees and shivery all over. "The girls…" she whispered feebly, unsure how much longer she could stand up without falling.

"Upstairs," came his hoarse reply. His hands gripped her hips, holding her in place as the hot, moist heat of his mouth feathered kisses at the hollow of her throat.

Shards of unbidden desire spiraled through her with stunning velocity. Liquid heat pooled between her thighs until she was throbbing, aching for his touch, carnal urges filling her loins.

She wanted to grind her hips against his, wanted to feel the hard length of his body pressed intimately against hers. Her entire body trembled, quaked with need.

"Please, Reese..." At the abject desperation in her voice, she bit back a sob. She didn't want to want him like this, didn't want to reveal her weakness to him—her inability to separate herself from the role she'd been cast to play. "Please...stop...no...more."

Reese's head jerked up, Alex's protests dousing the conflagration that had been burning every inch of him with a bone-chilling, Arctic blast. He felt like a man in the grip of a fever who'd been thrown in a bathtub full of ice cubes.

Though a bead of sweat trickled between his shoulder blades, he didn't so much as blink, but watched and waited for some sign from Alex.

She was shaking like a cold, wet kitten. She looked dazed and confused, her eyes wide, her lips parted. Her breathing came fast and shallow, her expression wary and guarded as though she feared his advance.

With a muttered curse, Reese slid his hands to her shoulders and straightened his arms, setting her away.

"Don't worry," he reassured. "I know no means no. You have my word I'll never force myself on you again. If you're afraid—"

"Again?" She frowned and shook her head as if to clear the cobwebs. "Again?" she repeated when he didn't respond, her eyes narrowing into accusing slits. And then her hands balled into fists. "I can't believe you have the gall to *say* such a thing to me, much less *think* it." Her eyes searched his, unmasked pain reflected in their shadowy depths. "Kitty, yes. But you?" She spun away, reached for a dishcloth and started to wipe down the counters.

"Alex?" He stared after her, uncomprehending. "I'm sorry—"

"I *know* you're sorry, Reese. Sorry you have to marry me. Sorry you have to kiss me and pretend to like it. Don't you think *I'm* sorry, too?" she cried. "I am. More than I could ever tell you."

He felt the slow, twisting of a knife in his gut. She didn't want to marry him, didn't want to kiss him, didn't want to have to pretend to like it. What she wanted was to be a mother. And only he could give her that.

"I'm going to marry you," she confirmed, giving voice to his own thoughts. "I'm going to help you raise three darling little girls. We're going to live under the same roof and act like we're in love, even if we have to practice ad nauseam until we get it right. We're both adults. We know what we're doing and why we're doing it. Am I missing anything?"

"Not a thing." His voice was unsteady, and it echoed oddly in his ears. He had promised—*on his brother's grave,* he had promised—to stop being an ungrateful bastard, to stop seeing the glass as half empty instead of half full, to get the damn chip off his shoulder, not merely cover it up.

Yet here he was, feeling as if he was bleeding to death, instead of embracing all that was good and all that was right. And as she had so many times before, Alex saw right through him, clear to his true fear.

"Then for heaven's sake—" she smacked the dishcloth on the counter, her eyes beseeching him "—won't you please get it through your head I don't hold that night against you? If I did, I damn sure wouldn't be marrying you, Reese Collins, under *any* circumstances.'' Her cheeks flamed, and her chest heaved, as if reeling from a marathon that took every ounce of her strength to finish.

They both sagged against opposite counters.

Until that moment, Reese hadn't realized how badly he'd needed to hear her words, or how long he had waited.

She knew him so well. Too well. Not well enough.

Throughout the years, every time he'd replayed the events of that night, trying to pinpoint where and when things had gone awry, he'd always wondered: had alcohol blurred the line between taking advantage of a friend and forcing himself on her?

Reese pinched the bridge of his nose. He wanted to savor the gift Alex had given him in agreeing to marry him. But he knew the demons that had chased him for an entire lifetime wouldn't suddenly disappear because he chose not to look over his shoulder. They would lie in wait and spring on him in the middle of the night.

*You're going to lose her. You know you will. Nothing good lasts forever. Especially not for you.*

He knew it, and he had to face the possibility one day Alex might, too. He could only pray she would stick to her promise for the girls, that she wouldn't leave come hell or high water. Because both were headed their way.

# Chapter 8

"Did you tell Aunt Alex Grandma and Grandpa are coming to visit?" Jayne asked, two arms sticking up from beneath the blue bedcovers in anticipation of a hug.

"Nope, but you just did." Reese gathered her small form in his arms, pecked her button nose and adjusted the blue pinstriped comforter over her. In the corner of the room, Albert curled into a furry ball by the radiator.

Reese stood and noted Alex's troubled expression, but before he could say anything, Jayne's arms poked back out.

"Aunt Alex."

Alex's gaze shot to Reese. When he smiled and nodded his encouragement, she took a step forward and appeared to assess the mechanics of the situation before bending down and embracing his youngest niece.

Jayne's little arm curved around Alex, and something tightened in the area of Reese's heart—a rightness of the moment that caught him by surprise and soothed any lingering doubts he was indeed doing the right thing in marrying Alex, as far as the girls were concerned.

"Goodnight, Jayne. Sleep tight."

"Aunt Alex? When I wake up in the morning will you still be here?"

"Yes, I will." She stroked Jayne's hair. "And lots of mornings after, too."

"Only weekends, right?"

Alex's knowing gaze flickered to Reese, and he knew she remembered what he'd said about Leslie. Pursing her lips, she smoothed Jayne's hair from her forehead. "No, honey. Not just weekends. Every day—after Uncle Reese and I get married, that is."

Her eyes lit up. "Really?"

"Really. I'm going to live with you and your sisters and Uncle Reese. And on weekends, and maybe longer in the summers, we can come out here to the lake. But we'll stay together—all of us, all the time. How does that sound?"

Jayne glanced at the sleeping cat. "Albert, too?"

"Albert, too."

"Goodie." Jayne snuggled under the covers.

"You know where Uncle Reese is sleeping, but you can come in my room, too, if you need anything. We'll leave the hall light on, okay?" She reached for the bedside lamp, waiting for Jayne's nod before she clicked the switch.

Reese straightened from the door frame where he'd been leaning, watching their exchange.

Who would have guessed the bookish Alexandra Ricci had such maternal instincts? Though uncertain of her actions, she was a quick study with a natural affinity for sensing and responding to the girls' needs. They had taken to her—in a very short time—in a way they'd never taken to Leslie.

Not that it surprised him.

Leslie didn't have a nurturing bone in her body. The emotional detachment that had proved an asset for his first marriage had become a liability for parenthood. In sharp contrast to his ex-wife, whose outward charm camouflaged an aloof spirit, Alex had all the trappings of an ice princess, when in reality, she was anything but.

Alex thawed around the girls, allowed them to glimpse her true colors…and heightened his own curiosity about the range and depth of her emotions.

Reese jammed his hands in his pockets and waited for her at the doorway. She lifted her gaze to his as she passed, her expression once again troubled.

They walked down the hall without saying a word, the floorboards creaking underneath their feet. He liked the fact they didn't have to resort to small talk to fill the silence.

Around the corner, a cushioned window seat overlooked the backyard where moonbeams danced across an ice-covered lake, and a pale half-moon hung in a star-studded sky.

"Beautiful." Alex tucked one leg beneath her as she sat down.

"Yes," he agreed, his gaze on her face.

Alex's father had always said his daughter was different. She was. Because of him. He had raised her with his own goals and ambitions, his own hopes and dreams, and he had made them hers. Alex had not sprung from the womb in her father's image—he had molded her that way.

For months after they'd met, Reese had never seen beyond that tightly controlled image. Until the first real belly laugh when she nailed him in the back with a snowball, the first scream of victory when he sunk the winning free throw for the varsity basketball team, the first sniffle during what he'd considered an overrated chick flick.

And when he compared those rare glimpses of Alex with the rest of the girls he'd dated, he realized she wasn't less emotional, less feeling, less compassionate. She was more. And when he kissed her in the kitchen, it all came back to him. The challenge, the discovery, the rush of her response, the blow of her rejection.

He closed his eyes and shut out the memory.

"Reese? Do you want to sit down? There's room."

He surveyed the space beside her and leaned his shoulder against the wall instead. "I'll stand, thanks."

He'd pushed his luck enough for one night, still hated to think about the way she'd trembled in his arms, as if she couldn't wait to get away from him. She obviously didn't relish any kind of renewed or sustained intimacy with him, even something as innocent as kissing.

Innocent? Desire pulsed through him at the memory of the way her lips had slid against his with tender, hesitant exploration, as if tasting and fitting their shape to her own, brushing back and forth as if she wanted more.

But she didn't—she'd told him to stop.

With implacable resolve, Reese vowed to keep his distance when they were alone. He'd promised to wait until she was ready, and he would. Even if it killed him.

"So." Alex pulled an afghan over her legs and stared out at the winter night. "When are they coming?"

He didn't need clarification, knew she referred to his parents. "A week."

She nodded. "I see."

"They'd like us to join them for dinner Friday night at the Sherwood Inn. My mother specifically asked—"

"I'll bet she did."

He looked down at the crown of her head, at the silky strands of her hair shimmering like mink in the moonlight. She appeared so small in the big window, her arms wrapped around her legs. His protective instincts kicked in, wanting to shield her from any and all unpleasantness.

"We don't have to go if you don't want to."

She drew a breath and appeared to consider, resting her cheek against her knee. "This is going to sound really strange, but I almost want to see her. I need to. There are things I've wanted to say over the years, but I haven't been able to get past the contrasting images in my mind."

"Ah." He tipped his head back. "You mean the polished and overly gracious Kitty Collins and the ugly, mean-spirited drunk."

She nodded. "It would be nice to reconcile the two."

"I understand," he said; but in truth, he never had. Never had been able to reconcile the words and actions of the woman who had willingly adopted him and given him a permanent place in her family, yet resented him at times as if she'd had no choice. "I ought to warn you. She'll probably try to talk you out of marrying me."

"I doubt that, seriously."

"Be prepared."

She lifted a shoulder. "If she does, she'll give me the perfect opening into what I have to say. You're always harping on my segues." She gave a crooked smile.

"I don't harp."

"You harp, Reese."

"Yeah, well you prod."

"Because you dodge."

"I don't... Okay, I do. But I have my reasons."

"Your reasons—" she lifted her foot and poked him in the stomach with her toes "—drive me nuts."

He caught her heel before she could pull back, cradled it in the palm of his right hand. Without thinking, he stroked her calf, then closed his eyes and let her go.

"*You* drive me nuts, Alex." He shoved his hands back in his pockets.

Her eyes widened, then narrowed. She frowned and pulled the afghan over her legs again.

"About what I said earlier…wanting our parents to believe we're in love." He rocked back on his heels and considered her. "Think you can convince Frank?"

She bit her lip and nodded. "How about you? Think you can convince your folks?"

"Definitely." He thought back to the kitchen, to the way his body responded to hers. "By the time I'm through, they'll think I've been pining away for you all this time."

"Fancy that." She gave a tight smile and looked away.

"So how's your schedule looking tomorrow?"

"Tomorrow? I usually head over to the lab on Saturdays while it's quiet. Why?"

"Skip the lab. Marry me at Hendrick's Chapel."

Her gaze shot up. "*Tomorrow?* But what about the marriage license? And the minister? And—"

"I've got connections."

"What about our parents?"

He shrugged. "We'll call them tonight. If they want to come, they can."

"It's awfully short notice, Reese."

"Better than no notice."

"True. Kitty won't be pleased."

"I'm more concerned about Frank."

She toyed with the edge of the afghan. "He'll understand."

"What about you? Are you up for eloping? I could take the girls shopping for dresses—"

"No, I want to. I mean, would it be all right if I…"

He grinned. "They'd love it."

"I've long had a theory shopping's linked to the X-chromosome."

"No argument here."

She gave a shy smile. "All right then."

"Yes?" Reese raised his eyebrows.

"Yes, you have a date."

"A date." He whistled softly through his teeth. "Hot damn—no curfew this time." He winked.

With a nervous laugh, her hand fluttered to her throat. "I, um, we'd better say good-night before I change my mind." She pushed the afghan away and came to her feet.

"Alex." He reached out and grasped her elbow. "Do me a favor? Don't even joke about changing your mind, okay?"

She moistened her lips and nodded once, the stars glittering in her luminous brown eyes.

"Thank you." He leaned down to plant a chaste kiss on her mouth, but she turned her head, and his lips brushed her cheek. He told himself it was better that way, better she enforced the limits, so he didn't inadvertently slip.

He forced himself to take a step back, followed by another, forced himself not to think about Alex all alone in her bed, or to imagine her in his. Then he started down the hall, needing to put distance between them and fast, before he thought about those exact things and a whole lot more.

After all, this wasn't any woman. This was Alex. He wasn't supposed to have these thoughts about her.

"Reese?" her soft voice came behind him.

"What?" He shoved a rough hand through his hair.

"I…I was wondering…"

He drew a breath and turned around. Big mistake. She looked ethereal as an angel with the silhouette of her gentle curves outlined in the pale moonlight. And when she glanced toward her bedroom, then back at him, a shot of one hundred proof desire surged through his body.

*Don't do this to me. Don't tempt me with things I can't have.*

She clasped and unclasped her hands, as if wrestling with indecision. Finally, she bowed her head. "Never mind. Goodnight, Reese."

He swallowed and turned down the hall. "Goodnight."

A baby's cries broke the still of the night.

Instantly alert, Alex sprung from her bed. "Coming, honey! Mommy's coming!" As she ran down the hallway, the cries grew more insistent. Heart pounding, she threw open the nursery door and gasped in horror.

The cradle was empty. Her baby was gone.

"No," she whimpered as a bolt of pain ripped through her midsection. Doubling over in agony, she fell to the floor in a shuddering heap. "Please, no."

But the cries continued, ringing in her ears like a siren. Like a telephone.

The telephone!

Alex's eyelids flew open, her bleary gaze focusing on the digital clock by her bedside. Two o'clock. Her body drenched in a cold sweat, she groped for the receiver. "Hello?"

"Alexandra?"

"Daddy." She raised a trembling hand to her face, as if her father could see her, and swiped at her errant tears.

"How's my favorite physicist and future Nobel prize winner?"

She sniffled and lifted the pillowcase to dab at the remaining moisture. "I was about to ask you the same question. Where are you?"

"Los Angeles. I just checked messages—"

"And you heard mine."

"It's true then? You're marrying Reese Collins?"

"Yes, Daddy."

"Are you *sure* this is what you want? Three young girls are going to be a handful. Your schedule will be severely limited. Your research may suffer."

"Working mothers are hardly an endangered species. In fact, I met several at the faculty holiday party last week."

Her father chuckled under his breath. "You speak as if you're an ordinary woman, Alexandra. Need I remind you you're anything but? My dear, you have a gift. One doesn't use a sledgehammer to crack a peanut. Your contributions to the field of physics have been extraordinary. And for someone your age... The Nobel is truly in your future— it's just a question of time."

She laid her forehead against her palm. "I know that, Daddy. I'll work it out, I promise. I won't let you down."

"You never have."

Her throat tightened. "The, uh, ceremony's tomorrow at Hendrick's Chapel. Four-thirty. I'd like you to be there."

"I don't know if I—"

"I'll understand if you can't make it on such short notice." She tried to hide her disappointment.

"Alexandra, does Reese know what happened?"

"He knows I can't have children."

"And the rest?"

She closed her eyes. The rest...

When she'd told her father of her pregnancy, he had reacted as expected. After an initial flicker of surprise, he had calmly and collectedly explained the ramifications and urged her to consider the pros and cons of a teenage, unwed mother raising a child in today's society.

When she could no longer live in the emotional void

she called her home, she had run across the street, escaping to what she'd always considered normalcy.

Even with Reese gone, his home represented a safe haven. His parents had always been so kind to her. His mother, the picture-perfect image of sugar and spice and everything nice—everything "normal" little girls grew up to be. Everything Alex wanted to be for her own child.

And so she had made the decision to tell Kitty before she told Reese, to assure her she would raise her grandchild to the best of her ability without forcing her son into a situation he wouldn't have chosen, and to ask if she might solicit her opinion whenever she needed an expert.

But while everything had gone as expected in her own home, never in a million years had she foreseen the scene that greeted her at Reese's.

She had suspected something was off when Kitty opened the door, teetering slightly. But she'd displayed her usual grace in inviting Alex inside, exhibiting no other signs of inebriation. Only when Alex summoned the courage to tell her the true purpose of her visit did she metamorphosize into the nightmare that haunted her nights forever after.

*"I was afraid this was going to happen. I'm so sorry. You did the right thing coming to me. Of course I'll help you. Don't worry about a thing."* Kitty started toward the phone. *"We'll make arrangements for a private adoption."*

*"No!"* Alex edged back, curling her arms around her stomach in reflex. *"That's not the kind of help... I'm keeping my baby."*

*"I understand. You're very emotional right now. You haven't thought through the logistics yet. But you will. You have a chance to make something of yourself. You can't*

*throw your entire life away because of one damned mistake.''*

*Tears sprung to Alex's eyes. "Is that how you felt when you were pregnant with Jeff? That you'd thrown your entire life away? That you'd made a...a mistake?''*

*Kitty blinked. "That was different. I was married to Clay. He was steady and secure. Reliable. Dependable. Reese...is none of those things. He isn't fit to raise a goldfish. You can't expect him to willingly give up—''*

*"No, I don't. And I would never ask him. I don't need or want to be anyone's responsibility. It's true we didn't plan for this, but I will never, ever regret having this baby.''*

*Kitty's eyes turned glassy and vacant. "You say that now, but you have no idea. You'll see when the time comes, when you don't bond with it. When you want to and you try to, but you can't, no matter what you do, no matter how long you wait. Every time you look at that face, all you see is lost opportunity and wasted chances and the selfish, self-centered man who stole your—''*

*"That's enough, Kitty.'' Clay entered the room just then, walking toward his wife, one hand outstretched.*

*"I'm not drunk. Don't tell me I'm drunk!''*

*"Kitty. Honey. Come on. Let's get you to bed.''*

*"She's carrying his child, Clay!'' She let out a sob of anguish, clutching for his arm as she neared collapse. "We have to do something!''*

*His eyes registered shock, though his voice remained calm. "Alex, if you'll stay right here. I'll be back in a minute. My wife isn't feeling very well...''*

Alex had taken that minute to slip out the front door, never to return. Not when a sober Kitty called day after day, trying to apologize, to explain herself, to appeal to her with "reason.'' Not when Reese returned from college for the holidays, or permanently after the funeral. Not once in fifteen years, for any reason.

Until now.

And now, a past that started as a tiny snowball began its descent down the side of a mountain, swiftly gaining mass and velocity, with the kinetic energy to wipe out an entire village.

"Alexandra?" Her father's sensible voice came through the receiver. "I asked if Reese knows about the rest."

"No," she whispered.

A deep sigh. "And you're going to enter into holy matrimony with these lies hanging between you."

These and more. But she couldn't tell her father that. He would never understand, never approve of their marriage of convenience.

"I don't know how I can tell him, Daddy. Everything happened so long ago. Is there really any reason to dredge it up again?"

"You tell me. Marriage is a sacred union. Not to be entered into lightly."

She pursed her lips and gripped the phone tighter, the shame of deception rushing in her ears.

"I trust you will do the right thing, Alexandra. Just keep one thing in mind. A wound can't fully heal until it's properly cleansed."

"Aunt Alex? What does A-N-T-I-B-I-O-T-I-C-S mean?" Jayne asked, copying the word from the label of Elizabeth's prescription onto a lined sheet of paper.

"Antibiotics fight infection," she explained, handing Elizabeth a glass of milk to wash down one of the pills.

Jayne stared at her with a blank expression.

"Um, the doctor wants to make sure Elizabeth doesn't get any bad germs that could make her sick."

"Oh." Jayne nodded, latching onto the new explanation. "Special medicine."

"Exactly." Now why hadn't she thought of it like that? *Know your audience.*

Elizabeth drained the glass, rinsed it out and put it in the dishwasher. "Okay, ready."

"Wait." Alex grabbed a napkin from the holder and dabbed Elizabeth's mouth. "Milk mustache."

"Gone?"

"Yes. Beautiful. Go on." Alex tingled with nervous excitement as the girls, dressed in matching blue velvet dresses, fluttered into the great room where Reese awaited the unveiling of their selections.

"Well, well." He raised an approving eyebrow. "Who are these dazzling young ladies and what have you done with my nieces?"

The girls giggled as they curtsied and spun around.

"We picked blue because it's your favorite," Nora said.

Alex beamed. "Aren't they precious?"

"And how." Reese handed Nora a plastic bag bearing the name of a drugstore. "For all three maidens-in-waiting."

She peered in the bag. "Cameras!"

"Disposable. You're going to be the official photographers."

"Great!"

"So what's in Aunt Alex's bag?" He stepped toward her.

She stepped back. "None of your business."

"Come on. Just a peek."

"No!" the girls shouted in unison, sandwiching between Reese and her like little referees breaking up a fight.

"Ahhh." Reese staggered back, pinching the bridge of his nose as if he were in excruciating pain.

"Reese? What's wrong?" Alex dropped the garment bag in her haste to rush to his side.

"Nothing. It's nothing. I just had this vision of life with four women in the house."

"You phony!" Alex smacked his arm.

"Careful. That's my bad arm."

"You had me worried!" She smacked the other one.

"That's my other bad arm."

"You're still a pain," she mumbled under her breath.

Reese opened his mouth as if to retort, then closed it again. But Jayne piped up. "Yeah, but he's *your* pain."

Their gazes met and held in a silent exchange of sorts.

Her pain—that he was. From day one, and now, until eternity. At that thought, something fluttered in her stomach, lost and forgotten dreams beating like butterfly wings. She shivered and forced herself to turn away.

"Alex?" Reese's voice came behind her, the deep, rich timbre tempting her, as always, to believe against all logic. He leaned close and whispered in her ear, "Don't forget your costume. Two and a half hours to showtime."

Just like that, the butterflies stopped fluttering.

"Thank you. I won't." She forced a smile, scooped up the bag that held her wedding dress and ran from the room.

At the sting of tears, she quickened her stride, taking the steps two at a time. Upstairs, she pushed her bedroom door shut behind her and collapsed on her bed. And though she told herself there was no reason to let Reese's words affect her, no reason to be upset, they did, and she was.

*Marriage is a sacred union. Not to be entered into lightly…*

Their marriage was a sham, built on a foundation of ever-increasing lies. Soon, they wouldn't know where one lie stopped and another started. She recalled a line from

Shakespeare about the "tangled web we weave when first we practice to deceive."

"Alex?" A knock at the door. Reese's voice, tinged with concern. "Everything all right in there?"

"Everything's fine." She straightened and tried to pull herself together.

"Just checking. I don't want anything to go wrong at the last minute."

"No, no. Nothing's going to go wrong." She rubbed her temples and took a series of deep breaths.

"What's your estimated time to departure?"

"Give me five minutes." She closed her eyes and started to recite the periodic table of the elements.

Two hours later, Alex surveyed her appearance in the full-length mirror of the changing room at Hendrick's Chapel. Elizabeth, Nora and Jayne surrounded her, taking turns helping with her hair, her makeup, her gown.

At their insistence, she wore her hair pinned up with baby's breath, ringlets of curls spilling down. Elizabeth did her makeup with a surprisingly professional hand, using colors Alex selected from a cosmetics ad in *Vogue*. Her gown was a simple silk and lace cut, ivory colored with buttons down the back and a small bow in the curve of her spine.

Jayne beamed. "You look like a fairy princess."

"She looks like Belle," Nora gushed, "from *Beauty and the Beast*."

Elizabeth drew a festive-colored bag from the hallway and handed it to Alex. "For you. Something old. Something new. Something borrowed. Something blue."

"You made this for me? Yourselves?" Alex's hand lingered over the tissue, noting the care with which the girls had arranged the gifts. Without warning, a river of maternal emotions flowed through her—so alien, so natural, so unexpected.

It hit her at that moment—the sheer magnitude of what was about to happen. In mere minutes, she would walk down the aisle and stand beside Reese Collins. She would promise to love, honor and cherish him for all her days. She would become his wife, and he would be her husband, and the girls would be theirs together.

And though she'd pictured it a million times, never had she believed it possible. And despite the fact it wasn't a real marriage, she had only to look at the expressions on the girls' faces to know it wasn't *all* pretend.

"Thank you. Elizabeth, Nora, Jayne…thank you," she whispered, to the girls, to the heavens, to whatever powers had brought her here today. "I am so lucky your uncle asked me to marry him."

Click. Flash. Jayne took a photo.

"Aren't you going to look inside?" she prodded.

"Yes. Yes, of course." Alex blinked and stuck her hand in the bag, withdrawing the first object. A pale ivory handkerchief.

"Something new," Nora told her. "But the lady at the store said it's just for show, not for wiping tears so bring tissue, too." She opened her pocketbook to display a travel-sized tissue pouch.

"I-it's lovely."

"Keep going. What's next?" Jayne peered in the bag.

"Don't rush her."

"That's okay." She smiled and reached inside the bag again, this time taking out a small embroidered satchel.

"Something borrowed," Jayne announced. "That's the purse Mommy wore on her wedding day. Look inside."

Alex pulled open the drawstring to reveal a tarnished penny and a blue hair ribbon. Old and blue.

"Those were hard," Elizabeth explained. "We didn't know what else would fit in there."

"It's perfect. Everything is—"

"Uncle Reese!" Jayne squealed.

Click. Flash.

Reese's broad shoulders filled the doorway, and Alex's breath stilled in her lungs. He looked so devastatingly handsome in his tuxedo it hurt her eyes to look at him.

"You can't be in here!" Nora tried to shove him back out the door. "It's bad luck to see the bride before the wedding!"

"Sorry." Reese covered his eyes, but not before Alex registered his stunned expression. She didn't have time to contemplate whether it was good or bad before he said, "Your father's here. He'd like to give you away. He wasn't sure if you—"

"He's here?" Tears stung her eyes. "Yes. Oh, yes. Please, tell him to come down." She hastily dabbed at the corners of her eyes as she watched him disappear through the doorway. "Oh, dear," she mumbled. "I don't know what's wrong with me today. I can't seem to get a hold of myself. My father absolutely cannot see me in this condition."

"What condition?" Nora asked, pulling a tissue from her pocketbook. With an innocent smile, she handed it to Alex.

"Thank you, sweetie. You're a lifesaver. I'm afraid my father doesn't approve of these displays of emotion."

"But it's your wedding day. All brides cry on their wedding day. Mom cried."

"Yeah, lots," Jayne chimed in. "She's crying in all the wedding photos."

"Happy tears," Elizabeth explained. "Mom said it's

okay to cry sometimes. You shouldn't keep it bottled up inside you, or else you'll explode.''

What must be bottled up inside her father? Alex had only seen him show the barest flicker of emotion one time—when he'd rushed his pregnant daughter to the emergency room, and the doctors didn't know whether she would live or die. Then, she had seen her own pain and fear reflected in her father's eyes, though his expression remained guarded otherwise.

Afterward, she had been too weak, too physically and emotionally depleted, to think straight. Even so, she had the vaguest recollection of lying in that hospital bed, attached to all those tubes and monitors, and wondering if her father would have allowed himself to cry if *he* had lost the only child he would ever have.

Alex scrunched up the tissue she'd wrung into shreds. ''I didn't know your mom very well,'' she told the girls, ''but I knew your dad, so I know she must have been very special.'' Drawing a steadying breath, she turned her solemn gaze to each of them one by one. ''I want you to know I won't ever try to replace your mom, but I will love you,'' she vowed, ''as my very own daughters.''

*As my very own daughter.*

She spread her arms in invitation, as she'd seen Reese do when the girls came home from school. Nora was the first to dive into her embrace, followed by Jayne, then Elizabeth.

Something swelled inside of her. Something that had always been there, waiting for the right time, the right moment to emerge. Something that felt like the Tin Man's heart, the Scarecrow's brain, the Lion's courage and Dorothy's homecoming all rolled into one.

Click. Flash.

''Alexandra,'' a deep voice boomed from the doorway.

"Daddy." Her eyes overflowed so quickly she had to turn aside to regain her composure before facing her father. He didn't understand her reasons for keeping the truth from Reese, but he would, once he saw how happy she was and how happy she could make Reese and the girls.

"It's her wedding day," Jayne explained in her defense. "She's allowed to cry."

Alex laughed and smoothed her dress. "Thanks, honey. I'm fine. Really." She gave Jayne's shoulder a reassuring squeeze, then crossed the room to embrace her father. "It's so good to see you, Daddy."

"Alexandra." He awkwardly patted her on the back, took a few steps back and cleared his throat. He stood a few inches taller than she, but his commanding presence added another foot. He wore his thick, silver hair in a short, military-style crop that made him look more like a retired army general than a physicist.

"Doesn't she look beautiful?" Nora prompted.

"Indeed," her father agreed. "She looks lovely. As always." Had he ever commented on her appearance before? If he had, she couldn't remember. His eyes were tired, which might have explained why they appeared to soften when he smiled. "She looks like her mother on our wedding day."

Now he had *never* said that before, she knew for a fact, and this wasn't her first trip down the aisle.

"Thank you, Daddy. You're a sight for sore eyes." She wanted to tell him not to go away again, that she'd missed him terribly, and wouldn't he please stay for a while.

Instead, she took his arm and tried not to read too much into his uncharacteristic show of emotion, knowing he would not appreciate hers. "Allow me to introduce my three nieces. Elizabeth, Nora, Jayne. Girls, this is my father."

After everyone said hello, her father stepped forward and took a small jewelry box from his pocket. "I've brought you something."

"What is it?"

"Go ahead. Take a look."

Inside, she found a gold chain with a floating sapphire in the shape of a teardrop.

"Mom's." She lifted the stone with reverence, having recognized it from the wedding photo her father had tucked away in the lower right-hand drawer of his desk.

He nodded. He had kept all her things, boxed them up and put them in the attic. As a little girl she would sneak up the pull-down staircase when he wasn't home, spending hours rifling through the boxes, trying to get to know the woman who had died giving her life.

To her knowledge, her father had never ventured up the stairs. She suspected he'd stashed his wife's possessions out of sight to eradicate the pain of losing her. Out of sight, out of mind.

*...A wound can't fully heal until it's properly cleansed.*

"I only recently found it," he said, as if he knew the direction of her thoughts. "She would have wanted you to have it on this day."

"I...it's beautiful. I don't know what to say."

"Will you wear it?"

"Yes, of course." She turned around and let her father fasten the clasp around her neck. Peeking at her reflection in the mirror, she glimpsed him looking on. If she wasn't mistaken, she would swear that was pride in his eyes.

"I have always supported your decisions, Alexandra," he whispered. "And I will continue to do so."

She swallowed thickly and laced her fingers together. Then, before she could think better of it, she succumbed to the urge, pivoted and wrapped her arms around his waist.

"Thank you, Daddy. That means so much to me."

Over his shoulder, the girls smiled from ear to ear, and Nora reached in her pocketbook to ready the next tissue, while upstairs, the organist started to play.

As Alex readied the girls, she marveled again at the strings Reese had indeed pulled. He happened to play racquetball with the chaplain, who managed to sneak them in between previously scheduled ceremonies. They had half an hour to get in and out, so they needed to hustle.

The girls walked down the aisle in ascending order. Since they were pressed for time, they'd agreed not to strew the petals from their baskets, so they wouldn't have to worry about picking them up.

At the organist's cue, Alex took her father's arm and drew a deep breath. The university's old-fashioned chapel was immense, with soaring ceilings and pews so long even mildly claustrophobic people avoided sitting in the middle.

Today, the aisle seats were plentiful. All empty except one in front—the one where Clay and Kitty Collins stood, watching her entrance.

# Chapter 9

**R**eese had already seen her once. He didn't think she could steal his breath a second time.

He was wrong.

When had she become so damn beautiful? He wanted to rub his eyes to make sure he wasn't hallucinating, but he couldn't seem to move.

His one-time best friend was walking down the aisle, her eyes on no one but him, and all he could do was stare back as a dumb, happy grin spread across his face and his bow tie threatened to cut off his circulation.

It wasn't the dress or the makeup or the hair. It was *her* and the way she looked at him, the way she had always looked at him—as if he mattered.

He didn't want that look ever to change, but one glance at his mother reminded him he'd tempted fate enough for one lifetime. He had no business holding out for more favors.

*Do you have any idea how fortunate you are, Reese?*

*You shouldn't even be here. You shouldn't be living and breathing. You shouldn't exist. Yet here you are.*

Yes, here he was, about to marry the most amazing woman he'd ever known, a woman likely to go down in the annals of history right next to Marie Curie, a woman whose enigmatic smile gripped him like no other.

A woman with whom an undeserving man hoped to share not only his name but his life.

He swallowed as Alex slid her hand into his. It was cold and shaking, so he gripped it firmly. She raised her gaze and smiled, and his chest tightened so painfully he couldn't breathe—again.

A dozen thoughts raced through his mind. He wanted to promise her the world to repay her, to assure her he would never do anything to make her regret her decision to marry him. But such vows seemed sacrilege in a house of God, where his soul lay bare to the truth. So he turned instead and faced the altar and repeated the vows they had chosen.

When it came time to kiss his bride, he thought, "Let the show begin."

He took Alex's face in both his hands, gazed adoringly into her eyes and lowered his head. He expected her to stiffen, thought for sure she'd hold still and allow him to do what he wanted without protest, without participation.

Instead, she stretched up, her hands circling to the back of his neck, her fingers threading into his hair. She returned his arduous look with one of her own, and a tremor quaked through him. A definite eight on the Richter scale.

His mouth whispered over hers. Once. Twice. Three times. Enough, he told himself. The deed was done. But then Alex leaned even closer, applying a bit more pressure, and he was the one to stiffen. Her lips were soft and moist and tempting beyond reason. When they fell open in silent invitation, he bit back a groan as blood pounded through his veins, turning his mind to mush and other places to stone.

It was pure insanity to think for one second this was anything but an act, but when Alex's tongue slid against his, he forgot to think. He angled her head and kissed her back, drinking in the intoxicating sweetness that was hers alone.

One second, they were standing center stage, and in the next, the entire world narrowed to encapsulate the two of them in the spotlight. Gone were the props, the audience, the theatre. Gone were his custody papers, her infertility, their agreement. Gone were mistakes of the past and fears of the future. For one heart-stopping moment, all that remained was the woman in Reese's arms and his unquenchable thirst for her.

"Woooo!"

"Uncle Reese!"

"Aunt Alex!"

His eyes flew open. *What had he done?*

Beneath his lips, Alex laughed. He felt her shoulders shaking and drew back to find her smiling up at him, her embarrassment warring with self-confidence.

She was pleased with herself, and she had every right. She'd done one hell of a convincing job—so convincing, he'd nearly bought the ruse, and he was in on it!

From the corner of his eye, he glimpsed the girls' smiling faces and quickly plastered a grin on his own face.

The chaplain winked at him before addressing their guests. "It's my honor to present Mr. and Mrs. Reese Collins."

Applause broke out from the pews, echoing in the rafters overhead. Their family descended upon them, and Alex clutched Reese's hand.

They were in this together no matter what.

Alex stooped to hug her new nieces, impressed she had made it through the ceremony without giving herself away. But one look at the ring Reese had picked for her, and she wasn't sure how much longer she was going to last.

It was a plain gold band, but inside, the inscription had their names and the wedding date. It looked real. It felt real. But it wasn't. And kisses like the one they'd shared at the altar didn't do much in the way of helping her to remember that.

Mind over matter, her father's expression seemed to say. *You're so close, Alexandra... Tough cookies don't crumble.*

"Hello, Alex."

Just the sound of Kitty's voice made Alex bristle.

Kitty Collins was tall, elegant, and bubbly like the finest of champagnes in a hand-cut crystal flute. She had pale blue eyes, frosty blond hair and a flawless complexion. No one would have guessed she owed her appearance to a fine salon and a skilled plastic surgeon, but then, there was a lot no one would have guessed about her.

"Hello." Alex murmured the obligatory greeting and attempted to move past her.

But Kitty moved faster, grasping both Alex's arms. "Congratulations, dear." She leaned forward and kissed the air to the side of her cheek.

Alex held her breath, as if the woman emitted toxic fumes, and was grateful when she didn't try to prolong their contact. "Thank you." She sidled by at last.

"Reese." Kitty lifted her face in anticipation of her son's kiss, embracing him at a socially acceptable distance. "We took the liberty of booking the honeymoon suite for you at the Greencrest Manor."

"That wasn't necessary, Mother."

"Judging from your message, I didn't think you had

time to make prior arrangements. I apologize if I've duplicated efforts. Tell me, are you in need of a sitter?''

Reese and Alex exchanged glances.

"If you are," Clay offered, "your mother and I will be happy to stay with the girls."

Alex shook her head. "Thank you, but no—"

"Alexandra." Her father touched her sleeve. "May I have word with you?" Drawing her aside, he raised a bushy eyebrow and pinned her with his no-nonsense gaze. "Today is your wedding day. There will be time enough for *this* later. Have you or have you not made overnight accommodations?"

"No, but—"

"Then take Clay and Kitty up on their offer."

"Daddy, you don't understand."

"Explain it to me tomorrow. Right now, the father of the bride has arranged for a small reception at Nikki's Downtown. I, too, hope I haven't overstepped my bounds, but you have to understand as parents, we want to do something besides show up at our children's wedding. Can you do this for us, Alexandra?"

"I can do it for you." She gave a determined smile. "I've missed you, Daddy."

A crimson stain crept up her father's neck and into his cheeks. "Very well, then." He grasped her hands, patting them as he nudged her toward her groom. "Why don't you and Reese work out a plan of action and let the rest of us know what you decide."

Alex filled Reese in on her conversation with her father. Since they hadn't made definite plans beyond the wedding ceremony and knowing the girls would delight in any and all festivities, they agreed to Frank's generous offer.

"The Inn's up to you," she said. "If you're uncomfortable about leaving the girls with your mother…"

"I'm not." Reese couldn't explain to Alex his mother was different with Jeff and Jeff's children, different with everyone but him. He couldn't admit he was the sole target of his mother's ugliness when she used to drink, that the alcohol had brought out her true feelings about him.

He blew out a breath and draped a casual arm around Alex's shoulder. "Let's do it. It'll probably look strange if the newlywed couple doesn't jump at the chance to be alone on their wedding night."

"That's what I thought." She gave a halfhearted smile, as if the prospect of spending the night alone with him didn't thrill her any more than it thrilled him.

"Buck up, buckaroo. It'll be over before you know it."

"No, it won't. This is just the beginning."

They exchanged miserable glances.

"Uncle Reese! Aunt Alex!" The girls smiled and waved from the balcony. They looked so happy, so content.

Their good cheer warmed Reese's heart. He turned to Alex, saw her eyes mist as she smiled and waved back. His gaze captured hers, asked a silent question. She looked again to the girls and gave an answering nod.

With a breath of determination, they straightened their shoulders and forged ahead, as if all was right in the world and they couldn't be happier.

Across the room, the mother of the groom twirled a straw in her glass of sparkling water and charitably conversed with the father of the bride. Alex had long questioned the source of Kitty Collins's charity when her heart so obviously defied her actions.

She caught Kitty's eye across the room, narrowed her gaze and noted with satisfaction Kitty's glass froze short of her lips. Good, let her see her new daughter-in-law as a force with which to reckon if she chose to make trouble.

As expected, Kitty recovered with practiced grace, smiling and raising her glass, but Alex didn't return either gesture. She would not be so easily handled this time around, would not turn a blind eye to Reese's suffering.

After an awkward moment, Kitty seemed to realize there would be no easy truce between them and turned to speak to the closest available party, who happened to be Elizabeth.

From the sidelines, Alex watched her work the room—no matter the size of the gathering, Kitty was always working. Every few minutes, she would glance up, her gaze inevitably locking with Alex's. Finally, as if she could no longer bear the silent accusation in Alex's frosty glare, she excused herself and started toward her.

Alex knew she had but one opportunity to stand her ground, to set the precedent for all future interactions, to show Kitty the impressionable, easily intimidated girl she once knew was gone. She'd had fifteen years to practice. With so much at stake, she had no room for error.

Drawing a deep, calming breath, she inclined her head. "Hello, Kitty."

"Alex." The corners of her mouth lifted as if by invisible pulleys. "I was hoping you would eventually mingle my way."

Alex clenched the stem of her glass a little tighter. "I don't know if I could ever mingle your way. You have a style all your own." The words were out before she could stop them, as the rumble of a long-dormant volcano.

*Don't blow. Not now. Stay calm.*

The pulleys lowered the merest fraction, then raised back into place without missing a beat. "I suppose even a backhanded compliment is more than I deserve. I know you see me as some sort of horrible monster, but the truth is—"

"Please." Alex held up a hand. Kitty had to know she would not tolerate disparaging remarks about Reese in her presence ever again. "I'm not the one who needs to hear your explanations." She glanced across the room and caught Reese's eye. Noting his concerned expression, she lifted a hand and smiled, letting him know she was okay.

Kitty's mouth tightened. "My relationship with my son is more complicated than you think."

Understatement of the decade.

"I'm not trying to make excuses for my behavior," Kitty continued. "I had a severe drinking problem, as you know—that's not an excuse but an explanation. I've been sober almost two years."

"I heard. Twenty-three months, eight days, and seven hours. Congratulations."

"Thank you. Alex, I…" She glanced down at her hands, then drew a breath. "I want you to know how very sorry I am for the manner in which I expressed myself to you, but you have to know, I had legitimate reasons for questioning Reese's suitability as a parent."

*But.* Of course there was a *but.* Kitty always had a reasonable explanation for everything…why she wore dark glasses, why she had headaches, why she needed to spend the day in bed. And Reese, ever grateful to Kitty for taking him in, bore the weight of those reasonable explanations.

"You're apologizing to the wrong person," Alex said.

Kitty grasped her hand. "You were children having children. You couldn't have handled the responsibility. Reese certainly couldn't have…"

Alex's stomach tangled in painful knots. Her hand went limp and slid from Kitty's grasp. "What a lovely wedding gift." She willed her voice to remain steady. "Tell me, does proper etiquette require me to thank you now or later?"

"Alex." Kitty looked aghast. "I didn't bring this up to be cruel but with the hope you would understand—"

"I don't. I never have. Tell me, why does a woman magnanimously adopt a child, then hold him to unrelenting standards all his life? Why must he work twice as hard as his brother to win his mother's favor? And even then, why does she expect him to prove himself over and over?"

Kitty paled beneath Alex's undeniable accusation.

"If you still think Reese couldn't have handled the responsibility, you don't know him any better now than you did then. If you *just once* took a good look at the person he is, instead of the archetype you've cast him to be, you'd see your son, *my husband,* is one of the most admirable men on God's green earth." Her voice was thick with conviction. "And since Reese and I are no longer children, I will *not* understand you questioning our suitability as parents." She let the words hang between them, ominous and challenging.

Their meaning registered as expected. "I assume you haven't told Reese what happened," Kitty said, as if on cue.

Alex didn't move a muscle, didn't flinch, didn't look away. "Only that I can't have children."

Kitty nodded. "Your secret is safe with me."

"Yes, and I know why—because I'm not the only one who kept the truth from him. You have just as much at stake."

Kitty didn't—or couldn't—meet her gaze. If she'd intended to use her knowledge as a bargaining chip for the girls' custody, she was sorely mistaken.

"You know, for years, I *was* afraid you'd tell Reese, even as recently as last night. Then my father gave me some sage advice." She drew strength from the man who'd backed her decisions no matter what, who'd always tried to do his best by his only child. "He said a wound can't fully heal until it's properly cleansed, and I realized he was right, as usual." She squared her shoulders in determination. "Reese and I aren't going to have secrets this time around. When the time's right, I'm going to tell him everything."

Kitty's eyes took on a distant look. "There's never a right time. The longer you wait, the harder it gets."

"I don't expect it will be easy." Indeed, her doubts seemed to have undergone mitosis and multiplied in the past week; but talking to her father had halted the process, allowed her conviction to steadily increase and catch up. Alex knew what she had to do. "I'll find a way," she vowed.

"Yes, I believe you will." Kitty's voice held a touch of envy. "You're a better woman than I, Alexandra Ricci."

"Thank you." She accepted the compliment in the spirit it was given. "And it's Alexandra Collins." With a smile of confidence, she raised both her chin and her glass. At long last, she had said exactly what she'd wanted.

"Dance with me." Reese's new wife tugged at his arm.

He lowered his glass, one eyebrow raised in question. "But you don't—"

"It's a special occasion." She turned and signaled her father, who in turn signaled someone outside the door. A moment later, the opening bars of Eric Clapton's *Wonderful Tonight* drifted from the overhead speakers. "My pick. I hope you don't mind."

"It's perfect." His hand slipped to the small of her back, guiding her onto the dance floor. With a casual smile, he leaned down and grazed her jaw with his lips. "Don't look now, but everyone's watching."

She smiled back and laid her cheek against his chest.

"I saw my mother cozying up to you," he whispered, his lips brushing her hair. "Everything okay?"

She closed her eyes. "Everything's fine."

"Good." He pushed aside a tendril of her hair and traced the curve of her neck with the back of his finger. "Did she say anything about the girls' custody?"

"Not exactly, but I have a feeling…call it cautious optimism…that she might be about to change her mind."

He'd call it a damn miracle, if they pulled it off. His arm drifted over her back as he rocked back and forth.

"You sure you're okay with taking my name?"

"I'm sure. It'll be easier with the girls."

Whatever her reasoning, he was glad. Since she hadn't taken Tom's name, he'd assumed she wouldn't take his either. Leslie hadn't. But Alex had suggested it, and she wouldn't get any arguments from him.

"Reese," she murmured. "There's something I've been wanting to say…ever since the holiday party. I wanted to tell you then, but I was so nervous, caught up in my own…"

His hand stroked up and down. He didn't want her to be nervous around him. "What did you want to say?" he coaxed.

She lifted her gaze, and his gut pulled tight at the look in her eyes. "I'm so proud of you. Everything you've accomplished. Everything you've become. You were an incredible boy, and now, you're an extraordinary man."

Reese swallowed—once, twice. He couldn't find his voice around the sudden tightness in his throat.

Alex lowered her lashes and picked at imaginary lint on his sleeve. "I…I know I was your last choice, but it's an honor to be your wife. Leslie's loss is my gain."

He lifted her chin with the curve of his finger. "You

were my first choice," he admitted, his voice hoarse. When push came to shove, she always was. Because he trusted her more than he'd ever trusted another individual. "I just didn't want to take advantage of you again."

Her eyes filled with tears she blinked back. "You never did. You never made me do anything I didn't want."

At her words, Reese bent his head and caught her lips in a long, lingering kiss—not because they had an audience, but because it felt as vital to him as his next breath.

Her hands slid around the back of his neck, and her tongue slipped into his mouth. A flame of desire ignited low in his belly, spreading through his limbs like a wild fire. He kissed her back with a restless hunger, then broke off before he started groping her in front of their family.

"Damn, woman." His voice sounded ragged, his breathing choppy. "Where'd you learn to kiss like that?"

A stain of a blush crept into her cheeks. "Sorry. I got carried away." She laid her cheek against him again.

"I liked it," he admitted, his hand drifting to the back of her neck, idly stroking his thumb over the soft skin as he struggled to catch his breath. "I liked it a lot."

"Really?"

"Really."

"So…" She lifted her shoulder in a tiny shrug. "Does this mean I get a spot in your little black book?"

He chuckled, tipping his head back. "Sweetheart, you *are* my little black book."

She drew back and searched his gaze. With an enigmatic smile, she reached up and touched his cheek. "Remember our promise—no one leaves this time. I'm holding you to that."

He took her hand, turned his face and kissed her palm. "You're the mother of my children. I'm not going anywhere."

The music stopped. Neither of them moved.

After a moment, Alex's hand fluttered to her throat. "I—I could use some more champagne, please. If you don't mind…"

"Sure." With reluctance, he let her go. "Be right back."

They stayed at the reception another thirty minutes, playing their newlywed roles to the hilt. When it came time to leave, Reese scooped his bride into his arms and carried her out the door to a round of cheers. The instant his feet hit the lobby, they both heaved a sigh of relief.

Reese eased Alex down, sucking in a sharp breath as her body glided against his. Her eyes darted to his, then slid away. He steadied her on her feet, then strode toward the coat closet, struggling to get back his equilibrium.

All this role-playing messed with his mind big time. What was real and what was videotape? Did actors have this much trouble getting out of character at the end of the day?

He handed his ticket to the clerk, retrieved their long, cashmere coats, and stuck a tip in the glass. Then he waited a full minute, trying to ground himself in reality, before heading back and helping Alex with her coat.

"Wait here. I'll get the car."

She nodded and took a seat in an overstuffed chair in the lounge. He watched her reflection in the glass as he pulled on his coat and scarf. She smoothed her skirt and clamped her hands together, her back straight as a pin.

She didn't look any different, didn't appear the least bit affected by the past hours' charade.

Because nothing had changed, he told himself as he shoved out the door. He and Alex had acted all lovey-dovey, as agreed, for the sake of their families. Beyond that, Reese had no business reading anything into anything.

Not the way she reached for him, the way her hands lingered for no apparent purpose, or the way her eyes appeared to take on that bedroom quality, focused on no one but him. Definitely not the way she kissed him, the way her tongue meandered into his mouth, though no one but he would know, or the way her lips curved in a lethal combination of shyness and seduction afterward.

None of it.

Reese left the canopy of the restaurant and headed out into the latest winter flurry. Though the roads were recently plowed, the Suburban was blanketed in a few inches of freshly fallen snow. He blew on his knuckles and opened the door to a mini-avalanche, leaned over the front seat and turned the keys in the ignition. Blasting the defrost, he let the engine warm while he scraped the windshield.

Big, fat snowflakes continued to fall from the sky. He hadn't checked the forecast. Were they in for another lake effect storm? He hoped not. That was all he needed—to get snowed in at the inn with his new wife. *You swore you wouldn't touch her until she was ready—put your money where your mouth is, bud.*

He climbed inside, tossed the ice scraper into the back seat and slammed the door with more force than intended. He turned on the radio and eyed Alex's overnight bag on the passenger seat. What were the chances she packed baggy, shapeless sweats?

Alex pulled a white silk robe over a matching nightgown and tied the sash. With shaky fingers, she reached for the doorknob and opened the bathroom door.

Decorated in French country style, the spacious honeymoon suite boasted a sitting area in front of a marble fireplace, three walls of windows and a huge platform bed.

Candles of various shapes and colors lined the window sills, flanked by red and white poinsettias. A heavy quilt covered the bed, the sheets turned back to reveal rose petals strewn over the pillowcases. On each bedside table sat baskets of more petals, their faint fragrance lacing the air.

Reese stood facing the far windows, his back to her. He'd untucked the tails of his tuxedo shirt, and his feet were bare on the plush carpet.

A slow, languid heat spread through her body at his partial state of undress and her first glimpse of the everyday intimacy they would share as man and wife.

"All yours." She padded into the room.

"Thanks." He turned from the windows and started for the vacated bathroom, a wad of red flannel bunched in his hand. Halfway there, he glanced up, his stride faltering an instant before resuming.

She didn't know what she would have read on his face had she kept looking because the instant their gazes met, hers swept across the length of his body.

He'd unbuttoned his shirt, and his undershirt stretched taut across a muscular upper chest, the planes of his hard stomach, and the tapering of his narrow waist.

She looked away in a sudden rush of heat. He was only the most attractive man she had ever known. Did it surprise her she could handle such potent virility only in small doses, like the first sips of good cognac?

She dove for the chaise lounge and her overnight bag, fumbling with the contents until she heard the door close behind her. Exhaling, she took a bottle of lotion to the vanity table, sank onto a ruffled stool and smeared a blob on her legs.

At the sound of running water, she rubbed harder and faster, trying to concentrate on the task so as to keep from imagining the sight on the other side of the wall.

It didn't work.

Her skin tingled as she capped the lotion and replaced the bottle. When the shower stopped, she surveyed the bed and ran a nervous tongue over her lips, trying to figure out the logistics of how they would get through the night.

She thought of crawling in, burrowing under the covers, and feigning sleep, but she didn't know which side of the bed Reese preferred, which side would be hers.

It was a strange thing not to know. They knew each other so well, on so many different levels, yet on others, they were complete and total strangers.

She rubbed her arms and rounded the foot of the bed. Moonlight shone through the naked tree limbs, casting long shadows, like bony fingers, across the rug. She walked to the window, her steps halting at the sound of the bathroom door opening behind her.

Light spilled from the doorway, and she spun around, stopping short at the sight of Reese's bare chest, her breath catching in her throat. He wore only the pajama bottoms low on his hips, and a towel draped around his neck.

Caught staring, she grasped the first words that popped to mind. "N-nice pjs."

"Thanks. I don't usually..." He shifted and glanced around the room. "They were a Christmas present from the girls." His hair was damp from his shower, and she smelled the familiar scent of soap and shampoo and something else—something entirely his.

The remembered scent brought with it a remembered ache, so powerful her heart thundered in her chest, and she took an involuntary step backward, followed by another, until the window sill hit the back of her knees.

She grasped the ledge to steady herself. Behind her, the frigid marble chilled her. In front of her, Reese's gaze warmed her like the heat from a fireplace. Her eyes flickered toward the bed and then back to Reese, and she moistened her suddenly dry lips.

He followed her gaze to the bed, and she noticed the sudden tension that crept into his posture.

"Alex—"

"Reese—"

"Go ahead."

She chewed her lip, trying to come up with the right words to put them both at ease, but not even a script could make this act any easier. "I—I've never really bought into this wedding night hype," she ad-libbed. "How about you?"

"Hype?" He frowned.

"You know, the expectation that the bride and groom must consummate their marriage immediately following the ceremony."

"Right." He tipped his head back. "*That* hype."

Alex clasped her hands together to keep from shaking. "Of course, the origin's understandable. We can trace its roots back to the days of rampant virginity before marriage. The wedding night was like a ribbon cutting ceremony. But in this day and age… Well, we're hardly virgins."

"Hardly."

"So we shouldn't feel pressured to…you know."

Reese raised an eyebrow. "Make love?" His voice was deep, husky.

A wave of longing crashed through her body. "R-right. I mean, that is, unless you—"

"I wasn't planning on it." He gave a casual shrug, eyeing her curiously. "Were you?"

"Me? Oh, no," she lied, pulling her silk sash tighter around her waist.

Reese tugged the towel from around his neck, scrunching and scrutinizing the plush cotton as if looking for defects. "It's not a big deal."

"No, of course not." She forced a smile, though deep inside, she felt something break, felt the jagged edges stab at her heart.

What had she expected? For Reese to deny the truth, to get down on his knees and declare a change of heart, to profess his undying love for her?

Had she dropped one-hundred IQ points in the past five hours?

She knew what she was getting into, knew their reasons for marriage had nothing to do with each other and everything to do with the girls.

So why was it becoming increasingly difficult for her genius brain to retain these simple facts?

She turned then, and stared unseeing out into the night, afraid to shed even one of the tears that had welled in her eyes, for fear if she started, she would never have the control to stop. She wrapped her arms around her waist and tried to calm the ache in her stomach.

Why did it hurt so much to know Reese didn't want her?

She wasn't ready. He wouldn't push her. He would be a gentleman, true to his word.

Reese glanced around the room. It sure would have been easier if they weren't in the honeymoon suite of a romantic country inn. The snap, crackle, pop of seasoned birch blazed in the fireplace. The soft glow of candles illuminated the windows. The magnum of champagne chilled by the bed.

The bed.

"I hope you aren't tired yet." He did *not* want to get

in that bed with her until he was sure he'd fall asleep within thirty seconds of his head hitting the pillow.

"Not especially." Her voice sounded like it came from further away than the window.

Reese eyed the bed again. "Want some champagne?"

"If you're having some."

He'd drink the magnum if it would put him to sleep, but he knew what happened the last time they got drunk together. Tonight, he'd play it safe.

Better safe than sorry.

Reese popped the cork, poured two flutes of bubbly and handed one to Alex. "So, what should we drink to?"

"Let's see... We covered health, happiness and prosperity at the reception. We promised to love, honor and cherish at the ceremony. How about a short-term toast this time?" She raised her flute. "To getting through tonight."

"Hear, hear."

Their glasses clinked.

Alex took the first sip and wrinkled her nose. "Good, but the bubbles tickle." Her tongue flicked to the corner of her mouth to dab at the moisture.

Reese tried not to stare, forced himself to look around the room. "Got any ideas for killing time?"

"TV? Cable? Maybe there's a movie."

"I'll check." He sprawled out on the couch, remote in hand. Hey, this wasn't so bad. Maybe he could sleep here and give Alex the bed.

In his peripheral vision, he saw Alex move to the vanity. With every move of her gently rounded hips, the nightgown swished behind her, giving her a regal air.

She placed her champagne on the glass top and sat down on the stool. Stretching, she reached behind her head to pluck the pins that held up her hair. The reflection of the mirror revealed her robe had gaped open, and Reese glimpsed the swell of one creamy breast through the slit.

He bit back a groan and took a gulp of champagne. Damn it, wedding nights weren't supposed to be spent watching TV!

If things were different, if she'd given him even the smallest indication she was anywhere close to ready, he would have crossed the room and eased the robe and gown from her shoulders. He would have kissed the delicate column of her neck and kneaded the tender mounds of her breasts until she arched and wriggled against him. He would have carried her to the bed and laid her atop the rose petals and made sweet, incredibly slow—

"See anything you like?"

Reese choked on his champagne, then realized Alex couldn't see him with the angle of the mirror. "Ah, still looking." And he was—with rapt fascination—as each hairpin plunked onto the vanity and each silken lock unraveled like a spool of ribbon.

He felt like a voyeur but couldn't seem to turn away. He'd never seen a woman take down her hair, never imagined anything so innocent could look as erotic as a striptease.

And then he remembered, in all the years he'd known Alex, he'd never once seen her with her hair down. Always, she'd worn it either in a French braid or a ponytail or else a knot on her head.

He hadn't known what he'd been missing.

Curls spilled onto her shoulders and down to her waist. A man could get lost in all that hair. He wanted to be that man. He'd only touched stray locks between his fingers, but a handful would be heaven. He imagined burying his face in the softness, pictured long, silky strands fanned across his chest.

Alex glanced over her shoulder and caught his eye before he could look away. "Nothing good, huh?"

"Oh, I'd say there's lots of potential." He expelled a harsh breath and clicked the remote a few more times. "Just trying to remind myself patience is a virtue." One that didn't make the Top Ten on his list of personal attributes, unfortunately.

As if sensing his frustration, Alex sighed and turned around, her expression sympathetic. Reese imagined what it would be like to wake to this sight every morning, or if he'd ever manage to sleep.

"We could play cards," she offered. "There's a deck on the desk."

Reese tossed the remote aside, needing to move around to keep the circulation distributed throughout his entire body, not just his central regions.

He found the cards and shuffled them, wondering if he might interest Alex in a game of strip poker when she resumed with the brush. Midshuffle, he forgot what he was doing, and half the cards spilled on the floor.

Alex heard the noise and laughed. "Don't tell me. I know. It's not your fault. Your fingers are too big."

"Nah, I just use that excuse to cover my incompetence."

Her contagious laughter dissipated some of the tension in the room. Some. Not all.

"I'll trade you," Reese found himself saying.

"Trade me what?"

He held out the deck. "Shuffle. I'll brush your hair."

Brown eyes searched his, as if trying to gauge whether or not he meant it. She hesitated a moment too long. He'd dropped his hand when she extended her brush.

She froze, and a deep crimson stained her cheeks, as if realizing she'd miscalculated and ended up the butt of a joke. And though he'd half-intended the offer in jest, it suddenly became imperative Alex understand he would never laugh at her expense.

"A little faith, sweetheart." He took the brush from her hands and replaced it with the deck of cards. "We're talking brushing—not braiding. Basic father-daughter bootcamp. I can do this drill in my sleep. Turn around."

She eyed him with stunned disbelief.

"Turn." He made a circular motion with the brush.

She obeyed and cut the cards. They arched into a perfect bridge.

"Show off." Reese glided the brush through her hair. "Too rough?" When she shook her head, his hand smoothed over the path of the hairbrush. "Wow, it really is as soft and silky as it looks," he whispered in awe.

Alex laughed. "You sound like a commercial for shampoo."

"And you look like the model." He met her eyes in the mirror.

Her cheeks flushed, and she lowered her lashes. "Thanks."

"Alex, I…" He glanced at the bed and gave a silent oath. He must have been insane to insist on sharing a bed. What red-blooded man could sleep in the same bed with her and stay on his own side?

He'd thought the king-size bed at home would be big enough, but judging from this one, they'd need two king-size beds, each with its own separate, unconnected bedding.

Hmmm…what were the chances of a furniture store having an answering machine? He could leave a message and get an order in for delivery first thing Monday morning, so he wouldn't have to spend one more night in a damn torture chamber with his new wife.

"It's okay if you want to go to sleep," Alex offered, misinterpreting his anxious expression. "We don't have to play cards."

How stupid would it look to request a rollaway in the honeymoon suite?

"Actually, I'd rather watch TV. Do you mind?"

"No, I brought some academic journals. I can read in bed."

"Fun." He handed back her brush, trying to keep the frustration from his voice. Didn't every bride spend her wedding night curled up with a hot essay on the evolution of something-or-other? He flopped back on the couch.

Alex frowned, looking at the bed. "Reese?"

"What?"

"Which side do you usually sleep on?"

"The left."

She started to move.

"No, the other left. If you're in the bed."

She stayed put, pressing her fingers to her temples. "Reese?"

"What?" he snapped.

She sat on the edge of the bed, the long, straight line of her back to him, one spaghetti-strapped shoulder exposed where the robe had slipped. "Are you angry with me?"

"No." He deliberately softened the edges of his voice, pulled a soft, nubby blanket from the back of the sofa and carried it to the foot of the bed. "In case you get cold."

"Why don't you come to bed, too?" She brushed her hand across the pillowcase, gathering the rose petals and putting them in the basket on the bedside table. "You can watch TV while I read. We can get used to…sleeping together."

"Right." Reese combed a hand through his hair.

God help him. He was going to die.

# Chapter 10

Alex didn't know how long she lay on her side with her back to Reese, listening to the smooth, even pattern of his breathing. Such a melodious sound, one she had longed to hear on so many nights, so many years ago. A sound she didn't think she would ever hear again.

Slowly, she rolled onto her other side, careful not to shake the mattress too much.

Reese lay on his back, one arm slung over his head to rest on the pillow. The exposed biceps was so perfectly shaped it almost looked fake, as if someone had stuffed a big ball of gauze, or a tennis ball underneath his skin.

She remembered how little boys would prop up the underside of their arms to make the muscle appear bigger. Hesitantly, she reached out and dusted the tips of her fingers over the smooth flesh.

Heat emanated from his body like electromagnetic waves, prickling her fingertips and transmitting energy up her arm and down through her body.

She levered herself up on one elbow and drank in the sight of his body, relaxed in sleep. So beautiful, so compelling…like the sunset over Lake Ontario that drew her gaze even when she knew better than to stare.

Before she could think better of it, she grazed the length of his upper arm, sliding her fingers along the curve of his shoulder.

She remembered sitting on the rocks at Mallard Lake and watching him swim across the lake, the fading sunlight glistening on the well-sculpted muscles of his shoulders. Those memories had fueled many a schoolgirl fantasy.

But this wasn't a dream.

She trailed her knuckles along the column of his neck, his cheekbone, his jawline. Late night stubble prickled against her already sensitized skin.

As a teenager, the grace of his body had mesmerized her. She'd wanted without knowing what she longed for, felt a cataclysmic yearning for something she couldn't define. How could she act upon impulses she couldn't even name?

She traced his collarbone and the hollow of his throat, feeling his pectoral muscles with the rise and fall of his chest beneath her palm. The sheet bunched around his waist, and her fingers drifted toward it, whispering over the expanse of exposed skin with heightened longing.

She wanted to continue her exploration, wanted to do things she hadn't dared before, but how could she act upon desires that weren't returned?

She was supposed to be asleep. With her soliloquy on the hype of wedding nights, Reese couldn't believe Alex would consciously do what she was doing.

Her hands wandered all over his upper torso with the ease and familiarity of an old lover. With his luck, she was probably dreaming and would soon awaken to realize her mistake. In the meantime, what harm would it do to enjoy her sweet torture as long as it lasted?

Or so he thought. Until her hand drifted lower. With purpose. Like a flame burning a trail of gunpowder, heading straight for one undeniable target.

He held his breath and told himself he had to wake her, to extinguish the fuse before the imminent explosion, but for the life of him, he couldn't do it. Not when the target was hot and hard and aching for her touch, when he wanted her hands on him so badly he could taste it.

He'd been without a woman too long, he told himself. It wasn't Alex. Any woman would have had this affect on him. And yet, when he cracked one eye open and read the fascinated expression on Alex's face, something unfurled in his chest, something that felt way different than run-of-the-mill lust.

Lust, he could deal with. This, he balked at giving a name or even acknowledging its existence. He couldn't.

Wide-eyed and pensive, Alex's gaze roved over his body, as if calculating the odds of taking some action.

Reese wanted to take action all right. To hell with odds. He wanted to wrap his hands around her waist and haul her astride him. He wanted to peel off every stitch of her clothing and guide her hips over his as they found a perfect fit. He wanted to let her ride him as he caressed her to a fiery pitch.

He wanted all these things and more, but before he could act on any one of them, her hand was gone, her back turned, her decision made. His body cried out in silent protest, and he bit back a groan of pure, unadulterated agony.

As unsatisfying as their last encounter had been for her,

he didn't blame her for having reservations. But he wanted to show her it would be different this time.

He wanted to show himself.

The bed dipped, and he heard the rustle of her robe, followed by the creak of hardwood under the thick carpet. She walked to the window and braced both hands on the ledge. First came a sniffle, then a defeated droop of her head.

Something was wrong. Very wrong.

Reese sat up halfway, bracing his weight his elbows. "Alex? What is it?"

She spun around, swiping a hand across her face. "Sorry. Did I wake you?"

"No." He pulled himself upright. "What's wrong?"

"Nothing. A touch of insomnia. It'll pass."

"Bull."

"Pardon me?"

"You've obviously got something on your mind."

She sighed. "It doesn't matter, Reese."

"It matters to me." He tossed the covers back and came to his feet. Whoever choreographed this three-act musical of theirs, he wanted his money back. "Come on, Alex. Just because we're married doesn't mean we can't talk anymore."

She frowned and stared somewhere around the area of his chin. Finally, she admitted in a small voice, "It's the hype. I—I still don't buy into it, mind you…but I have to admit it feels…odd, you know, to start a life as man and wife without…"

"Without…?"

She shook her head, waving her hand in dismissal. "It's late. I'm overtired. My brain's in meltdown."

Reese's throat tightened. "Without making love?"

She closed her eyes as if the thought distressed her beyond words and turned toward the window. "You know, everything's so garbled in my head. Garbage in, garbage out. I'm not thinking straight. This isn't like me."

"You think too much."

She gave a pitiful sniffle. "That's like saying you breathe too much."

He stared at her slumped shoulders, the rigid line of her back, the curve of her bottom. He was afraid to touch her, afraid not to. "This is harder than you thought."

She nodded.

One chance. He would give her one last chance. He steeled himself. "Do you want out, Alex?"

"No. Not at all. It's not that. I'm having a little trouble getting through tonight. I'll be fine...tomorrow."

He stepped closer and cupped her shoulders, his thumbs slipping beneath her hair to stroke the tender skin at the base of her neck. "Is there anything I can do to help?"

She gave a strangled laugh and let her head fall against his chest. "Can you will the sun to rise any faster, so we can get this night over and done with?"

"I wish I could, but I don't think it would help. Like you said, this is just the beginning."

A long moment of silence stretched between them.

"Then I want to begin," Alex said in a voice so soft he almost didn't hear.

His hands stilled. "What exactly are you saying?"

"I—I changed my mind. I think we should consummate our marriage tonight."

He cleared his throat. "I, uh, don't have a problem with that."

Alex nodded. "We should get the first time behind us."

Reese wasn't about to argue this wasn't their first time when she sounded so devastated by the prospect of a repeat performance. Searching to find "a spoonful of sugar to help the medicine go down," he found himself saying, "It might not be so bad if we keep pretending."

"Pretending?"

"Just for tonight. We could rewrite our past and our present. Even our future."

She turned her head to the side, her gaze searching his. "What would we pretend?"

"The usual. That we're in love. That we always have been, and we always will be."

"I don't know, Reese... I'm afraid..." She shook her head. "I don't want to disappoint you."

She had to be kidding. The fact that she wasn't, unleashed his protective instincts. Leaning down, he enfolded her in the circle of his arms, his cheek against hers, wanting to soothe her worries and self-doubts.

"You couldn't disappoint me, Alex."

"I have before."

In that moment, he realized she had carried her own baggage from that night so many years ago, and it seemed more imperative than ever they created a new memory to eradicate the old.

"Close your eyes." Reese swept his fingers over her eyelids and up to her temples. Rubbing gently, he coaxed, "Relax. Stop analyzing. Just listen to my voice and let yourself believe..."

Her hair fell like a silken veil between her shoulder blades. He scooped a handful off her neck and brushed his lips across the sensitive flesh. "I have loved you from the first moment I saw you..."

She gave a soft cry of incredulity. "With my knobby knees and my nose in a book."

"No, with your incredible smile that turned my insides to mush." He pressed warm, moist kisses along the column of her neck, peeling back her robe to expose one creamy shoulder. His hand skimmed her collarbone. At her low, throaty sigh, he slid the spaghetti strap of her gown aside and nibbled a path to her shoulder. "You turned me into an addict. I would do anything to see that smile. Again and again." He punctuated each *again* with a gentle nip.

Alex's head rocked forward. "You were the kindest boy in the entire neighborhood. So cute with that dimple, and so smart."

"Even though I could never compete with the ever-fascinating world of science…" His hands glided over her rib cage, and she gripped his thighs, bunching the flannel of his pajama bottoms.

"I have loved you—" Her voice trembled "—since the day you chose me to play on your team."

The air stilled in Reese's lungs. *World. Stage. Men and women. Players. He and Alex. Role-playing.*

He told himself he didn't want or need Alex's avowals, but the words sounded so sweet on her tongue, he couldn't help but want to taste them. And so he dipped his head and swept his mouth over hers. She opened eagerly, her hand curving around his neck to hold him to her.

One night. He would let himself believe the farce for one night. But no more. No more…

Reese groaned and pulled her more fully against him. Her bottom pressed against his arousal, and he heard her swift intake of breath.

"Reese…?" She knew he wanted her. There was no denying it. He waited for her to pull away, to show any sign of protest, but she didn't.

"We started as friends…" His hand slipped beneath her robe, cupping the fragile flesh of her breast. Rewarded with a soft moan, he continued. "But we grew into more."

"Yes, more." Her nipple hardened into a tight bud he rolled between his thumb and forefinger. She trembled, her breath coming in short gasps. "Reese, do you remember the first time we made love?"

"Yes." He bowed his head, rubbing his cheek against her hair. Would they ever succeed in forgetting that night?

She turned in his arms then, stretched up and laced her fingers through his hair. "It was at Mallard Lake." Her eyes searched his, daring him to let reality encroach on their fantasy. "We went camping," she coaxed, as if trying to jar his memory. "And I was cold."

He smiled. "You climbed inside my sleeping bag."

"You offered."

"You didn't say no."

She lifted her hand and caressed the side of his face. "I never said no to you."

He caught her wrist. "You should have."

"I didn't want to." Her soft breasts pressed against his chest, and he was overcome by the need to feel her bare flesh against his.

His hands reached for her robe and slid the fabric from her shoulders. It pooled to her feet, revealing a matching, low-cut nightgown that drew his gaze to the lush curve of her breasts.

He dipped his head and rolled his tongue through the supple valley in between. Her skin tasted sweet like apples. He remembered the bottle on the vanity and grew even harder as he envisioned Alex rubbing the lotion over herself slowly, without missing an inch of skin.

Her hands dug into his upper arms. "I didn't know how much I wanted you until that night. I couldn't put words or action to what I felt. It was all so foreign."

Reese stood and brushed his lips over her forehead, her eyelids, her nose, her lips. Then, ever so carefully, he lowered the straps of her gown. The fabric slipped to her waist, baring her upper body to his seeking gaze. His stomach clenched, and he forgot to breathe.

Who needed air? A man could live on the sight that greeted him—two perfect scoops of vanilla ice cream, each topped with a succulent, ripe strawberry.

Hoping he wasn't drooling like an idiot, he glanced up and noted the deep crease between Alex's brows.

She stood stock still, looking somewhere over his shoulder, as a defendant awaiting a verdict…and preparing for the worst.

Uncomprehending, Reese's gaze lowered again, further this time, until he saw it. A horizontal scar, right below her belly, ran from one side clear to the other.

*I had a hysterectomy. Not by choice.*

Whatever happened, it must have been complicated to warrant such an incision. He couldn't even begin to imagine… Tenderly, he traced the line with his fingertips then dropped to his knees and retraced it with his mouth.

A muffled sob broke free, though no tears fell.

"Alexandra Collins." He lifted the hem of her gown and rose to pull it over her head. "You are the most beautiful woman in the world to me." His fingers trailed along the underside of her raised arms and down her sides, turning her skin to gooseflesh.

She shook her head as if she'd reached some limit in her mind and couldn't stretch her imagination any further. He took her hand, without breaking her gaze, and put it on the steely evidence of his attraction. "Believe it, Alex."

She gasped, her eyes two round pools of surprise, but instead of pulling away, her fingers closed over him through the flannel of his pajamas.

Reese gave a strangled groan, his mind riveting back to Mallard Lake when she had done the same thing without knowing any better. With the clarity of hindsight, he admitted, "I knew that night at Mallard Lake it was you I wanted to be with more than anyone else, you who made me feel accepted..."

"Yes," she cried, her eyes smoldering with passion. "For the person I was inside. Not the shy, awkward—"

"Outgoing, laugh-a-minute—"

"Geek."

"Jock."

They laughed, then stopped.

Alex's hand moved with purpose on his swollen flesh, wrenching another groan from him. "It was beautiful."

"Perfect." His hands slipped beneath the elastic of her panties and eased them over her hips. She wiggled and kicked out of them. At the movements of her shapely bottom in his hands, he restlessly pulled her closer.

She gave a tiny sigh of pleasure. "I dreamed of marrying you and having your children."

A guttural cry ripped from him, and he couldn't stop the convulsive jerk of his hips against her hand.

"Too much." He took her hand and put it on his shoulder, burying his face against the curve of her neck as he struggled to pull much-needed oxygen into his lungs.

She had no idea what she was doing to him, no idea how deeply she'd managed to burrow into his mind yet again, to the far recesses of his soul, to places he allowed no one.

*No one.*

His mind cried out to stop this game, to pull back before it was too late. His body screamed for completion.

He moved urgently, lowering his head to nuzzle her breasts, first one and then the other. Alex moaned softly, her hands plunging into his hair and holding him to her.

His mouth captured one taut nipple, suckling as a babe then flicking his tongue across the tip. She gasped and arched like a bow, her balance wobbling. He anchored an arm around her waist and moved to the other breast, repeating his sensual assault.

"Reese." His name was a plea, and when he lifted his head and looked into her eyes, he saw a reflection of his own bottomless need. "There's nothing I can't tell you."

"Nothing that would ever separate us." He dragged his body upward, the friction of their bare skin racheting up the flame under his already-boiling desire. And though his oxygen-starved brain protested he would never be the same again, he took her face between his hands, knowing he would surely die if he turned back now.

"Alex?"

"Yes?"

"I want you."

"I want you, too."

"Now."

"Yes, now." Her hands rubbed his upper arms, and he watched with wonder as she pressed her lips to his chest, slid her fingers beneath the waistband of his pajamas and drew the flannel over his straining arousal.

His lips found hers. Sighs mingled. Tongues tangled. They fell onto the bed, clinging to one another like two long-lost lovers reuniting after an unbearable separation.

Alex felt Reese holding back in his effort to lavish her with all the patient, reverent attention he'd been too rushed to give her that first time. It didn't matter he had no idea what that night had meant to her, how it had been perfect in its imperfections. She wanted to give him what he had given her—a new memory to cherish as she cherished the old.

Wanting to please him as he'd pleased her, her mouth and hands wandered everywhere, touching and tasting and doing things she'd lacked the courage and experience to attempt in her youth. His responses told her she was succeeding and gave her the confidence to keep going.

She draped a thigh over the hard plane of his stomach and rolled on top of him. Hungry eyes raked over her, and she bent to kiss the hollow of his throat, awestruck by the racing pulse beneath her lips.

Her breasts felt heavy and swollen in his hands, and when the sensitized nipples grazed the coarse hair of his chest, an unbearable, throbbing ache settled between her legs. She moaned and closed her eyes.

In one fluid motion, Reese rose and flipped her onto her back. His mouth dragged long, lingering kisses down the length of her body, fueling her desire until her every nerve ending quivered with frenetic need. And then his hands were parting her thighs, and a cry of protest escaped her lips.

Reese raised his head, stormy blue-gray eyes reflecting the shattering intensity of his own desire. "Please, Alex."

In a remote part of her brain—the only microcosm still functioning—an alarm sounded. Red alert! Danger! Proceed at your own risk! If she exposed herself any further, if she let down the last of her defenses, she would never recover this time. Never pick up the pieces and resume her life.

Never get over him.

"Please," Reese whispered again, his voice raw, earthy. And then, before she could respond, his head dipped, his gaze never leaving hers. His tongue found her—hot, wet and tender.

She gasped and arched off the bed. No more. She couldn't take any more. She hooked her hands under Reese's arms and tugged him over her. The heat and the hardness of him nudged against the silk and the wetness of her, and a muscle in his jaw bulged with the effort of holding back.

She didn't want him to hold back. He had to let go…before she did.

"Now." Her thighs moved restlessly against his.

"Not yet, sweetheart." He braced his weight on both hands, and the steel bands of his arms flexed as a bead of sweat dripped from his brow. "It's been too long. I won't last a second inside you. Let me satisfy you first."

"I'm satisfied." She reached between their bodies before he could roll away. Lifting her hips, she guided his entry and felt her own slick heat where their bodies joined.

"Ah, Alex…" He swore softly, and she moved again, wanting to erase the regret and self-blame from his eyes. "You feel so good. So damn good." He gripped her hips and inched forward, then retreated. "I don't want to hurt you."

"You won't. I'm ready, Reese."

At her words, his control snapped. With a low groan, he drove deep and hard, burying himself to the hilt.

"Yes," she cried, wrapping her legs around his waist.

They started slowly with whispers of encouragement, reacquainting themselves with the subtle nuances of one another. With each whimper of pleasure, they grew more bold, their tempo increasing amid pleas for more. Soon slick, sweat-dampened bodies rocked together in perfect harmony, mindless of all but the primitive dance of lovers.

Reese reached for her, but she caught his hand and shook her head. "Too much."

"Alex…can't wait…much longer…"

"Don't wait." She arched to meet his lips. "It's not the first time, or the last."

He moaned and gathered her in his arms, burying his face in her hair, as if he couldn't bear to let go.

But he had to. She reached for him. "Let go, Reese. Please, let go."

As though the decision was no longer under his control, fierce tremors wracked through him, and he gripped her hips. Plunging one final time, he erupted inside her, spilling his seed with a low, tortured groan of regret that told her just how much he'd wanted to take her with him.

Spent, he collapsed against her, then rolled to the side, taking her with him. "Alex." He tucked her into the curve of his arm. His breathing labored, and his hand stroked her hair. "You didn't..." he said after a time.

"Some women don't."

"Now where'd you read that?"

"Oh, I don't know." She traced the shape of his lips with her index finger. "Numerous sources."

He kissed her fingertip. "Your sources are wrong."

"And you're such an authority on the subject, are you?"

"I've conducted a bit of my own research."

"I don't want to hear this." She closed her eyes.

"I'll skip straight to the findings. All women can. Some women haven't, or don't regularly." He skimmed his fingers over her shoulder and down the length of her back. "I'm persistent. Trust me." He brushed his lips across her temple, then lifted her face for a long, lingering kiss before settling her back into the curve of his arm.

How she wanted to trust him—*him* more than anyone. But how? When it came to her innermost secrets, when it meant abandoning her hard-won control and stepping outside the fortress she'd built around her heart stone by precious stone, Alex trusted no one—not even herself.

Who better to understand that than Reese?

It was worse than Reese remembered, worse than the worst of his college hangovers. His temples pounded, his insides churned, and the acrid taste of bile burned at the base of his throat.

Careful not to awaken his sleeping wife, he untangled his limbs from hers and stumbled toward the bathroom.

With only one exception—Leslie—this was the point at which he untangled himself from a relationship. Experience had taught him it was far easier to be the one who walked away, instead of the one left behind.

Only this time, there would be no easy escape. Reese had made his proverbial bed; now both he and Alex would lie in it, together forever as man and wife.

He turned on the faucet, lifted the toilet seat and emptied his stomach.

After splashing cold water on his face for five minutes straight, he brushed his teeth and braced his hands on the edge of the basin, summoning the courage to look into the mirror. He already knew what he would see…

All his life, Reese Collins had avoided serious relationships. When it came to women, ''serious,'' by his definition, meant the combination of physical and emotional.

For the most part, he'd succeeded. Retaining emotional distance with the women he dated, and even his first wife, had never posed a problem. Their relationships started as purely physical, and they stayed that way until they ended.

Alex had been the opposite. She'd started out his tutor— a whiz kid with whom a physical relationship had never entered his mind. So he'd let down a few barriers he might not have otherwise, never sensing the danger, until it was too late.

Instinctively, he'd kept their relationship platonic, pushing aside all thoughts of anything more. He would not, could not think of Alex as anything more than a friend. Or so he'd thought.

And when he crossed that line, all bets were off.

He'd felt it then, as he'd felt it last night. His worst fear had come to life. He was that little boy again—the one he never spoke about. Weak, vulnerable and needy.

He hated it, despised himself for feeling that way, felt physically ill the morning after. And he knew, even before he lifted his gaze to the mirror, what he would see reflected in a grown man's eyes—the despondent hunger of a little boy who wanted more than anything in the world for someone to see him for who he was, and to love him anyway.

Alex sensed the change in Reese almost immediately. He said the right words and made the right gestures, greeting her with a long, deep good-morning kiss and an intimate fondle of her breasts. But he didn't touch her hair or her face, his gaze didn't linger and his easy grin wasn't as "easy" anymore—as if it required greater effort.

"Hungry?" he asked, reaching for the guest services binder. "I can order room service while you shower."

He'd already showered and dressed. She had awakened to the sound of running water. "Just coffee, thanks." She pursed her lips and eyed him warily as she cinched the sash of her robe at her waist.

He looked up, met her gaze and put down the menu. "Alex, about last night…"

She wrapped her arms around her stomach and braced for the worst.

He seemed to register her protective stance and spread his hands. "It was incredible," he admitted. "*You* were incredible."

Alex felt her heart swell with his praise, certain he could see everything she'd ever felt for him, everything he'd ever meant to her, reflected in her eyes. She wanted to tell him, tried in vain to find the right words, but all she could manage was, "You, too."

"Yeah, right." By gradual degrees, he took on the casual air of a man who'd lived through his fair share of morning afters. "Thanks for playing along." He sat down and draped an ankle over his knee. "You're a good sport."

*A good sport?*

Alex's smile froze. Her entire face felt as though it had turned into a plaster cast, and if one muscle so much as ticked, the mold would crack for certain.

Without a word, she turned for the bathroom and closed the door behind her. No tears. She would not cry. Sagging against the wooden barrier, she pressed the heel of one hand to her mouth and gasped for air.

Last night, Reese had made her feel wanted and cherished—*loved*—as she'd never felt before. And in his arms, she'd found a peace—with the world, with herself—she'd never imagined could exist.

Now, she couldn't salvage even a fraction of the feeling. Not when Reese had thanked her as if she were a lowly hooker with whom he'd bartered for a trick.

Damn him. Why did he have to ruin it?

## Chapter 11

"Penny for your thoughts," Alex prodded, disquieted by the oppressive silence on the drive home.

Reese shrugged and peered out the windshield. "Looks like clear skies. Hope it'll stay that way until my parents take off. They're predicting another foot tonight, but you know how that goes."

"They're leaving tonight? Don't they have a wedding next weekend? I thought they'd stay through the week."

"Dad's got a golf outing, and Mom won't miss Tuesday night bridge for anything."

"For a minute, I thought you were going to say bingo."

He raised an eyebrow. "My mother?"

"Good point." She smiled; he didn't. "So, what do you and the girls usually do on weekends?"

"I don't know. Any number of things. Play outside. Play inside. Go places. Read. Do homework."

"Have you ever done science experiments with them?"

"No, can't say I have."

She nodded. "That's what my father and I used to do on weekends. I know some good ones the girls might like. Fun and educational, too."

"Whatever you want, Alex."

What she wanted was him—the Reese she knew, not this impassive stranger. She stared at his profile, noting how all the small changes added to a lot. With each passing moment, bittersweet memories of the previous night tasted far more bitter than sweet.

She didn't like this new Reese. She wanted the old Reese back. The one who joked with her and tried to make her laugh. The one who initiated conversations, who didn't speak only when spoken to. The one she'd loved with her heart and soul into the wee hours of the morning.

*Where was he?*

Please, she begged the heavens, bring him back. Make it real.

But reality wasn't part of the deal in their make-believe marriage. If she wanted to maintain even the slightest semblance of her pride, she needed to remember that. She couldn't afford to forget. And so they rode the remainder of the trip in silence—not the companionable kind, not even the angry kind—but the kind between two people who shared no bond greater than mutual convenience.

Once home, the girls flooded into the mudroom, welcoming them with barely contained enthusiasm.

Nora grasped Alex's hand and swung it in the air. In a singsong voice, she chanted, "We have a surprise for you."

"Yes, we do." Jayne joined in, lunging for Reese who doubled over to intercept her. "Grandma and Grandpa got them at the store, and we helped…"

"Jayne," Elizabeth warned.

"What?" Jayne's eyes widened with innocence. "I didn't tell."

"You almost did."

"Did not."

"Did, too."

"Ah, home." Reese tipped back his head and smiled—really smiled—for the first time that day.

*It'll be all right. He'll come around.*

"How about you give us thirty seconds to get out of our coats and boots, and we'll be right in, okay?"

"Okay." Elizabeth hugged her uncle and pried her sisters loose from Alex.

"Where are Grandma and Grandpa anyway?" Reese asked.

"Inside. They said not to pounce on you."

"That went over real well." He winked.

"Well, we *missed* you," Elizabeth countered, her gaze encompassing both Reese and Alex.

"We're home now," Alex reassured, hugging Elizabeth. "And we're not going anywhere without you for a long time."

The apples of Elizabeth's cheeks rose, and she gave Alex a huge grin before shuffling off behind her sisters and closing the door.

Alone again, Alex felt the particles of air shift and regroup, as if she and Reese had invisible force shields between them. Having the girls around would help.

Maybe.

Reese hung their coats, shucked his boots and offered to help with Alex's.

"Thanks." She grasped the window ledge behind her, anchoring herself while he pulled off her boots. When she curled her toes, he took her foot in his hands and rubbed first one, then the other, never once looking up at her.

The right words, the right gestures, but something sorely lacked. Something had changed and not for the better.

Was this how he was with his girlfriends? Was this what she'd coveted all those years?

No, she wanted to scream. If she had to choose between friend and lover, she'd choose her friend, the man with whom she'd made love last night, not this stranger.

"Ready?" Reese straightened and pushed open the door, so she could precede him.

"Reese, I—"

"Surprise!" Clay and Kitty stood behind the girls in the foyer—Jayne holding Albert in her arms—reminiscent of a Christmas card pose.

Alex stepped inside, followed by Reese, and Nora skirted forward, holding a wedding album in both hands. "For you."

"You made this?" Reese asked, taking the album.

"It's lovely." Alex lifted the cover and drew back the tissue paper, her fingertips tingling with anticipation.

They had selected a full-length shot of Reese and Alex at the altar to grace the first page of the album. Reese held her hand, poised to slide the ring over her finger. She was looking up at him. He was gazing down at her. Love shone in both their eyes. Below the photo, the album's caption read: On This Day I Shall Marry My Best Friend...

"We should sit," Reese said, his voice gruff.

"Good idea." Alex gave a shaky smile.

Everyone headed toward the family room, except Kitty who lingered behind and caught hold of Alex's sleeve.

"We need to talk. In private."

Alex nodded. "After the album."

They spent the next hour looking through the album, piled on the couch with Reese's parents flanking them in adjacent armchairs. Each photo lent itself to a story, and the girls recounted in vivid detail what everyone was saying and doing at the time.

"Here's Uncle Reese pacing the hallways while Aunt Alex is getting ready."

"Yeah, he was real nervous."

"He asked us to make sure Aunt Alex was still getting ready and didn't slip out the back while he wasn't looking."

The girls erupted in a fit of laughter while Reese shifted uncomfortably and turned the page.

"Oh, look. Here's Aunt Alex crying *again*."

"Yeah." Jayne pointed one chubby finger at the photo. "That's right after she said how lucky she was that Uncle Reese asked her to marry him."

The girls made romantic cooing noises, and Alex imagined she turned at least twenty shades of crimson.

"Let's keep going," she urged, tucking a lock of hair behind her ear and ducking her head.

The next photo showed Reese walking into the dressing room and finding Alex. They both looked stunned in a dreamy I-can't-believe-you're-really-here kind of way.

Alex shot up, nearly stepping on Albert's tail and bringing Jayne, who'd nestled into her lap, to her feet. "Um, hot chocolate, anyone?" She settled Jayne into her vacated spot.

"Me!" sang the chorus of little girls.

"I'll help." Kitty followed suit.

"You know where it is, Mom?" Reese asked.

"Yes, dear. You keep going. We'll be right back."

As Alex followed Kitty into the kitchen, she was struck by recollections of the past, of the good times not the bad. With a pang of nostalgia, she recalled all the winters Kitty bustled them in from the cold, warming their coats in the dryer while she served up mugs of hot chocolate heaped with marshmallows on top the way they liked them. The instant they thawed, they'd run outside and start over again.

Once upon a time, Kitty had been the closest thing to a mother Alex had ever known. The disillusionment of youth, she thought as an overwhelming sorrow blanketed her.

In the kitchen, Alex opened a cupboard door and took down some festive, green-and-white pinstriped mugs. Kitty opened another and started to add some brown-and-white ones, but Alex said, "I think we have enough green ones, thanks."

Kitty's eyes cut to hers, giving her an anxious glance. "I know what you're thinking."

"Reese probably bought those ugly brown mugs thinking they were green?" She tried for levity, but Kitty made no attempt to dodge the subject.

"You're remembering how it used to be. It's difficult to realize I'm not the person you thought I was, to see me as Kitty, not that nice Mrs. Collins across the street."

Alex shrugged, though Kitty's accuracy pierced her heart. She didn't know what to say, so she took the kettle from the stove to the sink to fill with water.

Behind her, Kitty sighed. "As children grow up, they begin to see parents as people—peers instead of superiors. The mindshift is hard on parents, too, to have their flaws held up to the light, to account for their faults."

Alex bit her lip and turned on the water.

"You're right," Kitty said. "I'm not the person you once thought I was. I'm not the person Reese thinks I am either. I haven't told you everything…"

She turned off the water and peered over her shoulder.

Kitty raised a hand to her forehead. "It's difficult for me, even after all these years. But I realize you'll never believe I'm anything less than a monster if I don't at least

attempt to answer your questions." She met Alex's gaze.
"I gave a baby up for adoption once."

Alex's hand went slack, the kettle hitting the counter
with a thud. Pieces of the puzzle suddenly fell into place.
Her eyes widened, and her mouth formed a silent *O*.
"That's why..."

"That's why." Tears welled in Kitty's pale blue eyes,
her cool facade melting. "It happened before I met Clay.
I was older than you were, but the opportunities for women
were far more limited then, especially unwed mothers.
Needless to say, the pregnancy changed the course of my
life."

"Kitty, I'm so sorry." Her own eyes misted. "I had no
idea—"

She shook her head and waved her hand in protest. "I'm
not telling you this for sympathy. I'm telling you because
you're going to be raising my grandchildren, and I don't
want them picking up on your negative feelings for me.
I've never pretended to be perfect, but I've always tried to
do the right thing, to fulfill my responsibilities as best I
could. I've slipped more times than I can count—God
knows there are incidents I'll regret all my life—but I'd
like to think I've succeeded more times than I've failed."

Alex gripped the counter with both hands, not wanting
to jump to conclusions until...

"I'm dropping the custody suit," Kitty confirmed.

Alex's knees nearly buckled with relief. She felt the
sting of grateful tears and squeezed her eyes shut, sending
up a silent prayer of thanks.

"I was uncomfortable with the idea of a man raising
three girls alone—"

"You needn't be. Reese is an excellent father."

"All the same, I feel much better with you here. You

were like a daughter to me, and it pained me greatly when I thought my son had taken advantage of you.''

"He didn't. It wasn't like that *at all*. Reese and I...cared about each other very much. And while I certainly sympathize with what happened to you, it isn't fair to keep punishing Reese for things he hasn't deserved.''

"Punishing him for another man's sins.'' She gave a wry smile. "Yes, you made your position quite clear last night. Reese is lucky to have you.''

"It's the other way around—I'm the lucky one.''

"Perhaps you're both lucky, to have found each other. I do wish you both all the best.'' Kitty held out a hand, offering the proverbial olive branch. As she took it, Alex felt the first tiny, mending stitch in their relationship. "I'll tell Reese to tear up the papers. How's that for a wedding gift?''

Alex shivered. "It's wonderful. Thank you.''

"I'd like to ask something in return. I don't want what I confided in you to go any further than this room.''

"But...'' She thought of Kitty's closet alcoholism and the verbal abuse Reese had suffered. The revelation might show Kitty's behavior in a different light and help mother and son cleanse the wounds of their past. "It explains so much.''

"No.'' She said the single word with the authority of a parent who wouldn't tolerate any back talk. "And if you truly care about Reese, you won't intentionally hurt him.''

"I don't see how this would hurt—''

"It would. Our relationship is strained enough.'' Her voice was urgent, pleading. Her perfectly plucked eyebrows worried together. It was the same emotional button she had pushed fifteen years ago.

If Alex had cared anything about Reese, Kitty had advised her then, she wouldn't tell him about the baby. She wouldn't expect him to quit school, marry her and abandon his aspirations of a fast-track legal career. She wouldn't throw away her future.

All along, Kitty had been reliving her own past, her own forsaken dreams that still festered inside her. Reese had to know—it wasn't his fault. It was her—not him.

"Kitty, with all due respect, Reese is already hurting. He's been hurting all his life."

Kitty blanched, as if she understood where Alex was headed. "You think the truth will set him free."

"Won't it? And you and me as well?"

Kitty lifted a hand to her face as if to compose herself. "I need time. I'm not ready for this."

"There's never a right time. The longer you wait, the harder it gets." She repeated Kitty's words from the night before. "Reese needs to hear it from you and no one else," she allowed. "And you need to say it…to heal."

Alex turned her gaze to the window where the wind had kicked up snowdrifts and wondered how much longer she could put off her own confession.

Reese was ecstatic at the news Kitty was dropping the custody suit. The second they were alone, he swooped Alex off her feet, twirled her around and kissed her breathless.

They spent the next few weeks consolidating households and settling into new routines. For Christmas, they took the girls skiing in Vermont.

Unfortunately, Reese's unguarded euphoria lasted only through the New Year, which he and Alex celebrated in the Jacuzzi after the girls fell asleep. As before, Alex pulled back at the last minute, and Reese's barriers went up the very next day, leaving Alex to wonder if this time her heart might break in slow, painful pieces instead of all at once.

When school started, Alex took over supervision of the girls' afterschool activities, which allowed Reese more time for work and the possibility of pursuing partnership in a law firm. With her help, his participation in the girls' lives didn't suffer. He positively excelled at fatherhood, while Alex relished her second chance at motherhood. Recipients of two parents' devotion, the girls blossomed.

Not a day passed that Alex didn't think about their own daughter and wonder what it would have been like to share these experiences with her. Not a day passed that she didn't dread telling Reese what happened. And not a day passed that she didn't question whether she was compounding her wrongs by withholding what she'd learned about Kitty.

Within the year, she had allowed. She would give their new family a chance to bond, their new marriage a chance to solidify, before they faced what might prove their greatest challenge. But while their family flourished with each passing day, their marriage languished.

"Talk to me, Alex. Tell me what you want," Reese persisted when they made love. It seemed pillow talk was the only conversation he initiated anymore.

But Alex could find no words to communicate that what she wanted and what she needed were two different things.

She wanted to offer herself to Reese completely, but she needed to cleanse the wound. Until she did, she could not let go of the last remaining barrier around her heart. She was trapped in a vicious cycle of her own creation.

Every night, as she lay awake, she wondered…if Reese could grow to want her this much, maybe one day he could grow to love her. And if he could grow to love her, maybe one day he could find it in his heart to forgive her.

Then maybe, just maybe, she might even forgive herself.

* * *

Weeks turned to months, and winter turned to spring. In anticipation of her upcoming performance reviews, Reese helped Alex tailor her lectures to the common man and proved an excellent tutor on people skills.

"Earth to Alex. Come in, Alex."

"What? Oh, sorry. Did you say something?"

"You aren't at all into this, are you?" Reese closed the book with a sigh.

"No, I am. I am. I heard everything you said." She proceeded to regurgitate the past minute of his mock lesson verbatim. "See?"

While she'd grown increasingly confident in her ability to translate complex physics concepts into layman terms, she was increasingly discouraged by the lack of communication in her marriage. How could she solve the problems of the past when she couldn't even solve the problems of the present?

Reese frowned. "So, you're ready to run through your lecture one more time *in English?*"

He didn't talk to her anymore—not like he used to. He was most like himself when they were with the girls, but when they were alone, those blasted barriers went up as if set on an automatic timer, and try as she might, she could not get them to come down.

"Oh, Reese." She sighed and stared out the window with longing. "Do we have to?"

"Umm-*hmm.*" He narrowed his gaze. "As I suspected."

"But it's such a nice day. We suffered through an entire winter, and now the sun's shining, and the birds are singing. Are we nuts to be indoors?"

"You want to take this outside."

"No, I want to pick the girls up directly from school and go to the park." She stood up and wrapped her arms around his neck, pressing a series of kisses to his cheek. "What do you say? Please, please, please?"

"You learned that from the girls."

"They're very good at it."

"Yes, they are."

"So can we go?"

"Uh, hello?" Reese indicated the face of his watch. "We both have classes this afternoon."

"Shoot." She wrinkled her nose. "I forgot."

Somewhere along the way, their roles had reversed. Reese tried in vain to keep her attention on the task at hand, while she, equally determined, tried to distract him and get him to ease up and have some fun.

At the sound of the doorbell, she bounded toward the door. "I'll get it."

"I give up," Reese said behind her.

She peeked out the window. "I don't see anyone's car." She peered through the peephole in the mudroom, saw her father and threw open the door. "Daddy! What a surprise! Aren't you supposed to be in Alaska?"

"It's too cold."

"Uh-huh." She smiled. This was the second trip he'd cancelled. She suspected he enjoyed the adventures closer to home these days. "Say, you don't by chance want to teach my four-thirty class, do you? And get someone to cover for Reese as well?"

"Why? Aren't you feeling well?"

"Never mind. Come in, come in. So what brings you to this side of the street?"

"It's about your promotion, Alexandra. I cannot stress the importance of your upcoming reviews. You aren't far from tenure, and your student evaluations are pivotal."

Her smile melted. So much for a day in the park. "Can I get you a drink?"

"No, thank you."

"I think I could use one." A stiff one. "Why don't we go into the living room?" She took her father's arm and threw an anxious look over her shoulder. Reese gave her the thumbs-up signal. She wished for a fraction of his aplomb.

"How'd it go with your dad?" Reese drew patterns on Alex's stomach in bed that night, dipping lower each time.

"Fine." She caught his hand and laced her fingers with his. "The usual pep talk—three generations of Riccis, my higher purpose, the Nobel prize. Blah, blah, blah."

"Alexandra, my dear, you've been given a sledgehammer." Reese imitated her father's serious drone. "One doesn't use a sledgehammer to crack a peanut."

She laughed, then sobered. "I've missed that."

"Missed what?"

"Being your friend."

"What do you mean?" His eyebrows drew together.

She levered up on one elbow. "Don't tell me you haven't noticed things are different between us. Ever since we became…"

"Lovers?"

She nodded. "You don't talk to me anymore."

"I talk to you. When have I not talked to you?"

"It's not the same, Reese."

He sighed and rolled onto his back, one arm flung over his head. She slumped against her pillows. They stared up at the ceiling for a long moment during which neither spoke.

"I wish you wouldn't give me the silent treatment," Alex whispered. "You know how I hate it."

Reese closed his eyes. "You frustrate me."

"Well, you're not alone. It's not like you have some kind of monopoly on frustration."

"Oh, I know why *you're* frustrated. I'm working on it."

"Don't distract me with sexual innuendo, Reese."

"All right." He rolled over and nipped at her neck. "I'll distract you with the real thing."

Though her body shivered with longing, she forced herself to turn away. "Not tonight," she said, her back to him. "I have a headache."

"A simple no will suffice."

"You're shutting me out, Reese. I want to know why."

He groaned, and she heard him fall back against the pillows. "I wish you'd stop trying to crawl into my head. You're a physicist, not a psychologist."

At that moment, she was neither. She was a woman who was losing the man she knew, day by day, minute by minute. Fragments of age-old conversations replayed in her mind...

Reese, narrating his side of the story as to why his latest relationship had dissolved. Alex, murmuring sympathies and wishing him better luck next time.

Always, the same iteration—just when he and his girlfriend *du jour* started getting serious, he either broke it off or did something uncharacteristic to prompt the girl to dump him. She had recognized the recurring, self-sabotaging theme but attributed it to other girls—not her.

"To think I used to envy them." She gave a bitter laugh at the irony, unshed tears prickling her eyelids.

"Them whom?" The deep rumble of Reese's voice came behind her, and she realized she'd spoken aloud.

She contemplated evading the question—it would have been so easy—but evasion had turned into a way of life in the past months, and she was tired of it. So tired...

"Your girlfriends," she admitted, a hot lump of shame

like a fireball in her chest. "They had something I could never have, and I never realized how lucky I was to have something *they* could never have."

"Alex…"

"We were like peanut butter and jelly, you know. You were the jelly, of course—a different flavor for every mood and occasion. I was the peanut butter—pretty much the same each time…nuts on occasion." She lifted her shoulder in a show of indifference, while the first tear wrestled its way free. "Now, we're like anchovies and horseradish."

"Who's the anchovies and who's the horseradish?"

"It doesn't matter!" Her voice cracked, and a cascade of tears spilled down her face, plopping onto the pillow. "They're both horrid, and they're even worse together."

"Hey." Reese hooked one strong arm around her waist and hauled her backside up against him. "It's not that ba— My God, you're crying."

"It *is* that bad." She sobbed. "I want it like it was before. Please, Reese," she pleaded in a broken whisper, "I can't take this anymore. I just *can't.*"

"Don't say that." The desperate edge of fear tinged his voice. "Don't say you're calling it quits."

"I'm not! I just want you to talk to me again."

"I'm sorry," he choked out, burying his face in the curve of her neck. "Sweetheart, I'm so sorry. I didn't realize. I had no idea."

"You're my best friend, damn you." She pounded on his arm with her fist, helpless to downshift emotions now in overdrive. She felt the same as she had all those years ago when he'd up and checked out of her life. Only this time, she told him. "I need you. I miss you. I want you back."

"I'm here. I'm right here." He pulled her closer, planting kisses on her hair, her cheek, her temple. "I'm not going anywhere. I swear I didn't mean to hurt you. I never wanted to hurt you.''

"Then why are you shutting me out?'' she cried, wanting to believe him, unable to deny the facts. "Don't you *like* me anymore?''

"Of course I like you. I like you more than ever. Alex, I—'' He swallowed. "I've never felt this way about anyone. I don't know what to do, how to act. It's all so damned strange.''

"Just be you. The old you. *My* you.''

"Okay. That's what I'll do.''

"It doesn't have to change because we're lovers. We're still *us*.'' She sniffled. "We just have fewer clothes on.''

"Got it.''

"And *don't* shut me out.''

"Okay. I'll stop. Right now. Right this second.''

Alex drew a series of shuddery breaths as it dawned on her they were having a conversation—a real and meaningful conversation—in bed, no less. *She* was actually telling *him* what was on her mind, and he was responding positively. "R-right this second?''

"Right this second,'' Reese promised.

"And never, ever do it again?''

"Never, ever again. What do you want to know? I'll tell you anything. Just don't cry. Please, sweetheart. Don't…cry…anymore.'' He smoothed her hair, his voice sounding as though he'd run a great distance and was short of breath. "I…can't…stand…making…you…cry.''

She turned her head to gaze into his eyes. There, she saw a reflection of her own pain and suffering, but that wasn't all. There was a mixture of caring and desire—a mixture that stole her breath. "I have a question.''

"Ask. Whatever you want. Just ask.''

"Make love with me? Please? I changed my mind.''

"You'll never have to ask that one twice." His mouth swooped down, devouring hers in a long, deep kiss.

She matched his intensity, kissing him back with all the pent-up emotion in her heart. He drew her nightgown over her arms and head, then pulled her backside against him. He was already naked. She wore only panties.

His bare skin felt exquisite against her. She couldn't get close enough to him. She wiggled her bottom, trying to mold herself to the curve of his body. His arousal pressed against her spine. She reached behind her, but he groaned and removed her hand.

"Not yet." He flicked his tongue along her neck and nibbled her earlobe. His fingers splayed up her rib cage, his hand finding and cupping one of her breasts. It felt full and heavy, the nipple swollen and throbbing. When he squeezed gently, she moaned and arched her back.

He kneaded her breasts, first one then the other, and drew her closer, pressing his hardened length against her. She pressed back, her hips slowly rocking to his rhythm as liquid heat pooled between her thighs.

"Now?" she whispered.

"Not yet." His knee nudged her legs apart, and she opened willingly, rubbing her silky legs along the sinewy length of his. When his hand slipped down to cup her, she tilted her hips to thrust into his palm. He rubbed back and forth until her wetness soaked the fabric of her panties, dampening her thighs.

"Now, Reese." She had to divert his attention before she lost control, but when he slipped underneath the elastic and touched her heat, she was so ready for him, she gripped his arm and threw back her head. She could no sooner find the words to protest than she could slit her own throat.

"Reach for it, Alex." His fingers plunged into her, his palm grinding against her.

She gasped, sucking in a series of sharp breaths.

"Come on, sweetheart. Reach for me."

*For him.* His words were her final undoing. He embodied her hopes and dreams, her wishes and prayers, her life and her breath. Without him, she would never be complete.

A delicious, quivering sensation gathered in her loins, swiftly gaining momentum. Blood rushed in her ears, and rippled through her body. Before she knew what was happening, her hips were undulating in lightning quick thrusts, and a cry of sheer ecstasy ripped from her lungs.

Stars danced before her eyes, her body tingled all over, and her breaths came in short, ragged pants. She wanted to savor the feeling for all eternity, but then, reality encroached as it always did, sooner than she wanted.

She felt exposed, vulnerable in a way she'd never felt before. With a small whimper of mortification, she went perfectly still, mentally preparing for Reese's reaction.

Had she sounded like a banshee? Had she woken the dead? Or worse, the girls?

Taking small, shallow breaths, she closed her eyes and retreated to a safe place inside herself where it didn't hurt so much when she didn't measure up to the expected standards of mainstream society.

A minute passed, and nothing happened. Reese didn't stir or move a muscle, though his hand remained between her legs, holding her almost protectively. Alex pried one eye open, alert in the silence. She waited a full minute more. Sweat beaded her lip. Still nothing.

With caution, she turned her head, bracing herself for the worst. If he said he owed her, so help her, she would murder him in his sleep.

But masculine pride shone in his eyes. That, and something else. A raw, aching vulnerability, as if he'd been equally affected.

"Every woman can. Some women haven't," Reese whispered hoarsely. "Welcome to the other side. It's my honor to induct you, Mrs. Collins." Then he kissed her cheek with such tenderness, a lump swelled in her throat. "Do you have any idea how sexy you are?"

She choked up in earnest then. "Only you could ever make me believe that."

"Believe it." He rolled her onto her back, peeled off her panties and covered her body with his.

She wrapped her legs around his waist, welcoming him home. He slid into her easily, and right away, she felt the familiar pressure mounting. "Reese?" She clutched his arm.

"Go with it, sweetheart." He plunged, then retreated, one hand slipping between her legs. "Just let go."

"But you...?"

"I'm not going anywhere. In fact, I rather like it here. Right in this very spot..."

"Reese!" She clung to him as her back arched like a bow. He captured her mouth, anchoring her as the world spun on its axis like a top spiraling out of control. For the first time, she embraced the heady sensation of soaring without bounds, reassured her safety net awaited. Tremor after tremor gripped her, and then he was there with her, crying out his own shattering release.

She hugged him with her legs, cradling his head in her hands. In that moment of pure, unadulterated euphoria, she knew she was gone—absolutely, positively, irrevocably gone.

She could pretend she'd married Reese to repay a debt, or for the girls, or for a million other things. But in truth, she'd married him for one reason.

For herself.

And now that he'd slipped past her barriers and secured a permanent place in her inner fortress, she would never be the same again.

How would she explain about the baby? Would he blame her? Could she take that risk? God, she couldn't lose him again. She simply couldn't.

"*That* was incredible." Reese rolled onto his back, taking her with him, and tucked her against his side.

"I had no idea…"

"Now you do."

"Wow."

He chuckled. In the shadowy darkness, their breathing labored. He drew lazy circles on her back. She draped her leg over his and listened to the steady rhythm of his heart.

"Reese?" she asked after a time. "Why didn't you ever call me?"

"What? When? Did I forget—"

"No, not now. Before… All those years ago…"

There was a moment of silence, followed by a deep sigh. His hand stilled. "I didn't think you'd want to talk to me, or see me again."

"I did." She traced the strong line of his jaw with her index finger. "Very much."

"Then why didn't you call me? You could have gotten the number from my parents."

*Because I didn't want to force you into a situation you wouldn't voluntarily have chosen. Because I was in love with you and couldn't stand the fact you didn't love me back.* "Because I was young and stupid."

He caught her hand, laced their fingers together and brought it to his lips, kissing her softly. "No one could ever call you stupid, sweetheart."

How wrong he was.

# Chapter 12

Reese swished through the autumn leaves on Frank's front lawn, or Grandpa Frank's, as the girls liked to say. If they didn't hurry, they'd be late getting to dance class. Any minute now, Dr. Rothermel would pull in the driveway, and they still had to change.

Reese could hear them chattering and giggling inside even before he reached the door. They loved playing with the eccentric scientist. Alex claimed they'd mellowed him.

"You wouldn't believe what he lets them do," she'd said to Reese when she thought her father was out of earshot. "I was never allowed to do that."

"You never asked, Alexandra." Her father's voice boomed from the other room where he'd gone to retrieve a celebratory bottle of wine.

"You wouldn't have let me."

"*Au contraire*. You had only to ask."

"Sheesh. Now he tells me." Alex slumped against Reese, and he laughed and put an arm around her.

That afternoon, she'd received notification of her promotion—her performance had exceeded expectations, and she'd set a personal record on her student evaluations. They shared a glass of wine with Frank, then had their own private celebration.

If Reese stopped to think about it, the point of no return was when Alex came apart in his arms for the first time. Luckily, he didn't stop and think too much these days—he was living up to the promise he'd made his brother, taking each day at a time and being grateful for what he had. Truth to tell, life was pretty damned good.

Frank Ricci greeted him at the door wearing an apron with orange splotches. "Do you have time to come in?" he asked. "We just finished carving pumpkins for Halloween."

Reese grimaced at his watch. "How about a rain check? We're cutting it close."

"Sure. I'll round up the girls. You know they're announcing the Nobels this week."

"Yes, Frank. We know." Reese grinned. Some people counted down to the New Year in Times Square. Frank counted down to the announcement of the Nobel Prizes in Stockholm every October. "Tell the girls I'll meet them over there. I may have to tell their ride to go on and drive them myself." Reese dashed home and, by habit, checked messages once inside.

Beep. "Hi, Alex. Or Reese. I can't remember who's home today. Anyway it's Sara Rothermel. I just got out of surgery, and I'm running ten minutes behind—sorry! Oh, remember to send overnight bags—we're keeping the girls." Beep. Beep. Beep.

Lucky break.

The front door slammed as the tape rewound, followed by the mad dash of footsteps on the stairs.

"We're hustling! We're hustling!"

Reese grinned and opened the refrigerator to take out the pan of lasagna to put in the oven for dinner. The quality of meals had taken a sharp increase in the past ten months. His own skills had improved from watching Alex, though he didn't think he'd ever learn to throw things together in the mix-and-match way she did. She'd even gotten the girls into it, insisting cooking qualified as a science experiment, which made them all the more gung ho.

She'd imparted her zen for science on the girls. They loved to go to the library to check out new books on experiments for kids, though they all thought Alex should write one herself since she came up with the best ideas.

Reese wouldn't have been surprised if they turned out at least one scientist from the bunch. He'd put his money on Nora, who'd tagged along with Alex to the lab all summer and who'd been selected for a "gifted and talented" biology program aimed at giving exceptional young students a head start on advanced studies. She was currently hard at work on a hereditary traits project, which involved tabulating the traits of family members such as hair color, eye color, attached earlobes, color-blindness, double joints, widow's peaks, cleft tongues and skin pigmentation among others.

"Whoever comes up with the most traits wins a prize!" she'd proudly announced.

Reese chuckled, remembering her excitement. Their shy one was definitely coming out of her shell, and he couldn't have been more pleased. After sticking the lasagna in the oven, he turned on the timer, then popped open a can of soda and sat down for a long swallow.

Jayne came bouncing into the kitchen, "play" glasses perched on her nose. "Hi, Uncle Reese!" She flung her overnight bag to the floor and hopped onto his lap, diary and pencil in hand. "Whatcha doin'?"

"Unwinding. Want a sip?"

"No, thanks." She flipped open her diary. "How come Alex's baby doesn't live with us?"

"Uh, Alex doesn't have a baby, honey."

"Yeah-huh." She pointed to her latest entry, reading each word slowly. "Kitty wants me to give my baby up for A-D-O-P-T-I-O-N."

Reese choked and sputtered on his soda. Grabbing the diary from her hands, he re-read the sentence and felt the blood drain from his face.

A mistake. There had to be some mistake. Some simple, innocent mistake.

"What's that spell, Uncle Reese?"

"Where…where did you get this?"

"From Aunt Alex's diary from when she was a little girl." Jayne beamed, pleased with her ingenuity.

As if sucker punched, the wind rushed out of his lungs. He gasped and coughed, every muscle tensing with foreboding. In one swift motion, he lifted Jayne to her feet and sucked in large gulps of air. The diary clattered to the floor.

Jayne picked it up. "You okay?"

"Yeah. Sorry." He thumped his chest and willed his voice to remain neutral. "Shouldn't have taken such a big sip." With forced casualness, he put down the soda can and wiped his mouth. "Where did you find Aunt Alex's diary?"

"Under her bed at Grandpa Frank's. I put it back."

Just then, a car honked in the driveway.

"Jayne!" her sisters called from the foyer.

"Coming!" Jayne whirled and ran for her overnight bag.

Reese followed. "Why don't I hold on to that for you?" He indicated her diary.

"Thanks." Jayne handed it to him. "What's that word?"

"We'll talk about it later. You're going to be late."

"'Kay." She wrapped her arms around his waist and lifted her face for a kiss.

He bent down to oblige, then repeated the procedure in the foyer for Elizabeth and Nora. "Have fun." He waved as they left, then closed the door and leaned against it.

A pounding rhythm reverberated through his eardrums, as a judge's gavel slamming over and over. His vision blurred, and he closed his eyes. Like a video playback, he saw the penthouse he'd shared with Leslie, the Chippendale desk in the study, the file drawer...the insurance claim. He didn't think anything could have been worse than that moment.

Until now.

He stared at the flower diary in his hands, cracked it open to the page marked with a ribbon and rubbed his thumb over the sentence Jayne had copied from Alex's diary.

*Kitty wants me to give my baby up for adoption.*

No. Please, God. No.

It wasn't possible—Alex would have told him if she'd become pregnant. She would have called or written. She *wouldn't* have given up his child without telling him.

Would she?

Alex bounded up the front steps, hardly able to contain her excitement. In the mudroom, she yanked off her coat and boots, threw them on the floor and pushed into the foyer.

"Hello?" she called into the darkened house. Flicking

on the overhead chandelier, she jumped back in surprise to see Reese sitting on the staircase. "Reese! Geez Louise!" Her hand flew to her chest. "You scared me. What are you doing out here all by your lonesome?"

He squinted and lifted a hand to shade his eyes from the glare of the light. "Waiting for you."

She grinned. "Have you already heard?"

"Heard what?"

"Oh, good—you haven't. I wanted to tell you myself." She clasped her hands together, bouncing on the balls of her feet. "I have the most incredible news. You're never going to believe this. I can hardly believe it myself—" She glimpsed anguish in Reese's eyes before he schooled his features. Her heart leapt to her throat. "What's wrong?"

He rubbed a hand over his face. "Why do you ask?"

An eerie feeling stole over her. "I just had a flash of déjà vu…that day you got the custody papers in the mail… I was here. You were there." She frowned and stepped farther into the foyer. "Has Kitty done something?"

"Good question. I was hoping you'd have the answer." He stood and approached her, stopping three feet away, arms crossed, legs braced apart in a military stance. "Did my mother ever advise you to give a baby up for adoption?"

*He knew.*

Alex's heart lurched. She stumbled back as if he'd whacked her on the side of the head with a two-by-four. Spots danced before her eyes.

"Wh-what happened while I was gone?" she croaked, her gaze darting around the foyer.

"No one's home but us chickens." His voice sounded like granite. "A simple yes or no will suffice. Did my mother—"

"It isn't a simple question!"

*"Yes or no,"* he repeated, a skilled lawyer controlling the testimony of a reluctant witness.

Adrenaline pounded in her veins, carrying equal doses of fear, shock and confusion. "Please." She lifted a hand in desperate appeal. "I can explain."

Reese's arms fell to his sides. The muscle in his jaw bulged as naked pain glittered in his eyes. "I'll take that as a yes. You *were* pregnant with my child."

Tears sprung to her eyes. "This wasn't how I intended to tell you. Please, can't we sit down—"

"Your intent?" His fists curled, and his nostrils flared. "In fifteen years, you didn't think to tell me we conceived a child. You expect me to believe you actually planned to confess to giving it away?"

"No!" Alex lurched back, covering her mouth.

"I didn't think so."

"No, you're wrong. You can't possibly think—"

"No?" Steel-blue eyes widened in exaggerated confusion. "Where's our baby, Alex?"

She shook her head, releasing a cascade of tears. How she wished she could have told him their baby was happy, healthy and safe—that she was still alive. She tried to find the words to explain, but the connection between her left and right brain had short-circuited in her panic.

Reese stepped closer and trailed a finger down the path of her tears, his eyebrows lowering like hoods over piercing eyes. "Didn't think I could do it, did you?" His voice was rough as sandpaper. His hand moved to the column of her throat, his fingers wrapping around the back of her neck. "Didn't think I'd make a good father."

"Reese, no! Please—"

He smothered her plea with his mouth, as if seeking and finding and tasting her deceit. She knew he meant to force her to push him away, but instead of fighting him, instead of giving him what he wanted, she gave him what he needed.

Gripping his shoulders, she pulled him closer, holding onto him as if rescuing a drowning man. She kissed him with aching tenderness, trying to resuscitate him, to show him without words everything in her heart.

At his body's swift response, Reese shoved away in disgust. With her. With himself. With the cruel twist of fate that brought Alexandra Ricci back into his life and taunted him with everything that would never be his.

He'd forsaken reasonable prudence to have her, to hold her, to believe she was his. In all his life, he'd never allowed anyone close to him, never allowed himself to get attached, to risk exposing the darkness on his soul that marked him from birth as unworthy of unconditional love.

But being with Alex was the closest he'd ever felt to unconditional *acceptance,* if not love. And like a slow addiction, he'd let the barriers fall one by one, each day taking more and more, basking in the moment and closing his mind to eventual dependence. And the pain of withdrawal.

He'd been a fool to think it could be different this time. A bigger fool to delude himself their marriage was anything but a match made in mutual desperation. But to discover the very person who'd believed in him the most all those years ago had drawn the line at his parenting...

He'd never expected such a betrayal. His body felt cold and numb as a cadaver in deep freeze. He needed to bleed to know he was still alive.

"How could you?" he asked. "You, Alex, of all people. How could you do this to me?"

"I didn't. Oh, God. *I didn't.*" Her voice bordered on

hysteria. She shook her hands as if they'd fallen asleep and lost circulation. "It's not what you think—"

"Let's see, what do I think?" A deadly calm settled over him, as it did in the courtroom when he had to school his emotions against some horrific tragedy. He tapped a finger over his lip and paced the floor with the stealth of a cougar about to strike. "*I think* you must have gone to my mother and told her you were pregnant. *I think* she must have informed you I had the responsibility of a flea. And *I think* once you realized the truth about your ole pal—"

She covered her ears with both hands, shaking her head furiously. "I didn't give her up! I didn't give her up!"

*Her.*

Reese staggered back in shock and horror, as if she'd taken a blunt surgical instrument, slit him lengthwise and dissected his insides before his eyes.

Alex's face crumpled, and a choked sob ripped from her chest. Lowering her hands, she repeated, "I did *not* give her up. Do you hear me?"

He did, and his mind reeled with possibilities. Bile rose in his throat. Choking. Suffocating. "You…?"

"Miscarried. I *miscarried,* Reese. I…l-lost her." She wrapped her arms around her stomach.

"No." Reese shook his head, willing her to take it back, to say it wasn't so. At her jerky nod, agony unlike any other ripped through him with stunning velocity, as a thousand knives plunging into his heart and twisting. "She isn't…out there? Somewhere…?"

Tortured brown eyes lifted in paralyzed uncertainty.

*"Anywhere?"*

Covering her mouth with both hands, she shook her head.

Reese closed his eyes and swallowed what felt like razor

blades in his throat. His chest burned with grief, and his mouth tasted like ashes. His baby hadn't survived long enough for Alex to give her up. "My own mother…she knew all this time, and she never told me. *Why?* Why would she keep the truth from me?"

"Because she's your mother."

He gave a harsh, guttural laugh. "I see your point."

"No, you don't." Alex lifted her tear-drenched face. Her mouth opened, poised to speak when all of a sudden, her eyes widened, and a look of astonishment chased across her face. "Oh, my God. That's it." She covered her mouth. "The brown mugs… Nora's chart of hereditary traits…. It didn't sink in before. Kitty's color-blind."

"Lots of people are—"

"Eigh percent of males and point-four percent of females. Color-blindness is linked to the X-chromosome. It's very, very rare in women. Men get it from their mothers. *You* got it…from Kitty."

Reese stared at her in stunned silence. He didn't know her anymore. He didn't know anyone anymore. "What the hell would possess you to say something as twisted as that?"

"She…told me she gave a baby up for adoption…before she married Clay. She didn't want me to tell you…because your relationship was…complicated. She said she's…not the person you think she is."

*No way.* This wasn't happening. This was *not* happening.

"Kitty? My birth mother?"

"It all adds up…the sum of her parts."

Reese's head swam, and the room blurred. Reeling like a drunk, he lunged for the railing to steady himself. *How* could Kitty be his birth mother, the woman who'd given him up for adoption? How was it even feasible?

*Do you have any idea how fortunate you are, Reese?*
*You shouldn't even be here. You shouldn't be living and*
*breathing. You shouldn't exist. Yet here you are.*

He remembered her words. He could never forget them.

"Don't you see?" Alex said. "There's nothing wrong
with you. It was never about you."

Air. He needed air.

He could barely make out the door through the tunnel
of his vision. The distance appeared an interminable jour-
ney. He veered left and right but somehow made his way
there.

"Reese, please. Don't leave. You promised."

"I lied."

"Where are you going?"

"To see my mother. I'll be back tomorrow." With one
hand on the doorknob, he braced himself and forced the
next words past his lips, "Start packing. I want you out
of here before I get home."

"Reese, no. You can't mean—"

"It's over, Alex." He slammed the door, swiping the
single, angry tear that rolled down his cheek.

Three hours later in West Palm Beach, Reese cruised
past the upscale retirement community's security check-
point without delay. Alex must have phoned ahead and
given his mother fair warning. Hard to picture those two
in cahoots. Hard to picture the reality of his life with the
world tilted helter-skelter.

He'd wanted to be wrong about the baby, had wanted
Alex to prove him wrong. He hadn't wanted to believe she
could ever deceive him, that she could lie beside him,
make love with him, raise the girls with him and never
once indicate her lack of faith in his abilities.

And his mother, if she really was his mother...

He still couldn't grasp the concept, the plausibility. Too many questions remained unanswered.

Reese tipped the cab driver and slid from the back seat into the balmy night. He wasn't dressed for the tropical climate, still wore his jeans and a long-sleeved button-down. But he didn't plan to stay long.

His mother waited on the front porch. She stood when he approached and held out a frosted glass of lemonade. "Alex told me to expect you."

"Figures." He gave a sardonic smile, took the drink and drained it in a few swallows.

"How are you?"

"How do you think I am?" Tension strained every muscle in his body. He must have looked like death warmed over.

"Let's go inside."

"Yes, let's." Reese opened the door to a welcome blast of the air-conditioning. "Where's your accomplice?"

"Your father left for Sycamore an hour ago—Alex said she needed someone to stay with the girls for a few days."

He ignored the stab of pain. "Enough small talk." He searched his mother's eyes for something new and different, something he'd overlooked all these years, some indication of the hidden truth he'd never even suspected. But there was nothing. She looked the same as she always had. "Are you my birth mother?"

Kitty's gaze never wavered, as if she'd prepared for this question all his life. "Yes."

He blinked. In a bizarre sort of way, it all made sense. Her drinking, the ugliness the alcohol brought out, always directed toward him and no one else.

He sank onto the love seat like a deflated balloon. All his life, he'd envied natural-born children, and now, to find out he'd been Kitty's all along... He felt numb.

His searching gaze combed the room as if he expected to find the answers written in hieroglyphics on the walls. He summoned his voice but only managed one word: "Explain."

"Would you like another drink?"

"No."

"All right." Kitty perched on the edge of an ottoman, crossed her legs and drew a breath. "I suppose I should start at the beginning... I was a first-year law student at Stanford."

"You went to Stanford? But I thought—"

"This was before. Before Sycamore. Before I lost my scholarship due to round-the-clock morning sickness. Before no one wanted to give a pregnant, unwed woman a job, never mind a loan. Before I came home with a child who looked like the man who professed to love me, then wanted nothing to do with either of us. Before I gave you up because I couldn't handle my own unplanned life, let alone yours."

To his vast surprise, she slid from the ottoman and got down on her knees. "I'm sorry, son. I'm so sorry...for all the hateful things I said, for all the resentment I took out on you, for making you believe you were anything less than exceptional. I was wrong. I was so wrong." Tears welled in her eyes, overflowed in rivulets that ran down her face.

Reese dabbed at his own eyes. His chest felt tight, and emotion threatened to choke him as he listened to his mother explain how she'd arranged for a private adoption where all parties knew each others' identities.

"We planned to touch base when you turned ten. But when I tried to make contact, I discovered your adoptive parents had died in a car accident when you were three and you'd been bouncing around the foster-care system for seven long years. When I found out, I knew I couldn't turn my back on you. I brought you into this world. You were my responsibility. But I was ashamed to tell you the truth.''

She narrated Clay's steadfast support. ''I thought if we provided you with all the best life had to offer—a good home, a good education, all the extracurricular enrichment you desired—then I would have done my duty. But I failed you in the worst possible way.''

Reese's throat worked. ''You didn't fail me. I'm alive because of you. You could have…terminated the pregnancy.''

''That wasn't an option for me.''

''I ruined your life. *He* ruined your life.''

Kitty's face crumpled. ''No. *No.*'' She shook her head. ''That's what I believed, the anger and bitterness I carried for so long. So many wasted years. Wasted, railing at him, at you, at the heavens for being so cruel, for tempting and deceiving me with forbidden fruit, robbing me of the career I had fought, struggled and slaved for.

''The God's honest truth is no one ruined my life but me. Not by conceiving you but by living in the past, drowning in self-pity, believing I'd settled. I drank because I couldn't stand the person I'd become. I pushed you to fulfill my long-lost destiny. I was blind to everything I had—a husband who adored me and *two* remarkable sons.

''Jeff's death was a wake-up call. I could either continue down this path of self-destruction, or I could count my blessings. Even then, it wasn't until Alex held up a mirror that I saw myself—truly saw myself—through your eyes. And I saw *you* for the first time, through hers.'' She sniffled and swiped her nose. ''Even as a girl, she knew you were someone special, knew beyond a doubt you would make an excellent father. She was right, and you are.''

He clenched his teeth to ward the sting of salt pouring into his wound. "If she really thought that, why didn't she tell me about our baby? Why didn't she give me a chance?"

"She would have, if she'd carried to term. Surely you understand how difficult it was after her hysterectomy."

He shook his head, uncomprehending.

Kitty frowned. "Reese? What do you know about how Alex miscarried?"

He scowled and rubbed his hands on his thighs. It hurt like hell to say the words. "Just that the baby died before Alex could put her up for adoption."

"Oh, God." His mother's eyes widened. "Reese Collins, you need to get on the first plane out of here. I've said and done so many wretched things, but among the worst was standing idly by and watching you lose the love of your life. I'll be damned if I make that mistake a second time."

# Chapter 13

Alex hugged her pillow through the night and finally cried herself into a fitful sleep. When the first rays of morning broke, she tried to convince herself the previous night had been a bad dream, that life as she'd come to know it couldn't possibly end this way. But the emptiness on the other side of the bed echoed the emptiness she felt inside.

Her hand grazed the indentation on the pillow where Reese laid his head at night. Every night but the last.

Her worst fears had materialized. She would never forget the contempt in Reese's eyes. His forgiveness was never an option—she'd deluded herself with false hope.

Ten months of false hope. Ten months of heaven.

She threw back the covers and sat upright, then melted like a wax doll left too near the flame. Slumping against the pillows, she covered her eyes with the heels of her hands. How would she summon the strength to get through the next few months when she couldn't even get out of bed? Even Albert, who usually slept in Jayne's room, had curled at the foot of her bed, as if sensing Alex needed moral support.

*It's not just you and me this time... Whatever comes down the pike, we have to stick it out—for the girls... No one leaves this time. No matter what. I need your word.*

She had given Reese her word. He might have lied, but she hadn't. And now, she had to put one foot in front of the other for the girls, even if she wanted nothing more than to pull the covers over her head and die.

Later that morning, Dr. Rothermel dropped off the girls, and Alex forced herself to act natural. She told the girls Grandpa Clay had flown up for a visit and wanted to take them to a fall festival as soon as they could get ready. As they showered and changed, she took her wedding album into the family room and curled into an armchair.

Her hands shook as she turned the pages, but she forced herself to continue, to remind herself of why she'd done what she'd done...and why she had to do what she had to do.

She found herself returning to the photo where Reese had walked into her dressing room. The camera had caught them both off-guard and captured an expression for which they never could have posed. Everything Alex had ever felt for Reese shone in her eyes, and damn if his expression didn't mirror hers. Anyone who didn't know them would have sworn they were in love, for real.

"Hi, Aunt Alex." Elizabeth came into the room.

"Hi, sweet pea. Finished getting ready?"

"Yep."

"How about your sisters?"

"Almost." Elizabeth climbed onto the arm of Alex's chair, draped an arm across Alex's shoulder and rested her head against Alex's. Pointing to the photo, she said, "I always knew you were the one."

"Oh?" She curved her arm to stroke Elizabeth's cheek. "And which one would that be?"

"The one for Uncle Reese."

An ache tightened her chest. She swallowed and turned the page. "Look, here's one of you and Jayne."

"Umm-hmm." Elizabeth leaned over and flipped the page back. "Dad used to tell us this bedtime story about how he and Mom met and fell in love. Once I asked him how he knew Mom was the one, and he said it was because she understood him in a way no one else did—that's how he knew.

"So I asked if that's how it was with Uncle Reese and Aunt Leslie, too. But he said no, the only person who'd ever understood Uncle Reese was a girl who lived across the street. She was very smart, and she saw things in Uncle Reese that other people didn't see. Her name was Alex."

Tears welled in Alex's eyes, and she stared blankly at the photograph, at the bedazzled expression on Reese's face. "Your dad told you that?"

"Umm-hmm. And when we first met you, I just knew. That Alex was you."

"Thank you." Her voice was hoarse. She raised a shaky hand to Elizabeth's face, wanting to savor this moment for the days and months ahead. "I love you, sweet pea."

"Love you, too." Elizabeth hugged her with both arms.

Fifteen minutes later, Alex waved goodbye to her girls as they pulled from the driveway of the Tudor with their grandfather. "Have fun. Don't eat too much cotton candy!"

Her smile faltered when they disappeared around the corner. With leaden steps, she walked back into the house and climbed the staircase to her bedroom.

With mechanical motions, she closed her suitcase and with a last, sweeping glance around the bedroom, grasped the handle with two hands and hauled it off the bed. She took the first step down the stairs when the front door slammed open with a force that rattled the windows.

Reese stood in the foyer, looking ragged and worn as if he hadn't slept much more than she had. She wanted to run down the stairs and throw herself into his arms. She wanted to drag his head down for a long, lingering kiss. She wanted to tell him all the things in her heart, everything she'd kept bottled up for so long.

"Sorry," she said from the top of the staircase. "I—I'd hoped to be gone before you got back."

He appeared to sag with relief, then straighten with apprehension at the suitcase in her hands. "Here, let me help you with that." He started for the stairs.

"No, thank you. I can manage."

"Alex, we need to talk."

She nodded, descended the remaining stairs and put down the suitcase. Smoothing a hand over her hair, she led the way to the family room.

Reese waited for her to sit down, then took a seat opposite her. Strain deepened the lines that crinkled from his eyes and bracketed his mouth.

"How…how did it go with your mom?" She wanted to take his hands in hers, to squeeze them in reassurance and let him know she was there for him, that she always would be if he ever needed her.

He gave a deep sigh. "As well as could be expected, I guess." He raked a hand through his hair. "It's going to take time. And therapy. We're going together. We both have issues…with each other we need to work through."

Alex nodded. "I'm glad. I'm so sorry about how it came out. I wasn't sure at first, but the more I thought about it… I didn't tell you about the baby she gave up because I thought you should hear it from her, not me."

"I can understand about my mother, Alex. I don't like it, but I can understand. What I don't understand and what I'm still struggling with is our baby." He leaned forward. "What happened, start to finish? From the top."

She fingered the pocket of her cardigan, drawing strength from the age-old photocopy she'd placed there. "I'll tell you everything, but first, I'd like to request that you please not interrupt until I'm finished. Then, if you have further questions, I'll address them at that time."

He gave a curt nod. He'd coached her on interactive teaching techniques, and this went against everything she had learned.

She didn't care. She'd tried his way last night and failed miserably. She didn't want a repeat performance. She would own up to her actions, but she wanted him to understand those actions and not put words in her mouth.

"First of all, contrary to what you may think, I wanted our baby. I had *no plans* to give her up for adoption."

Reese's hands clenched, and his Adam's apple bobbed up and down, but true to his promise, he didn't interrupt.

"I went in for a routine ultrasound, and they found multiple growths—what they believed to be common fibroids, or benign tumors. Unfortunately, as the baby grew, so did the fibroids." She cleared her throat and laced her fingers together to keep her hands from shaking. "They…outgrew their blood supply and started to degenerate. The pain…was unbearable. I thought I would die. I thought she would die. My father rushed me to the emergency room. I begged the doctors not to go in—I didn't want to lose her. But they didn't have a choice—they had to remove the fibroids. They did, and in the process, I lost my baby and my uterus."

His gaze was fixed on her stomach, his eyes shuttered,

his expression unreadable. Quietly, he said, "I did that to you. I robbed you of the ability to have children."

"No, Reese. We made her together, and I have never regretted her creation. Never. Not even once."

His jaw pulsed, and his nostrils flared. "Why didn't you tell me you were pregnant? Why did you shut me out?"

"You didn't call. You didn't write…"

"*You* could have called. *You* could have written."

"What would you have done if I had? Dropped out of boarding school, given up your spot at Stanford, married me for the sake of our unborn child?"

Steel-blue eyes held steady with conviction. "Yes."

"I didn't want you to give up your hopes and dreams…"

"What about *your* hopes and dreams, Alex?"

She looked down at her hands clenched in her lap. "I always wanted to be a mother."

"You just weren't sure I'd make a good father…"

"No!" Her head snapped up. "I never doubted you for a moment. I have always believed in you, Reese. Always."

Vulnerability flashed in his eyes before he masked it. "Then tell me now." The muscle in his jaw bulged. "Tell me how it…felt…when you learned you were pregnant."

"How it felt? I…I can't describe it in words."

"Try." The single word had a hard, desperate edge.

Panic gripped her. She had to do this, had to find a way to express her innate knowledge. But how? She closed her eyes and tried to put herself back in the moment, a place she hadn't allowed herself to return for years.

"All my life," she began, "I knew there was something missing inside me. Something that made me…different from everyone else. But when I found out I was pregnant…I forgot." She glanced down at her stomach and rubbed the spot that once carried a child instead of a scar.

"There are words like miracle, completion and unconditional love, but truly, what I felt went far beyond that."

Without a sound, Reese rose from his seat and slowly lowered himself beside her. Not looking up, he covered her hand with his. It felt unusually cold, and she wanted to turn hers over, but she didn't dare move.

"Did you have...morning sickness?" he asked, his voice strained.

"Evening sickness."

"Bad?"

"Pretty bad," she admitted.

He frowned. "What about cravings?"

"Ice cream."

"Rocky Road?"

"Yes."

"What other...changes happened?" He was asking her to share with him now the things she'd kept from him then, and she could not deny him. Not again. Never again.

"I cried a lot...there was this one diaper commercial that got me every time. I fell asleep in my library carrel every afternoon...I'd wake up wearing the imprint from the edge of a book. I...gained ten pounds, mostly in my chest."

Reese's darkened gaze rose to her breasts, then to her eyes. "Did you...show?"

"Toward the end. My tummy got round. It became more real. *She* became more real." Alex swallowed around the lump in her throat and blinked at the sting of unshed tears.

Reese nudged her hand away and smoothed his own over her belly. "Tell me more."

She touched the edge of the photocopy in her pocket. "I loved...the idea of you and I together in one little body. I loved...the thought of watching her grow up to be her own person. I loved everything about her, every minute of every day that I carried her." Her voice cracked, and tears spilled unchecked down her face. "I love her still."

She took out the photocopy and handed it to Reese. "The photos eventually turn black, so you have to make photocopies... Baby's first sonogram."

At the anguished sob that tore from his lungs, a fresh wave of tears sprung to her eyes.

"I'm sorry, Reese. I'm so s-sorry. I...d-didn't mean to k-kill her." There, she'd said it, laid her true fear on the table. She braced for the blow, expecting him to order her out of the house, throw her suitcases onto the curb and tell her never to darken their doorstep again.

He tugged her toward him instead, enfolding her in the big, strong haven of his arms. "You didn't kill her, Alex. You didn't." Tremors wracked his body, and he buried his face in her hair. "It wasn't your fault. We...lost her."

She clung to him, wanting nothing more than to give and take solace, but she couldn't accept the generosity of his words so easily. "What if I'd done something differently?"

"You can't think like that."

"What if I hadn't moved around so much? What if I'd stayed in bed round the clock? Altered my diet? My sleep patterns? Something. Anything."

"Alex...

"If they hadn't gone in, I might have carried to term."

"If they hadn't gone in, you *both* would have died. A classic ethical dilemma."

"Now you know why I hate ethics."

Reese pulled back, his face damp with his own tears, naked pain clearly reflected in his eyes. "I would have made the same decision. I couldn't have lost you both."

"Oh, Reese." She lifted her trembling hands to his face. "I wanted her. I wanted her so much."

"I know you did. I know…" He shuddered and drew her into his arms again, rubbing his cheek against her hair. "I don't blame you, sweetheart. Please, don't blame yourself."

She wanted to crawl inside his skin, to hold him close and never let go. "When she died, I was so afraid of your reaction, so afraid of what you would think of me."

"Of you? Why of you?"

"Because when you carry a baby, you feel responsible, and when you lose that baby, you wrack your brain wondering what you could have done to prevent it. I've questioned myself for years. I couldn't bear the thought of seeing recrimination in your eyes, too. That's why I kept delaying and delaying. I'm sorry, Reese. I didn't mean to shut you out. I didn't want to hurt you. I was just so afraid."

His arms tightened around her, his hands drifting up and down her back in long, soothing strokes. "Shhh, it's okay. It's okay now. Everything's going to be all right."

For the first time, Alex believed it. In exonerating her, Reese had given her a gift more precious than any: the impetus to forgive herself.

"She has a grave next to my mother's," she whispered. "I take them both flowers…"

"Does she have a name?"

"No. I couldn't name her without you."

Reese swallowed thickly. "I'd like to name her Judith, after your mother. What would you think of that?"

"I think I'd like it…a lot."

"Yeah?"

"Yeah."

He released her and drew the sonogram between them. "Baby Judy."

She touched the edge of the photocopy. Their fingers

brushed, and her gaze flew to his, reading the unmasked remorse reflected there.

"I was a bastard yesterday."

"You were hurt."

"That's no excuse for what I did to you, the things I said. If I could take them back, I would. But I can't—I can only apologize and hope one day you'll forgive me."

"There's nothing to forgive."

"I don't want you to leave, Alex. You…you're…the best thing that ever happened…to the girls. Please stay."

She closed her eyes, torn between happiness Reese found her a good mother and sorrow his sentiments applied only to her qualifications for motherhood. She was ashamed that even after his forgiveness, she could still want for more.

But she would learn to live with that.

"I'm not leaving," she confessed, the truth she'd come to realize in the wee hours of morning. She wouldn't let Reese push her out of his life, the way he pushed everyone else who ever got close to him…the way he would push if, for some reason, he couldn't be the one to walk away. "I'm the mother of your children. I'm not going anywhere."

"But your suitcase…"

"New York. The city. I need something to wear." She dabbed her face with her sleeve. "They're awarding the Nobels in December, but you know it takes me a while to find anything. Tom's and my work with lasers was chosen," she added as almost an aside. "I'll be back—"

"Hold up. Rewind." Reese stared at her. "You won a Nobel prize?"

"Yes, my itinerary's on the—"

"You won a freakin' Nobel prize?"

"In physics, yes."

"Alex! My, God! This is incredible!"

"I'm pleased."

He frowned. "You don't look pleased."

"I am." She gave a tight smile.

Reese contrasted her blasé expression with the one she'd worn last night, when her giddiness had been a tangible thing.

*I have the most incredible news...*

He felt lower than slime. "Alex, this was your dream."

"Actually, this was my father's dream. My dream was to be normal, to marry the man I loved and raise his children."

"But he died," Reese finished.

"No, he didn't die." She rose from the couch and went to the window. "He's right here in this room."

Reese's heart lodged in his throat. She couldn't have meant... Could she?

Alex drew aside the curtain and pointed to her bedroom window. "I used to sit in that window seat and look out at your house and dream about belonging in a world like this, a world where I could be a wife and a mother." She closed her eyes. "*Your* wife, Reese. The mother of *your* children. *You* are the best thing that ever happened to me."

She dropped the curtain and turned to face him. "Now I'm living what I always believed was an impossible dream—far more impossible *for me* than winning a Nobel prize—winning a family with you. You and the girls..." She spread her hands, then lowered them to her sides. "You're everything to me, everything I've ever wanted. More."

Adrenaline pounded through Reese's veins, a barrage of emotions hitting him hard and fast. In disbelief, he stared at this woman who had always stood by him, no matter what, even when he said and did everything to drive her away.

"Alex…" He swallowed and took a step closer. "What you said before about being different… You're not the only one who's felt that way." He wrestled for the right words, for the confession he'd never voiced. "All my life, I thought there was something wrong with me, something I could never let anyone close enough to see. As long as I kept my distance, everything would be all right. No one would know. But kids, they force you to break your own rules. They crawl all over you and leave their footprints on your heart. Miracle, completion, unconditional love… You're right—those words barely touch the surface."

"You're the best father, Reese."

"Only you could make me believe that. Only you…"

"Believe it," Alex whispered, "but not because I tell you so. Because every day when you come home, those girls drop whatever they're doing and run to you. And so do I."

"Alex…" He bridged the distance between them. "You have no idea how much I love you. I've loved you ever since that night at Mallard Lake. Maybe even before that. But that was when I first realized it. And every day since you came back into my life, I only love you more. You're the most incredible, desirable woman in the world to me. I wake up in the morning and look at you sleeping beside me, and I wonder if I'm dreaming because I can't believe you're mine."

Tears coursed down her face, and she raised her hands to cover her mouth. "I never thought you would…"

"I never thought you would either." Reese brushed the pads of his thumbs beneath luminous brown eyes he couldn't imagine life without. "About last night—"

"It's over."

He placed a finger over her lips. "We're coming clean here." At her nod, he continued, "I couldn't see beyond my own pain. And you…even when I badgered you into a corner, you cut right through the garbage, to the heart of my true fear. You've always done that. You've always seen me for the person I am, and I was afraid one day, you weren't going to like what you saw. It was *because* I loved you, Alex—that's the reason I stayed away."

He framed her face between his hands. "That's the reason I shut you out after we were married. I was falling in love with you all over again, more than ever before, and I didn't know what I'd do if I woke up one morning, and you looked at me differently. Or worse, if you weren't there."

A myriad of expressions chased across her face. "Don't you know I could never leave you. You've been my hero for more years than I care to count. Nothing can change that. You're stuck with me. For better or for worse."

"I'll take you, sweetheart, anyway I can get you." He drew her against his chest and kissed her. "We can't shut each other out again. Nothing will be as bad if we face it together, and nothing could be worse than being apart."

"Never again." She wrapped her arms around his neck, and he kissed her again, this time with slow, sensual possession, wishing they didn't have to come up for air.

"When's your flight?"

"What flight?"

He drew back and stared at her, one eyebrow raised.

"Oh, right. That flight." Her gaze flew to the clock. "I have to leave in twenty minutes." She ran her fingertips over his lips. "Come with me. Please, it would really—"

"Yes." He kissed her fingers. "I'll go anywhere with you." He smoothed the hair from her face, then mimicked a reporter with a microphone. "So, Alexandra Collins, what are your plans now that you've won the Nobel prize?''

Her eyes sparkled with humor. ''Disneyland?''

''Very original.''

''Actually.'' She sobered. ''I'm considering a six-month sabbatical to spend more time with my family. I've been a career woman and a working mom… I'd like to try my hand at being a stay-at-home mom for a little while.''

''That can definitely be arranged.''

''Good, because in that time I also want my husband to choose the career path he truly wants, whether that's hot-shot lawyer, professor extraordinaire, both or neither. I'll hold down the fort, so whatever he decides, I'm behind him.''

Reese's stomach hitched, a knot of emotion tightening his throat. ''He's a lucky guy.''

''I'm a lucky girl.'' She smiled.

''And what will the father of the famous scientist think of this plan?''

Her smile widened. ''I'll tell him the sledgehammer's taking a vacation cracking peanuts. I've won a Nobel— my brain deserves a little R&R.''

''Hmm.'' He ran his hands down her sides, locking on her hips. ''Got any plans for your body?''

''Well if I can't interest my husband—''

''He's interested. I have it on good authority.''

She leaned into him. ''I love you, Reese.'' Tears flooded her eyes and clogged her voice. ''So much.''

He took her face in his hands and brushed the moisture with his thumbs. ''Is that why you're still crying?''

''Yes.'' She sniffled. ''Happy tears.''

''Peanut butter and jelly again?''

''Peanut butter and jelly forever.''

\* \* \* \* \*

# Look Who's Celebrating Our 20th Anniversary:

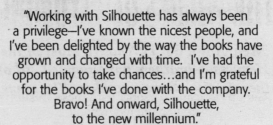

"Working with Silhouette has always been a privilege—I've known the nicest people, and I've been delighted by the way the books have grown and changed with time. I've had the opportunity to take chances…and I'm grateful for the books I've done with the company. Bravo! And onward, Silhouette, to the new millennium."

*—New York Times* bestselling author
**Heather Graham Pozzessere**

"Twenty years of laughter and love… It's not hard to imagine Silhouette Books celebrating twenty years of quality publishing, but it is hard to imagine a publishing world without it. Congratulations…"

—International bestselling author
**Emilie Richards**

INTIMATE MOMENTS®
Silhouette®

## INTIMATE MOMENTS®
### Silhouette®

INVITES YOU TO CELEBRATE THE
PUBLICATION OF OUR

# 1000TH BOOK!

And to mark the occasion, award-winning author

# MAGGIE SHAYNE

brings you another installment of

Look for

# ANGEL MEETS THE BADMAN

on sale April 2000 at your favorite retail outlet.

*And don't forget to order copies of the first six tales
about the irresistible Brands:*

**THE LITTLEST COWBOY,** IM #716 (6/96) $3.99 U.S./$4.50 CAN.
**THE BADDEST VIRGIN IN TEXAS,** IM #788(6/97) $3.99 U.S./$4.50 CAN.
**BADLANDS BAD BOY,** IM #809 (9/97) $3.99 U.S./$4.50 CAN.
**THE HUSBAND SHE COULDN'T REMEMBER,** IM #854 (5/98) $4.25 U.S./$4.75 CAN.
**THE BADDEST BRIDE IN TEXAS,** IM #907 (2/99) $4.25 U.S./$4.75 CAN.
**THE OUTLAW BRIDE,** IM #967 (12/99) $4.25 U.S./$4.75 CAN.

### Silhouette®
*Where love comes alive*™

# SILHOUETTE'S 20ᵀᴴ ANNIVERSARY CONTEST
## OFFICIAL RULES
### NO PURCHASE NECESSARY TO ENTER

1. To enter, follow directions published in the offer to which you are responding. Contest begins 1/1/00 and ends on 8/24/00 (the "Promotion Period"). Method of entry may vary. Mailed entries must be postmarked by 8/24/00, and received by 8/31/00.

2. During the Promotion Period, the Contest may be presented via the Internet. Entry via the Internet may be restricted to residents of certain geographic areas that are disclosed on the Web site. To enter via the Internet, if you are a resident of a geographic area in which Internet entry is permissible, follow the directions displayed on-line, including typing your essay of 100 words or less telling us "Where In The World Your Love Will Come Alive." On-line entries must be received by 11:59 p.m. Eastern Standard time on 8/24/00. Limit one e-mail entry per person, household and e-mail address per day, per presentation. If you are a resident of a geographic area in which entry via the Internet is permissible, you may, in lieu of submitting an entry on-line, enter by mail, by hand-printing your name, address, telephone number and contest number/name on an 8"x 11" plain piece of paper and telling us in 100 words or fewer "Where In The World Your Love Will Come Alive," and mailing via first-class mail to: Silhouette 20ᵗʰ Anniversary Contest, (in the U.S.) P.O. Box 9069, Buffalo, NY 14269-9069; (In Canada) P.O. Box 637, Fort Erie, Ontario, Canada L2A 5X3. Limit one 8"x 11" mailed entry per person, household and e-mail address per day. On-line and/or 8"x 11" mailed entries received from persons residing in geographic areas in which Internet entry is not permissible will be disqualified. No liability is assumed for lost, late, incomplete, inaccurate, nondelivered or misdirected mail, or misdirected e-mail, for technical, hardware or software failures of any kind, lost or unavailable network connection, or failed, incomplete, garbled or delayed computer transmission or any human error which may occur in the receipt or processing of the entries in the contest.

3. Essays will be judged by a panel of members of the Silhouette editorial and marketing staff based on the following criteria:

   Sincerity (believability, credibility)—50%

   Originality (freshness, creativity)—30%

   Aptness (appropriateness to contest ideas)—20%

   Purchase or acceptance of a product offer does not improve your chances of winning. In the event of a tie, duplicate prizes will be awarded.

4. All entries become the property of Harlequin Enterprises Ltd., and will not be returned. Winner will be determined no later than 10/31/00 and will be notified by mail. Grand Prize winner will be required to sign and return Affidavit of Eligibility within 15 days of receipt of notification. Noncompliance within the time period may result in disqualification and an alternative winner may be selected. All municipal, provincial, federal, state and local laws and regulations apply. Contest open only to residents of the U.S. and Canada who are 18 years of age or older, and is void wherever prohibited by law. Internet entry is restricted solely to residents of those geographical areas in which Internet entry is permissible. Employees of Torstar Corp., their affiliates, agents and members of their immediate families are not eligible. Taxes on the prizes are the sole responsibility of winners. Entry and acceptance of any prize offered constitutes permission to use winner's name, photograph or other likeness for the purposes of advertising, trade and promotion on behalf of Torstar Corp. without further compensation to the winner, unless prohibited by law. Torstar Corp and D.L. Blair, Inc., their parents, affiliates and subsidiaries, are not responsible for errors in printing or electronic presentation of contest or entries. In the event of printing or other errors which may result in unintended prize values or duplication of prizes, all affected contest materials or entries shall be null and void. If for any reason the Internet portion of the contest is not capable of running as planned, including infection by computer virus, bugs, tampering, unauthorized intervention, fraud, technical failures, or any other causes beyond the control of Torstar Corp. which corrupt or affect the administration, secrecy, fairness, integrity or proper conduct of the contest, Torstar Corp. reserves the right, at its sole discretion, to disqualify any individual who tampers with the entry process and to cancel, terminate, modify or suspend the contest or the Internet portion thereof. In the event of a dispute regarding an on-line entry, the entry will be deemed submitted by the authorized holder of the e-mail account submitted at the time of entry. Authorized account holder is defined as the natural person who is assigned to an e-mail address by an Internet access provider, on-line service provider or other organization that is responsible for arranging e-mail address for the domain associated with the submitted e-mail address.

5. Prizes: Grand Prize—a $10,000 vacation to anywhere in the world. Travelers (at least one must be 18 years of age or older) or parent or guardian if one traveler is a minor, must sign and return a Release of Liability prior to departure. Travel must be completed by December 31, 2001, and is subject to space and accommodations availability. Two hundred (200) Second Prizes—a two-book limited edition autographed collector set from one of the Silhouette Anniversary authors: Nora Roberts, Diana Palmer, Linda Howard or Annette Broadrick (value $10.00 each set). All prizes are valued in U.S. dollars.

6. For a list of winners (available after 10/31/00), send a self-addressed, stamped envelope to: Harlequin Silhouette 20ᵗʰ Anniversary Winners, P.O. Box 4200, Blair, NE 68009-4200.

Contest sponsored by Torstar Corp., P.O. Box 9042, Buffalo, NY 14269-9042.

# ENTER FOR
# A CHANCE TO WIN*

## Silhouette's 20ᵗʰ Anniversary Contest

### Tell Us Where in the World
### You Would Like *Your* Love To Come Alive...
### And We'll Send the Lucky Winner There!

Silhouette wants to take you wherever
your happy ending can come true.

Here's how to enter: Tell us, in 100 words or less,
where you want to go to make your love come alive!

In addition to the grand prize, there will be 200
runner-up prizes, collector's-edition book sets
autographed by one of the Silhouette anniversary
authors: **Nora Roberts, Diana Palmer,
Linda Howard** or **Annette Broadrick**.

## DON'T MISS YOUR CHANCE TO WIN!
## ENTER NOW! No Purchase Necessary

*Where love comes alive™*

Name: _____

Address: _____

City: _____ State/Province: _____

Zip/Postal Code: _____

Mail to Harlequin Books: **In the U.S.:** P.O. Box 9069, Buffalo, NY
14269-9069; **In Canada:** P.O. Box 637, Fort Erie, Ontario, L4A 5X3

*No purchase necessary—for contest details send a self-addressed stamped envelope to:
Silhouette's 20ᵗʰ Anniversary Contest, P.O. Box 9069, Buffalo, NY, 14269-9069 (include
contest name on self-addressed envelope). Residents of Washington and Vermont may
omit postage. Open to Cdn. (excluding Quebec) and U.S. residents who are 18 or over.
Void where prohibited. Contest ends August 31, 2000.

PS20CON_R